By Yael Goldstein-Love

The Passion of Tasha Darsky

The Possibilities

THE
POSSIBILITIES

THE
POSSIBILITIES

A Novel

YAEL GOLDSTEIN-LOVE

RANDOM HOUSE
NEW YORK

Published in the United States by Random House, an imprint and division of Penguin Random House LLC, New York.

RANDOM HOUSE and the HOUSE colophon are registered trademarks of Penguin Random House LLC.

LIBRARY OF CONGRESS CATALOGING-IN-PUBLICATION DATA
Names: Goldstein-Love, Yael, author.
Title: The possibilities: a novel / Yael Goldstein-Love.
Description: First edition. | New York: Random House, [2023]
Identifiers: LCCN 2022031697 (print) | LCCN 2022031698 (ebook) | ISBN 9780593446485 (hardcover; acid-free paper) | ISBN 9780593446492 (ebook)
Subjects: LCSH: Motherhood—Fiction. | Missing children—Fiction. | LCGFT: Paranormal fiction. | Thrillers (Fiction) | Novels.
Classification: LCC PS3607.O4859 P67 2023 (print) | LCC PS3607.O4859 (ebook) | DDC 813/.6—dc23/eng/20220712
LC record available at https://lccn.loc.gov/2022031697
LC ebook record available at https://lccn.loc.gov/2022031698

Printed in Canada on acid-free paper

randomhousebooks.com

2 4 6 8 9 7 5 3 1

First Edition

Book design by Debbie Glasserman

For Solly, and all your possibilities.
And J.S., for all of mine.

PART ONE

↔

*Perhaps, then, motherhood really is like a
secret space in a woman's brain, waiting
to be discovered.*

Adrienne LaFrance,
"What Happens to a Woman's Brain
When She Becomes a Mother,"
The Atlantic, January 8, 2015

Chapter One

That was when the worlds split.

When she was open on the table, paralyzed from the waist down. When they held her child up for her to see.

You, she thought, but the sight of him, twisted rigid in a howl that never came, cut off the thought.

Then he was gone. Someone had taken him.

Instead of his cry, there was the tinny hospital PA paging one neonatal team and then another.

Instead of his cry, the voices of competent, confident people creeping toward alarm.

A doctor's narrow head was bent in concentration, sewing her back into a body.

"What's happening?" she asked.

"They're trying," Adam said, from somewhere behind. Then he was just above and kissed her forehead. His lips felt dry and chapped.

The room was small, too small for all these people. She didn't know the situation but understood that it was dire. Someone had held her child up, then taken him away, and he hadn't made a sound yet, and the room kept filling with more people.

"It's cold in here," she said. "They need to wrap him."

"It's warm, Hannahbelle," said Adam's voice, but not from near her ear where she expected. "They've got him warm, don't worry, they're doing everything correctly."

He must have been straining to see, must have been craning, she could hear it in his voice. It was happening near the door, she was almost certain, somewhere past her feet, whatever they were trying, and the door was letting in a draft; she felt it blowing over her.

She didn't try to see. She wouldn't have been able to, her view partially blocked by the paper draping meant to shield her from an eyeful of her insides. But also seeing had never been a part of what they shared, she and this child. In their nine months together, she had only ever seen him for an instant: tiny body twisted rigid in a silent howl, eyes not yet open. That was seconds ago or minutes or hours and every second without oxygen killed more of him, the tiny brain that had been growing all along inside her, the one she somehow felt she knew, so much so that the unfamiliar look of him surprised her. The situation seemed to her quite obviously, quite awesomely a bad one, but also somehow muted, in the way that time mutes even the worst pain. It felt to her this had been going on for longer than the life she'd lived until now.

In the corner of her vision, something moved. She tilted up her chin and caught the blur as it moved past her. Held cradled in a nurse's arms—the blue-smudged lips, the way one tiny arm trailed as a doll's would. The clipped, efficient sorrow in the way the nurse grabbed at the arm and tucked it in. The clipped, efficient sorrow of the quiet that descended.

Then she was looking at the obstetrician's narrow head still bent behind the curtain, the hair so glossy black it cast its own strange dulled reflection of the overhead fluorescents.

"Is he OK?" she asked.

"Is he going to be OK?"

There was no answer.

Chapter Two

Eight months later, I stood on the top level of an open parking structure, watching fog roll in from the Oakland Hills and longing for a cigarette.

Jack was regarding me through heavy eyes. He looked like he could sleep.

I smiled at him, and then, unable to resist, though I knew it would perk him up and make a car seat nap less likely, I bent and nuzzled the top of his small head. The silky brown waves that tightened into ringlets near the base of his neck smelled of absurdly expensive baby shampoo mixed with a musk like a cat's just-licked fur. The smell soothed my nerve endings like nicotine.

Well, not quite like nicotine. It made no sense to stand outside a car, contemplating the view from the top level of an open parking garage, if you weren't smoking a cigarette. But so many of my habits were like this, obsolete cocoons of pre-baby behavior, the butterfly long gone.

"Get in the car, Hannah," I said out loud because when a day has already beaten you down before nine A.M., it's nice to have someone give you clear directions, even if it's yourself.

But I kept on standing there. The air was the perfect cool of one foot stuck out from sweaty blankets, and with the fog now burning off in the morning glare, I felt outside of time, outside of space in the best possible way, like at the airport. Just standing there was luxurious because there was no purpose to it. I was ignoring everything I had to face about this day. I was standing there simply because I wanted to and that felt better than sex, better than drugs. Slightly less good than a massage. Nowhere near as good as four solid hours of sleep.

But Jack was fiddling with his ear now. It was one of his more urgent Tired Signs and meant I had to get him in that car seat pronto to seize the glinting, flickering portal to a better dimension known in baby-sleep literature as the Tired Window. Reluctantly, I slipped the diaper backpack off my shoulder and started rooting for the car key.

I could tell right away it wasn't there. There was only one place I ever put it, in the side pocket that was a little too narrow to hold my phone, but still my hand kept rooting, hopefully, now in the main compartment, past clean diapers, hand wipes, spare onesies (always damp for reasons I had not pinned down), down into the substrate of loose Cheerios.

Jack had started mewling experimentally.

I trilled, "Mommy forgot the car key! Silly Mommy!"

My voice was pitched halfway between fun and seriously weird because I was trying to fend off an internal chorus of *fuckety fuck fuck*. I was imagining lugging the stroller all the way up and then back down four flights of stairs again. The parking structure extended only three floors up the low-rise, my therapist's office was on the seventh, and the elevator was broken because of course it was. It almost had to be on a day like this.

I felt in the diaper bag one last time, probing the refrigerated pocket where an empty, unwashed bottle festered, a relic of a time when I still hoped to convince Jack to accept something other than my breast. I did this even though I now knew exactly where the car key was: on the small side table in Dr. Goodman's office. I'd taken it out of the pocket in order to fish for the parking ticket, then put it down while handing the ticket over to be validated. I remembered this all very precisely, so precisely I almost felt I should be able to slip a hand into that memory and pluck the key right out.

I forced myself to picture instead the viable next steps. Up and down the concrete stairs again, four flights. Was there any way around this? I wasn't lazy, but Jack was a beast of a child, still 99th percentile in height and weight as of his last doctor's appointment, almost a different species from me; I very much doubted I'd ever in my life broken the 20th percentile. Jack's stroller added another fifteen pounds at least.

Options: I could try to take him out of it, risk his wrath. But he was so calm right now, still maybe looking drowsy. Like one of those magical creatures I saw in coffee shops, napping strapped to their mother's chests, as though caring for a baby might be as simple as starting to wear silk scarves, just a matter of getting the knots right.

"Right," I said aloud now. "Right," I tried again in a more cheerful voice. And then to Jack, "Mommy made an uh-oh."

Jack gurgled happily at this, recognizing the word. He didn't seem drowsy anymore, and this was mildly dismaying. It meant no car seat nap. The Tired Window flickering shut, a portal winked out of existence. No chance to start making phone calls, sending emails, sorting out the practicalities of the bombshell Adam had dropped on me that morning. But any frustration was mostly overwhelmed by my delight at Jack's sweet gurgle, at recognizing the great joy he took in discovering that within the buzzing, blooming noise always surrounding him there were patterns, little packets of sound that picked out little pieces of the world. It knocked my socks off, still, that babies ever managed to learn this, that he was learning it and I could actually see it happening.

"Right," I said again, and for a moment actually managed to feel fantastic.

But there was still the problem of the car key and the broken elevator, of my exhausted, aching body. The C-section scar that still felt raw and angry eight months on. And my giant baby who might at any moment become a writhing, wriggling, shrieking torque of impressive force, frighteningly uncontainable on four flights of concrete stairs.

Without him, I could knock discreetly at the heavy door, whisper "Left my keys," grab them through the tiny crack that Dr. Goodman would surely open—no wider—to protect the confidentiality of her next patient, then slip away almost as though it hadn't happened.

With Jack, I threatened to make a scene. A second scene actually. Because an hour ago, when Dr. Goodman had found me in her waiting room with a baby on my lap, you might have thought from her reaction that I was cradling a fresh-plucked eyeball instead of a fat-cheeked cherub. Which, fair enough, because baby-free was a condition that Dr. Goodman insisted on for treatment. It was why I came on Wednesdays at eight A.M., before Adam had to be at work. Dr. Goodman was a specialist in postpartum mental health, so you might have thought she could cut a mother some slack, but only if you'd never met her.

This morning, though, after her initial recoil of disgust, she'd been kind about my breaking her no-baby rule. She'd have had to be a monster not to be kind about it, given why I'd brought him: I'd woken at just past four to Adam crying at the foot of our bed, telling me he was leaving me. The words "shared custody" were uttered; this wasn't just a stressed, underslept father blowing off some steam. I'd known that things weren't going great between us, but I hadn't seen this coming. It was true that we hadn't yet been able to figure out how to transition from a twosome to a threesome, how to find each other within this new world order in which the complicated needs and wants and inner lives of two adults were entirely subsumed by the demands of a delicious-smelling tyrant. But Adam was not the sort of man to cut and run when things were difficult. Adam was devoted, often to a fault. To his students, his friends, his family, to Jack. He had been so devoted to me for the past seven years that there had been times his devotion made me hate him a little. Especially in the beginning— his utter certainty in our love seemed profligate to me, given the world as I perceived it: a place where nothing was ever certain. I believed in holding things lightly enough that you didn't mind when they inevitably slipped away. Adam believed in happily ever after. His leaving was like a square circle, it made no sense, but it was happening, so what could you do but roll with it? So I was rolling with it.

Well, mostly rolling with it. I had, after all, dragged Jack with me to therapy, thereby rendering the session all but useless on the day I probably needed it most. It's not that Adam wasn't willing to honor our agreement regarding Wednesdays at eight A.M. He was perfectly willing, eager even, urging me out the door as he bounced Jack a little too forcefully on his knee. But Jack's wide-eyed stare as he watched me go was beyond what I could stand. That startled look, his rosebud mouth a perfect O that seemed to ask, *How could you want to leave the perfect coziness of our union?*

It was always hard for me to walk away from Jack when he made that face, but today, with the world feeling newly hostile since my four A.M. awakening, it was impossible. Adam's bombshell reconfirmed my old belief that *of course* you should hold things lightly enough that you don't mind when they inevitably slipped away; I felt like an idiot for letting Adam lull me into his happily-ever-after bullshit. My devoted husband was leaving me, and the world was not to be trusted, as I had always known before I let Adam convince me otherwise. And now I had a child. A tiny, vulnerable, perfect child who I could not, for anything, hold lightly, and whose face asked, "How could you want to?" whenever I tried to step away, even for a moment, and so I couldn't want to. I couldn't want to be apart from him even for an hour. I wanted, I needed, his warm little body close, where I could keep him safe. So here Jack was with me, his mother, absolutely paralyzed by what surely had to be a profoundly simple problem to anyone with a well-slept brain: how to retrieve a car key that was waiting for you up four flights of concrete stairs.

I wheeled Jack down the parking ramp and through the sliding doors back inside the building, a soulless low-rise filled entirely with medical offices. I parked the stroller just inside the doors, below the sign—"We're working on it!"—taped at a slapdash angle on the brushed chrome of the door to the broken elevator. It was the right spot: impossible to see from the outside, shielded from the sun. I looked Jack over and considered covering the stroller's canopy with his blanket, a white rectangle of muslin spangled with pale stars in blue and gray. He smiled back. I didn't cover him. He liked to take the world in.

I swung open the door to the stairway, then stopped before stepping through.

Was leaving Jack here the obvious solution, or was it unthinkable? Was I crazy for contemplating it, or crazy for worrying? I knew that one of these was true, but not which.

I slipped into the shadowed cool of the stairway, then whirled and caught the door before it could click closed. I poked my head out into the fluorescent glare, back in, back out. Jack's face cracked wide; he laughed. He thought I was playing with him.

"Peekaboo!" I said.

It would take no more than three minutes. It was sane. *I* was sane, admirably sane, like a mother from the 1970s, or whenever it was supposed to be that mothers knew that worrying too much was almost as bad as not worrying at all. Like the kind of mother Adam wanted me to be. I started running up the stairs.

I knew how sane I was until I reached the first landing. That's when I pictured Jack below, waiting, eager, thinking we were still playing and trusting me completely. That open-mouthed smile, always halfway to a laugh if it wasn't already midscream.

Four flights of stairs with his torqueing, thrashing body against my tiny one; with my small, fat worm of a scab throbbing as though my muscles might spill out where I'd been split by the doctor's knife; with Dr. Goodman's look of rank distaste awaiting our arrival up above; but *that* was the sane choice. I saw that now and turned around.

I took the stairs back down two at a time. Grabbed for the door. Pulled it hard. Smile already plastered over my face—peekaboo!

And he was gone.

Before me was a long stretch of hallway, low-pile carpeting in an industrial shade of gray, bright light spilling from the windows at both ends. The same hallway I'd just left. But Jack wasn't in it.

I spun. Took in every inch of the empty hallway. As though I might see—what? Some person wheeling my child away? Some kidnapper who'd just been waiting for the moment a feckless parent left their child unattended in a low-rise medical building?

I was on the wrong floor. Obviously. I had popped through the wrong door in my anxiety to undo my mistake. This was very clearly the explanation, but as I raced back down another flight of stairs it felt as though the steps were pillowy and unsupportive, tipping me off them before I'd landed. I took the last step as a painful skid against the wide plane of my foot, then yanked open the door to the second floor so hard it hit the wall behind. The lump of fear in my throat swelled into a ball it was difficult to breathe around. No Jack. No Jack here in this hallway either.

I started calling out his name. I wasn't sure he knew his name, but he knew my voice, and wherever he was, maybe he'd answer with a cry. I was calling loudly enough that doors to the other doctor, dentist, or therapist offices should have swung open. They stayed closed. I hated them fiercely as I raced back up to the fourth floor, which was obviously the right one. I couldn't have overshot by more than one floor.

The same empty stretch of hallway. I had to grab the wall for balance.

Just to get my lungs to fill and my heart to beat the way it needed to, I had to give myself a talking-to. *Calm down, Hannah. The last thing Jack needs is for you to panic. That's how you end up leaving him alone for even longer on whatever floor you've left him.*

But panic was already edging in on my vision. I could see only a very narrow view in front of me as I raced up another flight of stairs. And then another. And another. And another. And then back down. Opening each door onto each identical stretch of hallway. Eight floors in all. None of them had Jack. My body felt like it was moving quickly, but to my eyes I was barely moving. As though the atmosphere were wrong, too little oxygen or else too much. Not *as though*. The atmosphere *was* wrong here. I felt it in the air, I really did: It was an atmosphere without Jack. Not that he was missing. More than that.

There was no Jack here. There simply was no Jack. I could feel it.

I missed the second to last step on the bottom floor and slammed onto the last one, ankle twisting underneath me. My cheek hit hard against cement. I lay there, cheek pressed to floor, my breath coming so shallow now I couldn't get the air I needed to push myself back up. Those first long minutes of Jack's life when they couldn't start him breathing, when the neonatal team kept on expanding, when the CPR wasn't working because they hadn't yet discovered the little plug of mucus inside his tiny airway. That blur rushing past me, a nurse holding a baby. Blue-smudged lips, arm dangling. I'd seen it. Adam swore I hadn't. Adam swore I couldn't have because it never happened. And of course he was right. Of course I hadn't. Because they'd found the plug of mucus in Jack's airway. They'd found it, and he was fine. He'd had just enough oxygen in his cord blood to carry him through those terrible ten minutes.

Still sprawled on the concrete beneath the banks of stairs, I caught my breath, counted to four, then counted to five as I exhaled. I realized I hadn't been thinking straight until now. I'd left him on the third floor. Of course I'd left him on the third floor, because that was where you came into the building if you were coming from the top level of the parking garage. How many times had I been in this building now, and somehow I'd forgotten this. Somehow I had skipped the third floor. I had to have skipped it, because the third floor was where Jack surely had to be.

I pushed into a crouch, then stood, and climbed back up two flights with a calm determination I didn't feel at all. I pulled open the door. And felt the breath knocked out of me. Another empty stretch of hallway lined with dead-eyed doors.

Except. Except! There was no sign on the elevator. I forced

my jelly legs to move and went to touch the smudged chrome. No sticky residue. There had definitely been a sign here. "We're working on it!" taped at a slapdash angle. Now there was no sign and it looked as though there had never been. This one detail relieved me so much I didn't even need to count to slow my breathing. It meant there was a mistake. This was all some mistake. I pressed the heels of my palms against my eyes, as though I could reboot the scene.

When I took my palms away, I was staring at my own blurred reflection in the sliding metal doors. I looked unwell. My hair was a wild halo of blond tangles. My cheeks were drained of color. My gray-green eyes looked hollow, gone. I had no eyes. My mouth was open.

I screamed. The scream was eaten by a siren loud enough to drown out my own thoughts.

When I opened my eyes again, I was exactly where I had been when I'd closed them, but somehow I was staring at the precarious, almost lunatic angle of "We're working on it!," and beneath that sign, Jack's face screwed red and tight. The siren blared, and then resolved around me as his wails. Judging from the register, he'd been at it for a while. Right here. Exactly where he hadn't been.

Chapter Three

Jack's screams grew even angrier as I lifted him from the stroller. But I grabbed him to me roughly, breathing in his salty smell, his animal heat, his small pounding heart against mine. I kissed his bulbous cheeks. Pressed my lips so hard against the squishy give of them that he let off screaming and started to laugh, and then to cry again in protest. Still I couldn't stop myself from kissing him. Those cheeks, the pink of them, the fleshy bounty, that stretched from just beneath his long brown eyes, Adam's eyes, to meet at my pointy chin. Those fat, fat cheeks, fed on my milk, on ground lamb and peas, on the watermelon he loved to squish between his fingers, on the bananas Adam pureed for him with avocado and yogurt and that he tried to feed me in his fists.

Fine. He was fine.

I shifted Jack onto my hip and fumbled for my phone in the bottom of the diaper bag, knowing I needed to call Adam and knowing I shouldn't. Knowing both simultaneously just like I knew what I saw in the delivery room, blue lips, arm dangling, and also knew I hadn't seen it. I pictured Adam earlier that morning. Hunched over himself, streaked by shadows, his voice cracking, a gentle man who had reached his limit. *I can't anymore, Hannah. I wish I could, but I just can't.*

His phone rang five times then went to voicemail. I tried again.

I tried a third time. Five rings then voicemail. I decided I might as well get the car key before I made a fourth attempt. I left the stroller in front of the elevator and started the trek with Jack up the concrete stairs. My body ached as if it really would split open at the seam.

The waiting room was empty, small blessings. I sank into a white leather bucket seat to catch my breath and then, since Jack was pawing at me, I unbuttoned my shirt and put him to my breast. I called Adam again and this time left a voicemail: *Everything's OK, but can you call me? We're still at Dr. Good-man's, and I think you need to pick us up.*

I pictured him listening to this message and feeling confirmed in his decision to go our separate ways.

But I was starting to feel calmer about whatever had just happened in the stairwell. Nursing Jack was calming me. The snuggly closeness. The oxytocin. Jack's big eyes gazing up at me from behind thick lashes.

My heart was still pounding hard enough that my left hand could actually feel the thumping through Jack's back. But as my milk let down, and his cheeks started flicking like fish's gills, his eyelids getting droopy, I felt my muscles unclench. I let my attention drift over the splayed magazines, the spinning fan overhead, the blond wood of the walls.

I jumped when the door to Dr. Goodman's office opened. I'd lost track of the time.

It wasn't Dr. Goodman emerging, but her nine A.M. appointment, a very pretty, very harried-looking woman who was always staring aghast at her phone when I emerged from my session, as though each and every Wednesday at eight-fifty she'd just received the worst news of her life. I averted my gaze to let her pass by in semi-anonymity, then shifted a drowsy Jack onto my shoulder and rapped on Dr. Goodman's door.

I meant to ask for my car key and skedaddle, but Dr. Goodman was the first to speak. I must have looked like hell.

"I've just had a cancellation. My hour is free. Come in?"

She held the door for me, which was very much not like her. Even less like her, she reached for Jack, which took me by so much surprise I handed him straight over. More surprisingly, he seemed OK with this arrangement.

I collapsed into my normal seat, an immensely comfortable gray bouclé Womb Chair, and let it all spill out, what had happened in the stairway. It felt like a relief at first, but by the time I reached the end I was starting to doubt my memory of the experience.

"It probably wasn't as dramatic as I've made it sound," I finished. "But it did feel terrifying in the moment."

Jack was still content on Dr. Goodman's narrow lap, one round cheek squished against the green silk of her shirt. His gray-and-white brindled lovey, an always-filthy square of nubbly fabric with the head of a cow sewn to one corner, was trailing down the black leather of her pencil skirt.

I glanced at the phone cradled in my lap to see if maybe I'd missed a call from Adam. I hadn't.

Dr. Goodman tilted her gorgeous head and said, "Seems to me that this experience bears a lot of similarity to what we often talk about in here. The car-swerve feeling."

The diagnosis on my reimbursement claims was adjustment disorder, postpartum onset, which Dr. Goodman had described to me as an insurance-friendly way of saying I was having a normal, human, difficult time in response to a difficult situation. But in this office, it was always the car-swerve feeling. Like when you have a near-miss on the road and seconds, minutes, maybe even hours later you're still waiting to feel relieved not to have died in a fiery crash.

Not because you aren't grateful to have escaped. And not because you aren't certain that you did, in fact, avoid becoming roadkill—you haven't lost your mind. But, rather, because you feel in a deep, primal, hard-to-describe way that the crash came *too close* to occurring. Because it didn't seem a simple yes or no in those car-swerve moments, did it? A simple it didn't happen or it did? Instead it seemed, in those moments, that the way things *could* have gone had some lingering reality, some awful stickiness that clung now to the moments carrying you away from when you might have crashed but didn't.

Or maybe, instead, it was as though *what could have been* was right there beside you for a while, separated by the thinnest of membranes, a shadow reality, a mirror reality, but still a kind of real. This sense, for as long as it lasted, could kind of fuck you up. That was the car-swerve feeling.

What I felt about Jack's birth was just like this, only it had been eight months and I still couldn't shake the feeling. Because I couldn't shake the image of the blue-smudged lips, the dangling arm. I'd *seen* it. And because I couldn't shake this memory, and the terrifying car-swerve feeling that came with it, I seemed unable to do the simplest things, such as leave my child for an hour so I could go to therapy on my own. Or hire childcare so I could get back to work. Every time Adam found a nanny share that seemed as though it might work out, I got the same panicked feeling I'd gotten this morning when I was trying to walk out our front door: I'd look at Jack's little face, which seemed to plead *Don't leave me,* and my stomach would clench with fear. So I'd tell Adam never mind, I'll stay home with Jack a while longer, and Adam would look at me with blank despair because it was hard work, apparently, finding these nanny shares, and because he couldn't understand the private paradox that gripped me: Of course I wanted to get back to work, use my brain, earn the money our family desperately depended on. But every time I tried to act on that desire, my instincts said I shouldn't.

This was the heart of most of my recent fights with Adam, this private paradox that Dr. Goodman and I called the car-swerve feeling. Adam had a different name for it: my Jewish Mother Overdrive.

↔

"But this felt so real," I said to Dr. Goodman now. "Like I was actually in a place where . . . like it had really gone the other way during Jack's birth." That Jackless atmosphere. A pressing in, a pain from all directions. A place that had no Jack.

A place that so easily could have been *this* place. Even the delivering doctor had said it, commending me: Jack would have died if I hadn't insisted on the C-section. She had tried to talk me out of it. That doctor with her glossy hair so black it reflected back the overheads, a doctor I had never met before that moment. Sitting at the foot of my stirruped bed, in a room where night and day and time itself seemed to have no meaning—I'd later piece together this was twenty-seven hours into my labor—she ran through all the standard reasons why a vaginal delivery was preferable, especially this late in the game. As if I had never bothered to do this most basic research about the most important thing my body would ever be asked to do.

Adam had been against me, too, wanting me to listen to the doctor. *Nine centimeters dilated, you're almost there,* as if impatience were the issue. *You can do this,* as though I were simply losing willpower, but I'd known, I'd *known.* Something wasn't right with the child inside me. There had to be a reason his heart rate kept on flatlining whenever I went through a long contraction. And to me, this didn't seem to bode well for the python squeeze of the main event. It wasn't like me to insist. But it also wasn't like me to be giving birth in the first place.

I insisted. I was right. And this had saved him. Those first ten minutes of Jack's life when they couldn't start him breathing, when the CPR wasn't working because they hadn't yet discovered the plug of mucus inside his tiny airway—it was the reserve of oxygen in his cord blood that got him through unharmed. If I had listened to the doctor, Jack would have gone through that reserve while I was pushing and then been starved of oxygen. He would not have been OK.

That thin membrane separating the awful way things could have gone from the way things actually went—that thin membrane was *me*. My instincts had saved him. So how could I ignore them now? This was what Dr. Goodman and I had so far figured out in our time together: The experience of Jack's birth was making it hard for me to know when my maternal instincts were a matter of life and death, and when they were just me being a nervous first-time parent.

I watched Jack's cow-faced lovey slip from his fingers. It slid down Dr. Goodman's pencil skirt and became a nubbly puddle on the pointy toe of one of her stiletto pumps. Dr. Goodman dressed like no one else in Berkeley. It was one of the things that made me trust her. She wasn't afraid to go against the grain. I reached to pick up Jack's lovey.

"Yes, but think about what you're describing," Dr. Goodman said, accepting the filthy square of fabric from my outstretched hand. "You were caught in a moment of terrible indecision. Do you lug him up the stairs, making a simple task into an ordeal, or do you quickly pop upstairs without him, allowing yourself freedom of movement but leaving him briefly unprotected? The moment posed a question that you find hard to bear: Just how powerful is your constant loving presence? Perhaps your mind supplied an answer, telling you that if you remove yourself even for a moment, he'll disappear."

"Are you saying that I scared myself on purpose? That I conjured all that as a fantasy to scare myself? I don't think so."

Dr. Goodman gave me one of her cold smiles. "Surely not consciously, no. But your brain is unusually good at finding ways to scare people. It's your job to be good at that. I wonder if just now your brain is working hard to scare an audience of one. What do you think? Does that resonate?"

My books scared people, it was true. That was the point of them. My books scared so many people, we'd been able to buy a four-bedroom house in the Berkeley Hills. And it was true that I wrote them most of all to scare myself. Just another way of dealing with a world that couldn't in any way be trusted. If you've already imagined her fangs and claws down to every bump and discoloration, then at least the beast in the closet can't surprise you.

I checked my phone again. No Adam.

"But why would I want to scare myself like that?" I asked.

Dr. Goodman nodded. "Now that's the question, isn't it?"

I closed my eyes. "I'm trying to remember what I was feeling just before Jack seemed to disappear."

I thought back. I did remember: I was feeling that Adam was right, that something was wrong with me. Whatever you wanted to call it, Jewish Mother Overdrive, the car-swerve feeling, adjustment disorder with postpartum onset, something was wrong with me, and if it was true that I was the membrane separating Jack from the terrible way things could have gone, all the many terrible ways that they still could, then Jack was fucked. So what was I feeling right beforehand? Panic.

And afterward, after I thought I'd lost him and then found him, a grateful calm had settled over me. I didn't usually love to nurse, but in Dr. Goodman's waiting room just now, while I was nursing Jack, I'd felt such an exquisite peace, not unlike the one that settled over me at the end of a scary book or movie, when the zombies have all been vanquished, the serial killer locked away. Briefly, all the terrifying aspects of the world have been concentrated down into one threat, and that threat has been soundly dealt with.

It was possible that Dr. Goodman was onto something.

"But this went on for minutes," I said. "It felt real. This wasn't my imagination run amok."

"It *was* real," Dr. Goodman said. "It happened. You were on the wrong floor, you couldn't find your son, and all that panic was very, very real. I'm not implying that you just 'made this up' the way a child imagines monsters under her bed. I'm suggesting that this was the car-swerve feeling but experienced with a visceral new terror, experienced *as and through* a visceral terror, maybe a full-blown panic attack. The car-swerve feeling as experienced through a panic attack. What do you think? Does it fit?"

"Can a panic attack feel like that?" I'd never had a panic attack before, but I had the impression that a panic attack felt like a heart attack. This felt nothing like a heart attack. "This didn't feel normal."

I flinched at my choice of words. *Not normal*: These days, the most damning assessment Adam could level at any person, thing, or situation. Among the things Adam deemed not normal: that Jack did not yet nap in accordance with the schedule Adam had drawn up for me to follow after reading a multitude of books on baby sleep; that Jack was not consistently sleeping through the night despite Adam's religious efforts at sleep training; that Jack still loved to breastfeed at eight months, did it for pleasure and comfort as much as for food, and refused to take a bottle. That Jack tolerated bathing only if we put his inflatable ducky tub in the middle of the kitchen floor. I sometimes had to bite my tongue to keep from asking where Adam's master list of normalcy was culled from. Was he tracking where all the world's babies took their baths? Adam seemed to regard Jack as a project that could be done correctly, a view I did not share, and so the broadest category that Adam deemed not normal was my every instinct as a mother.

"Shortness of breath. Tight chest. Tingly fingers. Derealization. As you've described it, I'd say yes, this sounds consistent with a panic attack."

"So you're saying this wasn't a—that I didn't just have a break with reality?"

"I wouldn't say that exactly. What I'd say instead is that this panic attack had marked dissociative features, not unlike a flashback. A panic attack in which your unconscious played fast and loose with what your conscious mind wouldn't allow."

"No way. There is no part of me that wishes I didn't have Jack."

Dr. Goodman arched a narrow eyebrow. "Is that what you heard me say?"

I must have looked annoyed, because Dr. Goodman bestowed on me one of her rare playful smiles and said, "Terrifying new therapist wants to know why you chose that chair."

I laughed. "Terrifying New Therapist Wants to Know Why You Chose That Chair" was a headline from *The Onion* that popped into my head whenever Dr. Goodman asked a certain sort of question, a question like "Is that what you heard me say?" I was surprised both that she remembered my once telling her about this, and also that I was laughing, given what had just happened in the stairway. I often laughed with Dr. Goodman; it was one more thing that made me trust her, and the fact that I was laughing now was reassuring because it made me feel more like myself, a person who used to laugh easily, even at the darkest aspects of life. Especially at the darkest aspects.

Feeling brave, I said, "It seems like you're not really considering that this could have been a full-on hallucination. That maybe I just had my first psychotic break, right here in your stairwell, and that I need immediate medical attention."

"I was wondering when you'd bring your mother up."

"Who said anything about my mother?"

"Well, were you just thinking about your mother?"

"Yeah, of course, I was thinking about my mother."

Dr. Goodman sat back, satisfied. Jack's head drooped down onto his chest. He'd fallen asleep against her.

"I wonder if you're scared of history repeating itself." She lowered her voice as Jack let out a sigh and sleepy shudder. "And that's affecting how you're interpreting what just happened. I'm not saying it was nothing. It was something. A doozy of a something from the sound of it. But one thing I can say with certainty is that you're not in the grip of psychosis."

I mulled this over, trying to decide if I was in fact afraid of history repeating itself. I was, I decided, but not in the way she meant it. I wasn't afraid of losing my mind, the way my mother had when I was a baby. But I wanted Jack to feel the world was safe and trustworthy and to have absolutely no aptitude for writing scary novels.

I had only one photograph of my mother. A fresh-faced laughing woman, holding a fat-cheeked baby, eyes flirting with my father behind the camera. One day she was that, and then she was the husk I'd met three times over my childhood before she disappeared for good.

"What makes you so sure I didn't just have a psychotic episode?"

"A hallucination that encompasses every sense modality? Reality testing otherwise intact? That's not how psychosis works. I think you're having one hell of a day. One hell of an eight-month stretch, actually, but now today, on top of everything, you've gotten this devastating wallop about your marriage."

I snorted, and Dr. Goodman leveled a look at me.

Tucking my legs the other way beneath me, I slid my eyes away from her and said, "No, yes, of course I'm devastated. But I don't think— Look, I'm furious at Adam. Because fuck him. But I'm even more furious at myself because, I mean, a man who at age forty still believes his childhood was perfect? Raised by a single mother since he was five, saw his father three or four times a year, at best, and his childhood was *perfect*. And I've told you about his sister, right? Nothing tees you up for three stints in rehab quite like a perfect childhood, but he insists, *insists,* that hers was idyllic, too, that it's something purely chemical in her brain. I should have seen this coming. I should have seen him coming."

Dr. Goodman had a piece of art in her office that I found immensely beautiful and comforting. It was at odds with the aesthetic of the office as a whole, which was also the aesthetic of Dr. Goodman's person—spare, modern, elegant, like the kind of upscale restaurant where you can never hear what anyone is saying. Bare wood floors, bare large-paned windows, furniture dominated by sharp angles, black brushed metal. There wasn't a throw pillow in sight. Even the book spines looked untouchable. There was the Womb Chair, softly curving, but I was pretty sure that was a joke meant to be appreciated by no one but Dr. Goodman.

The piece of art at odds with all this hung in the very center of Dr. Goodman's generous bay window. It was a large shimmering yellow orb, about the size and shape of a grown man's fist, that bounced and shivered as though alive, and shot off light. It was probably made of thousands of tiny beads, maybe amber. But what it looked made of, to me, was what would happen if you scooped a hand into the midday sun and discovered it to be the consistency of raw egg.

Actually, what it looked like was naked DNA. Adam had showed me naked DNA once, his face held motionless as he pulled the congealed nucleic acids out of an ethanol solution bubbling in a small metal pot.

I am not a spiritual person, but I had been moved in what I considered a spiritual way to see those yellowish, whitish, semitranslucent strands of DNA bouncing and glistening like an eggy glob of sunlight. We had just decided to start trying to get pregnant. Adam had been working on convincing me for years, but given my own experience of being parented, I hadn't been too keen. My mother's descent into madness and eventual disappearance, my father's depressed, distracted nonpresence, more a placeholder in a cardigan than an actual caregiver—this was not a legacy to build on. Agreeing to get married had been hard enough for me, given my passionate attachment to self-sufficiency.

But then, one Friday night a little over a year ago, we were making love. Not even really making love, just having sex, and only because we'd run out of the show we'd been bingeing. But the light of a full moon was spilling over us through the windows, and I could see Adam's face clearly, just inches away, such a kind face, such a loving face, a loving man, a man who loved *me,* and I got that feeling I sometimes got, as though we had dissolved into each other, as though we'd lost our borders. I'd had this feeling many times before, oxytocin scrambling my brain, the emotional equivalent of an optical illusion. But this time I had the feeling and it felt true. Something in me shifted: I wanted to make a baby. I trusted Adam. I trusted the world enough to do this. The epiphany lasted exactly eight hours. By breakfast, I was already wavering, trying to walk back what I'd promised in the night. Saying, look, I've got a book coming out in November so maybe let's start trying in the new year.

Adam didn't argue; he didn't point out that I was thirty-six and he was thirty-nine and time was not our friend here. Instead, he brought me to the science lab at the high school where he taught biology, chemistry, and AP physics. Somehow, he had known that this would work. Adam pulled DNA from that small pot, the eggy gorgeous holy purity of it, and I knew I wanted a child. Thinking *this*: This is what we're made of. Bouncing, glistening blobs of purity. I'd always thought the deepest truth was that we're on our own, but these coiled strands said otherwise: Two people twisted together, forever, to make a third. It wasn't rational at all—what did the shape or consistency of DNA have to do with existential truths? But somehow this loopy thought was an overwhelming joy, an expansive movement that felt like the purest distillation of what it felt like to love and be loved by Adam. A man who could meet my wavering with an act of such strangeness and kindness, of bizarre rightness.

An unremarkable little pot like you might use to heat spaghetti sauce, but out of it came—life. The kind of life I'd never considered possible before Adam. The kind of life he convinced me it was safe to want. A husband. A child. This child. Jack.

I glanced down at my phone again. No calls.

Hannah, I wish I could, but I just can't do it. You're not the Hannah I know. I miss her. But I was the Hannah he knew, the Hannah who had taken care of herself since she was old enough to tie her own shoes because she had no other choice. And now I was on my own again, and this time with an infant.

The DNA had lied to me, Adam had lied to me, I could depend on no one. But Jack, at least, could depend on me. That part I could make true.

Dr. Goodman was in the middle of explaining what to do if I felt another panic attack come on. I was concerned that I'd missed most of what she'd said, but the advice seemed pretty intuitive from the bits I'd managed to catch: Remind yourself it's a panic attack, close your eyes to block out overwhelming stimuli, use the tricks we've already been working on, the breathing, the muscle relaxation.

She had started writing, leaning with her right arm over a slab of reclaimed wood, while her left arm still supported my sleeping son. She handed over a prescription slip, but all it said was *Deep breathing, muscle relaxation, remember it's a panic attack, block out stimuli.* As our fingers met, Jack stirred. Dr. Goodman went on speaking.

"I'd also like to see you again before next week to monitor how you're doing. You can schedule a quick check-in appointment through my website. And, Hannah?" Jack's eyes popped open. He was opening and closing his mouth in a way that meant he was getting ready to start a scream. I began to reach for him, but then he burped and went back to looking contented. "Get some sleep. Please. Averaging four hours a night is not enough. I'm going to call in that prescription for lorazepam again. Fill it this time. I know you don't feel ready to wean, but you really don't need to with this medication. And if you still want to be extra safe about it? Sometimes the decision to wean gets made for us. The CVS on Telegraph?"

I nodded.

She said, "Try the deep breathing and muscle relaxation, get some sleep, and there's no reason to think an episode like this is going to happen again."

We sat in silence for a moment. Jack was staring at my face, but not with any expectation or request. He seemed to find it interesting to have this view of me.

"Someone's coming to drive you home?" she finally asked. "After a scare like that, I wouldn't recommend you drive yourself."

I leaned back, closed my eyes. I felt so tired I might have fallen asleep right then and there, and also so wired I wasn't sure I'd ever sleep again.

I opened my eyes and the room went wobbly for a minute, bathed in a burst of morning light. Then the sun passed back behind a cloud, the room went slightly dimmer, and Dr. Goodman came into focus. A fifty-year-old woman, unflappably secure in her own opinions and techniques, unwaveringly honest, often brutal in her assessments.

The car-swerve feeling as experienced through a panic attack. It made sense.

I leaned forward in my seat.

"Adam," I lied, and accepted Jack's sweet bulk from Dr. Goodman.

Chapter Four

Yes, it was a calculated risk to drive with Jack just now, when it wasn't outside the realm of possibility that I'd have another episode like I'd had in Dr. Goodman's stairwell. But what aspect of caring for young children wasn't a calculated risk? You continued to breastfeed while taking the lorazepam your shrink kept pushing on you for sleep because the studies, so far, indicated no adverse effects. You decided not to return the bottle of baby shampoo with the protective seal half removed because it really did seem as though the foil might have torn when you twisted off the cap. You fed your child solid food instead of keeping him forever on purees and juices like you secretly wished you could in order to remove all chance of choking. And there was no way I was going to call Adam a fifth time.

So up up up into the hills I drove now, winding with the switchback roads. The glittering bay, slashed by the elegant swoop of the two great bridges, one orange, one gray, spread out before me, then receded beyond the redwoods and eucalyptus.

I was halfway home when I realized I'd forgotten to pick

up the prescription for lorazepam Dr. Goodman had called in. I swerved into a U-turn, making a split-second decision based on naps, feedings, the regimented pockets of Jack's days—who knew when I might have another chance. The U-turn wasn't smooth, and in the rearview I watched Jack's little body thud against his car seat. His head hit the plastic side. I gasped, and as I evened out the steering, I tried to get a better look at him in the second mirror trained on him from the back seat. He wasn't crying. Why wasn't he crying? He looked stunned. His lower lip trembled. He met my eyes in the double mirrors. The way he looked at me. As though to ask: *I'll trust this if you say so, but are you really sure?*

I was not sure.

But we made it without another incident to the CVS on Telegraph.

Inside, while we were waiting for the prescription to be filled, there was a commotion in the "As seen on TV" aisle. Three cops pleading with an adolescent boy not to take his clothes off. He was slight, every inch of visible skin covered in grime, dressed in reasonably clean baggy jeans and a blue windbreaker that looked like they belonged to someone larger. His light hair was shorn down to the scalp; the scalp itself was bloodied in several places. He had a beatific smile on his face and seemed unaware of the two men and one woman talking to him, tentatively touching him. He was in communion with someone or something else. From the looks of it, the cat and dog on the package of a Paw Perfect electronic pet manicure device.

I turned back to the pharmacy, where the one tech on shift was speaking into the phone and frowning at her computer screen. She noticed me and held up an apologetic finger. I smiled, nodded, and continued bouncing to the tune of "The Teddy Bears' Picnic," which I was intoning softly into the velvet whorl of Jack's ear as though offering up a prayer to an angry god. Jack was fussing. He did not like being worn front-facing in the carrier. But I was feeling an aversion to the stroller after what had happened in the stairwell.

"Come on now, come on, let's find you a better spot," the female cop was saying. Her voice was deep. I suspected it wasn't her real speaking voice. It sounded too much like a male cop on TV. I looked away.

What were you meant to tell children about why some people lived on the streets? Were you meant to normalize it, sterilize it, or were you meant to keep it as strange for them as it ought to be for you? A society that takes so little care of its most vulnerable that human beings become like litter, something to step over, route around.

The pharmacy tech was waving me over to the window.

"I'm so sorry. Your doctor did call in the prescription like you said, but it somehow only just came through the system. It should be another twenty minutes for us to fill it. Can you wait?"

Jack released an extended shriek in answer. If this were a movie, the windows would have shattered. It was that kind of shriek.

"I think I can't," I said.

"Want me to ring those up at least?" the tech offered bravely, gesturing to my basket. I had never liked a person more than I liked this woman in this moment.

I tossed the items onto the counter. Baby shampoo, wipes, salt and vinegar potato chips; Adam could be subtly disapproving when I ate junk food, so my buying the chips, knowing I could eat them unjudged, was meant as an act of defiance, but in fact felt depressing. Jack went on shrieking. I barely managed to withstand the fifteen seconds before I could grab my items back and flee. People from every corner of the store were looking at us in concern and irritation. Whereas what was still going down in the "As seen on TV" aisle—*that* everyone was studiously ignoring. Was this the societal function of hating on mothers? To distract us from the fact that there was no one who could save us, no omnipotent mommy, only flawed systems and brutal chance?

I had somehow also ended up buying a Plen T Pak of Juicy Fruit.

In the car, I stuck one piece of gum after another into my mouth in quick succession as Jack tipped over into full meltdown mode behind me. I resisted the urge to look at his unhappy face in the rearview mirror. The initial burst of sweet from the gum sent a pleasant, gentle tingling all through my body. But it was gone so quickly.

I started the car, and this immediately lulled Jack into reverie. He hiccupped himself into silence, then began sucking the knuckles of his right hand. I took the opportunity to stick another piece of gum into my mouth. Near the store's entrance, the boy from the "As seen on TV" aisle was trying to shake himself loose from the three cops and why not, he'd done what they'd asked, he was out of the store now.

I felt voyeuristic for watching and apathetic for looking away. What if this were Jack? Would I want someone to watch or look away?

I clenched my jaw against a thought I felt approaching—an indifferent, merciless world; my son within it—and successfully deflected it. My reward: a burst of sweet from the fresh stick of gum now softening between my teeth.

As I backed out of the space, I heard a rap against the passenger-side window. I jumped, afraid I'd hit something, or, worse, someone, and saw instead the face of the boy from the "As seen on TV" aisle peering in at me.

He was a girl. A woman, actually. Not young.

My heart clenched like it always did. Every woman living on the street did this to me, for as long as I could remember, but specifically it must have been since I was six years old. That was when my mother went missing from the home where she had lived. The women didn't have to look anything like her for my heart to clench. Not that I knew what my mother looked like, really. I'd seen her only three times, but I did have that one photograph from before, of her holding me, grinning at my father behind the camera. She'd had a wide-mouthed smile, intelligent eyes with a naughty twinkle. She looked like someone I would get on well with.

I rolled down the window. The rush of air felt good.

"Did you need something?" I asked.

"You're doing so well with him." The smile the woman gave me was a jolt; open and kind and tinged with concern before it returned itself to a blank expression. Like she'd flashed her soul at me by accident. "Are you feeling the vibrations?"

"The vibrations?"

It was embarrassing to admit how good it felt to hear that someone thought I was doing well with Jack. Maybe especially this woman, who could have been my mother.

"Can you feel them?"

"I'm sorry, I don't think that I can."

She met this news with a look of such grave concern that I wished I had lied.

"You need to try. You'll be able to feel them once you open yourself up to their existence. That's when you'll hear the music. Do it now, don't wait. Please, don't wait."

"I won't. Thank you. I promise I won't wait."

She flashed her wonderful smile at me again, and I smiled back and handed her a twenty, which she didn't reach to take. She was still staring in at me and didn't seem to have any immediate plans for disengagement. But Jack was losing patience with his knuckles and making a face that I knew to be a prelude to a shriek, and so, apologizing, I raised the window, sealing us off again, and drove toward home.

↔

Our house was lower than the road, clinging to the hillside. Until you turned into the driveway, all you could see of it was the sprawling gables of the rooftop. I loved this house. I still had no idea if it was the smartest place to put the windfall from the movie they'd made of my second book, *The Cinders*, as several people had advised. My brain always turned itself to standby mode when people used words like "investment" and "annuity." But it seemed to me delicious irony that you could get five thousand square feet of light-filled home from a story about a serial-killing Cinderella who ultimately burns her kingdom to the ground.

Adam had been against our buying so much house. Big and showy was very much against the spirit of Adam. It was against the spirit of me, too, but not, it turned out, when it came to houses. This house, which we'd bought two months into my pregnancy, had seemed to me the embodiment of all that Adam had persuaded me to hope for: family, permanence, stability. Fantastical concepts given my experience in life before him, so it was reassuring to think these notions were real enough they could be rendered in wood, glass, and stucco.

It turned out, of course, they couldn't. Adam that morning: *I hope you don't think this means that I don't love you as much as I ever did.*

I made the turn, which was more a dip, into the driveway and caught sight of two hikers. It was an older couple. An Asian man with a chin-strap beard and a tall white woman with a profusion of frizzy hair, both dressed in birding beige, with identical Tilley hats and binoculars. I'd seen these two before. This must have been a favored trail for them. The woman always stared as though she thought I couldn't see her, which was a specialty of Berkeley residents of a certain age. It was possible she recognized me from my book jackets. Sometimes people did. People came up to me on the street occasionally, or at restaurants, and told me delightedly about the awful dreams I gave them. Every single time this happened it gave Adam a thrill. I actually had no idea how I felt about this kind of attention myself—probably mixed at best—because Adam's consistent thrill was so outsized and flattering that it commandeered my whole reaction. That expansive feeling of loving and being loved by Adam. His earnest generosity and sweetness. His sparkle and his charm. What had happened to that Adam? I hadn't seen him in many months and had no idea if he was gone for everyone or just for me.

I looked away from the birders into the rearview mirror, at the reflected image of the second mirror trained on Jack. He was asleep in his car seat, cow-faced rag held lovingly against his cheek. Amazing. I'd been sure that twenty-minute snooze in Dr. Goodman's office was going to count as his abysmal second nap. He never fell back asleep after a crap nap, never ever ever. This was unprecedented, a small gift from a terrible day.

I pulled the car up to the white stucco house with its wandering, vaguely Moroccan footprint, its blue-tiled entrance opened to the heavens, its succulent garden that, when not tended to, was capable of looking like a witch's curse, dense and high enough that, tucked behind it, we could sleep a hundred years unnoticed.

I put the car in park and let my head collapse against the steering wheel. My breath was coming ragged. The exhaustion of the morning was finally overtaking me. I could easily fall asleep right here with my head smashed against the steering wheel if I gave myself permission. For a second I considered it. But I also recognized that this was most appealing as a reason not to go inside. It had only been three hours since we'd driven off to Dr. Goodman's, leaving Adam in the house, but in that time it had assumed an abandoned look.

It was theoretically possible that Adam was still in there, grading some last few exams, making a banana and avocado smoothie and sticking it in the fridge as an afternoon treat for Jack. But, no, Adam had left me. Why would he be hanging around making smoothies? Smoothies would be a "Daddy's house" thing from now on; Daddy's house would be the site of all the wholesome parenting.

I couldn't tell whether I wanted him to be in there or was horrified that he might be. Both seemed equally repugnant options, and staying out here the only palatable choice. But I forced myself to open the car door, my body feeling heavy. My foot made a loud and grinding crunch against the gravel, but it didn't wake Jack from his nap. He slept through being lifted from the car seat, too, his body curled against me as I carried him toward the house. The weight of him helped to steady me. Maybe he would keep on sleeping. Maybe. Then I could sleep as well.

Silently, I padded across the shag-carpeted living room and down the two broad stairs into the kitchen. Adam was generally here or in the dining room if he was home, cooking, crafting lesson plans with books and papers and the makings of strange experiments spread across the table, or, lately, reading baby-sleep books and making me detailed three-nap-a-day game plans that I was constitutionally unable to execute.

He wasn't in the kitchen. But he'd done all the dishes before he left, which was exactly like him. Cleaned as well. The backsplash sparkled. The fridge gleamed. Sunshine streamed through a wall of freshly wiped down floor-to-ceiling windows, and because of the steep angle of the slope behind the house it looked as though the house were floating, as though Jack and I were in a soap bubble drifting off into the sky. Blown off by Adam, our filmy layer of protection about to pop. Adam, with his checklists and schedules and rigid ideas about what was normal and what was not, had made me doubt my every instinct as a mother. But I didn't know how to be a mother without him.

I headed toward another bank of stairs, the one that led up to the bedrooms. The house had been designed by someone very fond of stairs. There were six sets in total. When Adam and I first moved in we sometimes had to call to each other, laughing, not sure how to get from where we were to where we wanted to be.

In Jack's nursery, conveniently, the blackout curtains were still drawn and the white noise machine still running from last night. All I had to do was lay his sleeping body gently, gently, gently in his crib. My muscles twitched. I almost jolted him but didn't. The transfer was smooth and, miraculously, successful. I stood back and admired my handiwork, briefly, stupidly elated. Adam was a master of the crib transfer, but I'd never succeeded at one until now.

I drew the door closed with exquisite care, trying to avoid the smallest creak, and when that, too, was successful, I stood for several seconds outside the shut door hearing nothing but the pleasing whirr of the noise machine and enjoying my accomplishment. Thinking maybe I could do this.

But back down in the kitchen, I stood at the counter eating chocolate mousse cake directly from the tinfoil instead of doing any of the thousand things I should have taken the chance to do while Jack was sleeping. Adam had baked this cake for his own fortieth birthday last week along with a roast chicken and an heirloom tomato bread salad, a feat of time management that I'd regarded then as frankly heroic and now felt was slightly tragic. I was crying quietly as I ate it. The reality was settling deeper in: Adam had left me.

Adam, who laughed like a braying donkey and somehow looked sexy doing it. Adam, who the very first time I met him, invited into his AP classroom to speak about the physics I'd used in my strange, small, abysmally selling debut novel *Probability Lanes,* had introduced me to the audience—an audience of students so clearly bored by me before I'd said a single word, bored by the very concept of me, a boredom verging on outright hostility, that the only sane move on Adam's part would have been to disavow any responsibility for my presence, maybe even apologize and cancel the whole talk outright then and there—to that room, Adam had introduced me as his "favorite living writer." Not despite the anticipatory hostility but because of it. That was the kind of person Adam was.

I pressed the heels of my hands into my eyes. I made my mind a blank, and the crying stopped abruptly. These weren't the kind of feelings you could dip into during a baby's naps, when you had a few minutes to fall to pieces and then reconstruct yourself. These were the kind of feelings where if you tried to take a dip, before you knew it you were riptided out to sea.

My phone rang. I knew it was Adam before I pulled it out of my back pocket because his ringtone was "Bad to the Bone," which no longer seemed as funny as it had. I thought about not answering. I could just text something like *False alarm! We're home now,* and be done with it, pretend I'd never left that pitiful voicemail.

"Hannah." Adam's voice was extra gravelly, probably with worry and guilt, but what it sounded like was bored and sleepy.

Of all the things I loved about Adam, his voice on the phone was not one of them. He was forever reassuring people on the other end that they hadn't woken him. "I'm so sorry, I just got your message. Do you still need me to pick you up?"

"False alarm!" I said brightly, balling up the sweating tinfoil and walking it to the trash. "We're home now."

A long pause, filled with the particular clacking of Adam's keyboard. The space bar needed to be slammed since Jack spit up on it at two weeks old.

"OK, good." But he sounded annoyed. A hysterical voicemail for no reason: further proof that I was not the cool, collected woman he had married, not someone he could parent with productively. "What was the problem?"

I walked over to the wall of windows and stared down the slope with its tangled blueberry and towering pines. The sun was strong. It was almost midday. The eggy light falling over the backyard made me think again of Adam pulling DNA out of that ordinary pot, the gorgeous holy purity of those coiled strands. There was a part of me that wanted to tell him what had happened in the stairway, even though I knew he'd log it as further evidence that, of the two of us, only one was normal. The pre-Jack Adam wouldn't have done that. He didn't break the world down into normal or not normal. Yes, he enjoyed a spreadsheet and a kale salad, but he wasn't rigid. He was funny. He was playful. He didn't bridle at our differences, such as my preferring to work until three A.M. and sleep until eleven while he kept the hours of a frontiersman. He didn't disapprove of me back then for *not* worrying nearly as much as he did, about everything from our finances to climate change to my jogging after dark (he used to track my phone whenever I ran at night, which was both sweet and a little creepy) to whether every single guest had enjoyed themselves at a party.

The pre-Jack Adam would have heard about my panic attack and known exactly how to tame it into something I could tolerate about myself. I needed Adam. Who but Adam could get me through something as shattering as the loss of Adam?

I pressed my forehead against the cool glass of the window, bracing against the riptide of feelings that was coming for me now. What I needed was some space to feel, to think. To surrender to the current and then regain my footing. But Jack was awake. I could hear him crying.

And on the phone Adam was growing impatient. "Hannah? Hannah. Are you going to tell me what the matter was? I assume that Jack's OK?"

Jack wasn't fully screaming yet, but he was getting ready to go all in.

It was time to end the call and run upstairs, but I could feel my heartbeat in my armpits, and my tongue was weirdly large, so I started to count like Dr. Goodman had told me to at the sign of any panic. And then I staggered backward.

The wall, the windows, the slope were gone.

Chapter Five

Or, rather, I was.

I had been in my kitchen, staring out at my own backyard, and now I was somewhere else: up on the nearly vertical final incline of the Claremont Canyon, my favorite hiking trail. The whole of Berkeley, Oakland, Marin, and San Francisco spread out beneath me like a living map. I told myself that this wasn't actually happening, but it sure seemed like it was.

The ground on this stretch of the fire trail was treacherous: mud dried like continents formed in some primeval chaos and covered over in small, loose rocks, which were in the process now of sliding out from underneath me. I scrambled to get a purchase. But the harder I worked, cartwheeling my arms and bicycling my heels in an attempt to dig them in, the faster the small rocks were abandoning me. They made a hollow knocking as they tumbled. If I started really sliding, there was at least one hundred feet of sharp incline before the fire trail gentled out enough to stop a fall. I knew I was hallucinating. But that didn't make me any less afraid to lose my footing.

"Fall backwards, butt out!" came a familiar voice some ways behind me.

I flung myself backward, jutting my butt out like a shelf to catch me. It worked. I was sitting, stable. Moments later, Adam eased down beside me.

We were still a long way from the gentled grade, sitting in the middle of the fire trail, blocking foot traffic. My butt ached from the graceless landing, and all along my palms, blood was rising to the surface of small cuts. Now that I was no longer in danger of plummeting a hundred feet along a bed of jagged rocks, I was able to take in, as I hadn't before, the alarming sight of this favorite view of mine.

Something was terribly misfiring in my mind. And yet somehow it still felt almost good, sitting here with Adam. The late-morning sun was blazing, and even with my shaking hands made into a visor, his face was just a glare. But the easy feeling hanging in the space between us was strong enough to register against the deep, deep wrongness of every signal from my senses.

"You all right?" He was getting to his feet, taking it slowly given the grade. "We should probably clear the way."

Two people were approaching from the twisty path below.

I tried to move and found I couldn't. The moment of reprieve, bought by the pleasure of Adam's easy closeness, was spent. Now I was aware again that my heart was pounding, my tongue seemed extra large. Breath coming shallow. Pins and needles in my hands and feet. All part of the checklist of symptoms Dr. Goodman had rattled off that morning. *A panic attack, this is just a panic attack.* Inside my head I murmured the words the same way I said "You're OK" to a keening Jack. They sounded just as unconvincing.

"Hannahbelle." Adam's tone was unconcerned. "You coming?"

I couldn't get myself to stand. This was definitely more than a panic attack, no way around that. Panic attacks did not trick all your senses into telling you that you were somewhere you were most decidedly not. But even so the panic symptoms were getting worse. Chest tightening. Vision swimming.

And it was becoming impossible to ignore the pain, familiar from that morning, the Jacklessness pressing in from all directions. The Jacklessness was as palpable as the heat, as the sun beating down on my bare arms, on the dusty black skin of my yoga pants. And it hurt. It hurt all over.

"You two need a hand?"

The two hikers picking their way up the slope had nearly reached us. An Asian man with a chin-strap beard and a tall white woman with abundant frizzy hair. It was the man who had offered help. There was plenty of room on the trail to veer around us; he was asking out of kind concern. The woman was looking at me as though she recognized my face.

It occurred to me that I recognized them, too. Clad in birding beige, top-of-the-line Zeiss Victory binoculars swinging from slender, crepey necks, obligatory Tilley hats. It was the pair I'd seen just before turning in to our driveway. The Berkeley Birders of a Certain Age.

"Akio, don't bother these nice people," said the woman.

"You're not bothering us at all, but we're fine, thank you," Adam answered for us both with his good Canadian cheer. "We're sorry for the inconvenience."

"A rattler?" the man, Akio, asked. A strong Brooklyn accent.

"What's that?" asked Adam.

"A rattlesnake," Akio said. "Grace said your friend stumbled like something gave her a hell of a scare. We just figured a snake. It's a common way to lose your footing here."

"No," said Adam. "Just the good old-fashioned way."

Akio laughed.

"Let's go, old man," Grace sang playfully over her shoulder.

She was above us on the trail now. Akio shrugged at us and winked, then hustled to catch up to her.

"Thanks again," Adam called after them. "Enjoy the rest of your day!"

I looked up at my husband. The sun was finally off his face, and I could see his features in all their boyish glory. I was surprised by his expression. I'd been expecting the one I'd come to know so well over the past eight months, the one that said I was a problem he'd been asked to solve against his will. Instead, he was regarding me with simple curiosity, his face open and accepting of whatever quirk or whim or private crisis was keeping me stuck to this inconvenient spot. I'd forgotten he could look at me that way, with simple curiosity.

"Jack." I said our child's name out loud, and Adam's face, just a moment ago so open and accepting, shut tight against me. But not with disapproval. Not with impatient irritation.

He was crying.

So now I knew for certain what this hurt was. I'd named it just that morning in Dr. Goodman's office. But it was a different act to name it now, now that I was feeling it again. This hurt pressing in from every side—this hurt was grief. Real grief, not my knockoff, car-swerve version. And it had had time to settle in my muscles. In my bones. It had had time to settle into my vocal cords so that my voice sounded just slightly hoarser, just slightly harder than it should.

"But none of this is right," I said. "That isn't how it happened."

And now, like a pinprick from some other mind wrapped around mine, I saw it. Blue-smudged lips, a dangling arm, but the memory didn't stop there. In the sterile light, in the small delivery room, the nurse moves past me, and I see her tuck in my child's arm as she positions his tiny body over the sink. Because of the way she washes him, so carefully, I can almost believe there's been some terrible misunderstanding. Just as when she swaddles him and puts him in my arms, I can almost bring myself to believe his eyes will open. I look down at his perfect face and force myself to know the truth: He didn't make it.

Sitting in the middle of the fire trail, Adam crying quietly as he stood over me, I saw all this as a thing that I remembered. Imperfectly accessed, almost as though I were seeing the memory through thick fog, but still I saw it.

"I'm feeling that, too, today," Adam said. "Today is hard."

He would have been eight months today, I almost said back, but bit the words inside my mouth.

This was not my memory, this had never happened, and yet I could run it backward, too, in the other direction, before the nurse rushed past me. A man's voice saying *Call it, time of death four-thirteen* A.M., and the bustling neonatal teams, the voices of competent, confident people creeping toward alarm, all that frantic energy gone quiet. Nothing from something. I closed my mind against seeing any more.

Here it was: a way to reconcile that irreconcilable shard of memory, to make sense of the blue-smudged lips, that dangling arm. But this wasn't how it happened. My son had lived.

Adam was holding out his hand for me to pull myself to standing. I shrank back from it. Like Persephone eating the three pomegranate seeds that wedded her to death, I had the sense that if my skin touched his then I'd be stuck here. Inside this trick of my own mind. This false reality where it had gone the other way eight months ago. This Jackless horror.

Instead, I closed my eyes and put my head down on my knees, trying to do what Dr. Goodman had prescribed: Counting my breaths. Relaxing my muscles. Blocking out the sense impressions that threatened to spin me further into panic and keep me here for longer.

I yelped at the feel of a light touch on my shoulder. My eyes flew open in alarm, and I closed them again quickly, trying to shrug Adam off. But it seemed that Dr. Goodman's was the wrong approach. Her techniques weren't working. And intuitively I'd known they wouldn't. But there had to be some way to end this situation.

After all, my own mind was creating this. And I knew the worlds my mind created. Or rather, I knew the way my mind went about this task. It was the part of myself I knew the best, the part that wrote my books. I knew that if I were writing this experience in a book, I would give the protagonist some agency. There needed to be a way in and out, or it was just a series of events.

Then I was on my feet. Walking quickly down the slope, past the bench where we usually liked to stop to take a water break, past the long, brown treeless stretch we called the trudge. I could hear Adam crunching after me.

As I walked, I looked around me for some clue about the mechanism at play here, maybe a discrepancy like the sign— "We're working on it!"—that had been missing from the elevator that morning. But the sun was just exactly where it should be in the sky at eleven-thirty A.M. The dirt smelled of recent rain and, in fact, it had rained all last night, really gusting; these parched hills must have drunk it greedily.

Adam had caught up and fallen in step beside me. He slipped his rough, dry hand against mine, and I let him because his grip was steadying, both literally and metaphorically. And anyway whatever this was, it was no Greek myth; entangling our fingers wasn't going to entangle life and death.

But God, this scene was stubborn.

"Speaking of today being hard," Adam was saying. "Are you feeling up for tonight? I can go by myself. Or we can cancel. Stay in and watch TV and be sick with sorrow together. Your average Wednesday."

And here was my voice answering without my participation: "No, if I don't go eventually, they're going to think I hate them. And if I keep you from going, eventually they're going to start hating me. And anyway, I know you're looking forward to it."

Adam gave a smile that made me think of that one tuft of grass you sometimes see poking up out of a crack in a busy road, a sight that always filled me with equal parts hope (such remarkable perseverance!) and despair (such lousy chances). He *was* looking forward to whatever social occasion we had planned, probably dinner with Sundeen and Mary, or maybe with Joe and Ben, or maybe with all four of them. But, the smile seemed to ask, should he be looking forward to it? Was that allowed? I could see how the Jackless atmosphere weighed on him, too. It was an atmosphere we shared, an atmosphere for two. The way he moved. The way he spoke. Everything a little slower than it should be, even his sparkle.

"No one thinks you hate them," he said. "And no one could ever hate you." He raised our clasped hands to his mouth and kissed my knuckles. "It's against the laws of nature."

I felt one of my eyebrows rise without my say-so. I felt my mouth say, "Is that so, Mr. Bennett? Please tell me more about these laws of nature."

Who was having this conversation? It didn't feel like me. The words coming out of my mouth bore no relation to what I was feeling, to what I was thinking, to any intention I was aware of having formed.

Forming an intention, I kicked at a rock and sent a small avalanche cascading. I was able to do it, but it was hard. It took real concentration.

Our footsteps fell in sync, and an idea occurred to me. I could counter the lying memory trying to muscle itself into my mind—a newborn child dead in my arms—with one I knew was true. If I brought the actual and false in sync and coaxed my misfiring brain to see the difference, maybe I could end this.

I chose a memory at random, the first that floated to my mind: Jack yesterday at story time at the library. Fat little body sitting so alert on the bright-patterned rug that it made the other babies seem to be slacking on the job. When they sang the usual welcome song, each tiny person getting a verse to his or her own name, and they got to "Hel-loh-oh, Ja-ack," he'd done something I'd never seen before. Puffed his little chest out. Beaming. Swiveling his head around the room to look each of us in the face, as though to say *Me!* His fine curls achieving liftoff then falling gently each time he jerked to look at the next person. *Me! You're singing about me!*

"Do you think it'll ever just feel normal?" Adam asked. "To have fun, to live our lives? Will it always feel like on some level we're betraying him?"

"Dr. Goodman swears it will," someone said using my mouth. "And that when it does that'll feel like its own loss. Sometimes I believe her."

"It's hard to imagine it. Can you imagine it?"

I focused again on my true memory. Jack at story time. Delighted to his tiny core that he was a person in the world, a person with a name. His gummy smile. Six teeth, oddly spaced, that seemed to stand at bright attention when he grinned, each one proud to do its part.

It was working. This memory was having some effect. I could feel a kind of movement, a kind of wobbling in the corner of my vision, as though if I just looked over my shoulder fast enough, I'd see my kitchen.

But I could also feel that Adam was watching me, and despite myself I turned to him. I shouldn't have. With his eyes like that, big, wet, and frightened at the largeness of his feelings, he looked so much like Jack.

It was hard to turn away from Adam. Cruel to not be with him in his grief, even if my own mind had created both it and him.

But I did turn away, focusing my mind entirely on Jack, my Jack, a child who hadn't died in birth. A child who just this second was probably screaming bloody murder in his crib. There was a distinctive splotch of red that spread across his neck whenever he was screaming, the shape of it uncannily like a squid. I zeroed in on picturing this squid mark.

"Ow," Adam said, and I realized I was squeezing his hand too tightly as I tried to home in on Jack's squid mark in my mind. The strange wobble in my peripheral vision really did seem to become more pronounced the more vividly I pictured Jack going apeshit in his crib. His little face imploring: *Where are you? I'm alone.* I let go of Adam's hand. I focused. Jack upstairs. Jack starting to believe that I'd abandoned him. *I'm so alone.*

"Adam, something weird is happening," I heard that voice, not quite my own, not under my control, say. "I don't know how to describe it, it's almost like someone else is in my—"

Then I was back, standing at the kitchen counter, heirloom tomatoes bright as jewels in a bamboo basket, the sun beating down through the wall of windows. The phone was still pressed to my ear, and Jack was really letting loose upstairs. He sounded like a demon in the last throes of an exorcism.

"Hannah? You there?" Adam's voice sounded annoyed, impatient, worn down by trying to solve this problem that was me.

"I'm sorry, I've gotta go," I said, and hung up.

Chapter Six

Outside Jack's nursery, I fumbled with the doorknob.

Part of me was braced to find his crib empty. The whole room empty. No crib, no changing table, no diaper pail. Just his disembodied scream filling the space.

But inside the nursery, everything was exactly as it should be. It took my eyes a second to adjust, but already I could smell the bready scent of him. My gratitude felt like a kind of hunger, and I stumbled through the strange separate space that Adam said the baby-sleep books all insisted on, like the holy of holies in an ancient temple, the air alive with the whooshing of a white noise machine, the only light the green dot on the monitor. The climate held to a perfect 68 degrees.

Jack was sitting up in the criminally expensive crib I'd splurged on in a fit of consumerist anxiety. He had moved from shrieking to silently heaving with sobs. The second that he noticed me, he stopped. Smiled like *Oh, hi.*

"Oh, hi!" I said, and swooped him up, pulled open the blackout curtains to let in light, fell into the royal blue glider, put him to my breast.

He latched expertly. I disliked his staccato letdown sucks, a tickly sort of painful, but as soon as my milk released and he began to drink, I experienced the same relief I'd felt that morning in Dr. Goodman's waiting room.

Three minutes. That's how long the whole strange episode in the kitchen had lasted according to the clock on the oven. Three minutes during which I'd imagined that I was up on the Claremont fire trail; it seemed to me quite obvious, if I was being reasonable, that what had happened was that I had fallen asleep. Fallen asleep on my feet and had a terrible dream inspired by the panic attack I'd suffered in Dr. Goodman's stairwell. Or maybe what had happened in the stairwell had been a kind of waking dream as well, delirium caused by chronic lack of sleep. This one, though, was clear as anything— a nightmare grotesquerie of wish fulfillment: keeping Adam, losing Jack.

A thin white trickle dribbled from the corner of Jack's mouth. I used a finger to catch the drip before it headed toward his neck folds, where milk was always catching. He often smelled disturbingly of brie. He was staring up at me through his thick black lashes. He was perfectly contented. He was perfectly safe. He was perfect.

Perfect, fine, safe. The problem was entirely within me.

And the problem was I needed sleep. How long had Dr. Goodman been trying to hammer this point home? That I had to, *had to,* get more sleep than I was getting. The reason I didn't sleep much was, first of all, that Jack still wasn't sleeping through the night. Sleep training had never fully taken. But more than that, it was because some part of me was always listening over the monitor for his breathing. Even deep in sleep I was apparently listening, because I woke most nights fully alert, aware that his breathing sounded somehow different— louder, quieter, snuffling, absent. It didn't matter how many times this had happened before, or that each time I went to check on him he was fine, his tiny rib cage rising and falling evenly. Once the fear that he'd stopped breathing got ahold of me, I was in the grip of the jarring memory—blue-smudged lips, a dangling arm. Sometimes I got lucky and didn't fall prey to this cycle until three or four A.M. Other times it was closer to midnight. On really bad nights, I was asleep less than an hour before it happened. Those nights stretched like a fairy-tale curse, a hundred years until the dawn. But no matter what time of night it began, things unraveled in the same way.

I'd lie in bed next to Adam, fighting with myself not to wake him, doing my breathing exercises and progressive muscle relaxation, staring up at the slanted eaves of our bedroom, knowing what I'd seen during Jack's birth and knowing why I couldn't have seen it. Knowing both simultaneously.

Jack was feeding lustily. He always fed like this, with gusto. I watched him work, finding it reassuring after the awful image my brain had presented to me in the kitchen. That perfect still face lying in my arms, I hoped I could forget it.

If I was being honest, I usually didn't love to nurse, and part of me wondered why I still did it now that Jack was eating solids. It was like he was devouring me. As though there might be nothing left of me if he ever had his fill.

I'd confessed this to Adam when Jack was just a few weeks old, back when the feedings were never-ending and my nipples were always bleeding. That was why he'd gotten so hung up on trying to get Jack to take a bottle. To relieve me. But breast-feeding relieved me, too. It was at once a hateful devouring and a tremendous relief.

My phone lit up with Adam's face. I answered it reluctantly.

"Hannah, what is going on? Seriously."

"I'm tired, that's all. It's been a stressful day. I'm spent. In fact, I think I need to take a nap to keep on functioning."

"OK. I can come over."

I hadn't been expecting this. Or maybe I had. Maybe I had said it just to see whether he'd offer, but now that he had, I didn't think I'd like him here. His being here might make it hard for me to sleep. I'd be overwhelmed with feelings, and that wouldn't be restful.

"No. You can't just leave in the middle of a school day."

"It's lunch period. And then I'm giving an exam in tenth-grade chem. I can get someone else to hand it out and collect it. I bet Sundeen can do it."

"I can easily call someone else."

"Who?"

I mentally ticked through the candidates, none too promising. My friends worked during business hours or lived far away or had small children of their own to tend to or were not the sort of people any responsible parent would leave in charge of an infant. Also, I had confessed to none of them that I was anything but blissful in motherhood. I didn't want to have to explain to them even a small piece of what was happening before I had a beat to make sense of it myself.

Adam's mother lived in Ottawa. Timing alone ruled her out as an option, although I likely wouldn't have asked her even if she'd lived close. She was a nice enough woman. Aggressively conventional, which made perfect sense when you considered that she'd raised two small children on her own after her husband left her for another woman, and managed to cling to middle-class respectability despite having only a high school education. Her white-picket-fence conventionality was an accomplishment, no doubt about it. Which was why, before I'd had Jack, I'd grudgingly accepted her suspicious questions about why I chose *that* brand of ketchup and how I wrote *those* books. But now, in her disdain for anything unfamiliar, I heard the ancestral root of Adam's "not normal." The result was not that I liked her less. I didn't. But rather that, whenever

I spoke to her, I worried I didn't actually know my husband. This, it seemed, had turned out to be true.

My father was dead, five years ago now. As a babysitter, that might not even have been his most damning feature. When I was eight, he had planned to go to a weeklong conference in Croatia, leaving me home alone since this was during the school year. I had to be the one to tell him that this was actually against the law, and for good reason, because it was really quite unsafe. He'd been grateful for the information. He was a kind and gentle man and had a strong abstract desire to keep me alive and happy, but it was very hard for him to act on this desire in any concrete way, owing to his being both mind-bendingly impractical and locked in the profoundest grief over my mother.

I was just considering the possibility of asking one of the women from my mothers group—they wouldn't be surprised to hear I needed help, at least—when Adam said, "You know I wouldn't offer if I didn't want to. I'm happy to do it, truly. I was literally just sitting here missing him, so you'd be doing me a favor."

I closed my eyes, counted to ten. Good lord, I was exhausted. I was so exhausted I almost fell asleep trying to think of a good reason to refuse.

"OK," I said. "Come over."

↔

When Adam walked in twenty minutes later, I had Jack down in the living room in front of the fireplace. Jack liked to pull himself to standing using the bricks as handholds. He'd mastered this skill over a week ago, but still every time he did it, he regarded it as a triumph. Little face beaming. Chest puffed out. One wayward curl standing straight up from the left side of his forehead and doing its own chuffed swagger.

"We'll show Daddy!" I said, when I heard the scratch of Adam's key, but once Adam's face appeared, I felt defeated by the sight of him. His skin looked very white, almost glowing. Probably pasty from guilt and unease, but the blanched look suited his boyish prettiness. He'd always had a Snow White thing going on, black hair, pale skin, blue eyes. Which made me, I used to joke, all seven dwarves rolled into one, a small-statured provider of charmed real estate. Except I was also the one with the terrifying mother, so maybe I was Snow White, and he was Prince Charming. Or maybe he wasn't in this story at all.

"Thanks for coming," I mumbled, pushing myself up to standing. I winced. The shag of the carpet stung my palms as though the skin were covered with fresh cuts. I turned my hands up for inspection, surprised. The flesh was unmarred. Why did they hurt so much?

"I need to be back by two," Adam said, coming around the couch to get Jack.

They were wearing almost the exact same outfit, jeans and flannel, except Adam's jeans were a darker denim. Adam scooped Jack up and swung him high above his head. Both of them were laughing.

I averted my gaze as though this were the climactic scene in *Raiders of the Lost Ark,* when they finally open the sacred chest, and I was in danger of melted eyeballs.

On the way upstairs, I had to lean against the wall just to keep from slumping over and wasting my nap here on the steps.

This level of exhaustion erased any last lingering doubt about what had happened in the kitchen. My chronic lack of sleep had reached a tipping point. But my hamstring was throbbing for some reason. And my hands still stung as though they were scored with cuts. I turned them up again, but, no, there really was no sign of any damage. Strange, and it bothered me a little because hadn't I strained my hamstring and scratched my palms during that nightmare, when I'd fallen backward on the fire trail? But I'd also face-planted on the concrete in the stairwell of Dr. Goodman's office, and that was surely when I'd hurt myself.

I fell into bed and pulled the covers over me, already knowing that this would be a delicious sleep. The kind you can't resist and take great pleasure in not resisting. Like first-trimester sleep.

When I woke, the room was brambly with shadows and my dinky digital clock-radio read 1:47 P.M. I could hear Adam singing "Five little ducks went out to play." He was getting the words wrong, sweetly. Over the *dell* and far away. Adam was so unrelentingly competent a human being that it was touching when he made mistakes.

I stared up at the slanted eaves and felt a swell of love for Adam. I had to close my eyes to protect the feeling. I pictured him downstairs with Jack, nurturing him, adoring him. No matter what happened between Adam and me, that was always going to be true. The loss of Adam was terrible for me, but it didn't make Jack less safe.

And as for the other problem, my wayward brain, sleep really did seem to have restored me. In fact, I felt downright vigorous. Like I could run a marathon and write for eight hours straight and then turn with perfect, calm attunement toward my child.

I had to hand it to Dr. Goodman on this score. I should have been prioritizing sleep all along. Napping when Jack napped. Filling that prescription for lorazepam. I had been underslept for so long I'd forgotten what it was like not to be exhausted. How it could feel almost like a kind of superpower. And this was just from a two-hour nap!

I decided I would harness this new vigor and ride it through the rest of the day with Jack, make sure we had fun in blatant defiance of the badness of this morning. I popped into the bathroom to splash water on my face and moved some pieces of hair around in an effort to make myself look presentable, but that was a lost cause. I had creases in my cheek from the pillowcase and bags under my eyes it would take a lot more than a two-hour nap to send packing. If anything was going to make Adam feel like an asshole for cutting and running on our marriage, it wasn't going to be how hot I looked.

But something might bring him to his senses. Maybe it was the nap high talking, but as I headed down the stairs, I was feeling hopeful about *us*. I was starting to think I'd overreacted to Adam's announcement this morning. I'd been so out of it during our conversation, having just finally drifted off into something resembling sleep only to bolt up at the sound of crying, thinking it was Jack and finding that it was Adam. Crying at the foot of our bed, but what had he actually said? That he couldn't do this anymore, true, that a better man could but that he was too tired, so tired of talking me out of every possible fear that he was losing all ability to gauge what was worth being concerned over himself, and that he was going to stay in Ben and Joe's guest room for a while. Maybe he'd just meant he couldn't do this *for a while*. As in: Hannah, you need to get your shit under control or else I'll leave you for real. Whereas I had taken him to be saying: Hannah, I am leaving you for real.

I found Adam and Jack in the kitchen. Adam was spooning a banana avocado smoothie into Jack's mouth.

"Better?" Adam asked as I came down the two steps from the living room. He was smiling.

"Much. Thank you."

"Glad to hear it. Goodman was good?"

It was Adam who had suggested that I start seeing a therapist, when Jack was one month old. Adam, broaching the topic: "Is it possible that this is the first time a goy from Ottawa has ever pressured a New York Jew into therapy?" In retrospect, it was a sign of how shot his nerves already were that he'd been willing to fudge the facts in order to ease this moment with a joke: Yes, I'd spent my first year of life in New York City, where my parents were both graduate students at Columbia, and had lived there off and on during my twenties. But for most of my childhood my father and I bounced between dismal college towns as he went from visiting post to visiting post, unable or unwilling to publish without his far more talented collaborator, my mother. I was a Jew from Nowhere if we were being precise, and Adam almost always was.

I felt a jolt of guilt thinking about how shot Adam's nerves were, at least partly because of me. But even my guilt now made me optimistic. We were struggling through a difficult time, but surely we could find each other through this. I was in therapy, at his suggestion, and it was going well. Maybe we could go to couples therapy, too. We'd do whatever we needed to do. This wasn't the end of us.

"Listen," he said, and was I wrong or was the smile he was giving me a little hopeful, too? "I don't want to bring this up and run, but I also don't want you to be surprised. I got in touch with a mediator earlier today. They're going to be reaching out. Just so we can understand our options."

"Ah," I said. I was holding a smile steady on my face. The smile felt like a yoga position I'd had no business contorting into.

"Just to understand the legal end of it," he said.

"The legal end," I said. "Of course."

"I made a chickpea tikka masala that Jack should have for dinner. It's in the fridge in the red container. I made enough for you, too, if you want some. I'm trying to get him used to the taste of ginger this week."

"Ah," I said again.

I was still contorted into Smile Pose even though I felt like I might vomit. I tried to convince myself that Adam was just like this. It didn't necessarily mean as much as it would mean if someone else had contacted a mediator already. If there was something practical that might possibly need doing, Adam was already doing it. Like methodically acclimating his son to flavors week by week. Maybe this was just Adam methodically exploring legal options for our marriage.

But it was hard to maintain much optimism after that exchange, and so with Adam gone, I decided to take Jack out to get my mind off the fact that I was now awaiting a call from a mediator. We'd go to Baker and Commons café, eat something sweet at an outdoor table while we eavesdropped.

↔

Half an hour later, sitting under a cheery yellow and white striped awning, mindlessly devouring a reasonable week's worth of refined sugar in the form of a blackberry galette, I tried to convince myself that this was fun and festive.

It didn't feel fun or festive. The sun was bright in my eyes, the air nippy enough that I had on a scarf, but not my jacket, which would have made me hot. Accommodating to Bay Area weather required constant minute adjustments, kind of like a marriage, and given that my marriage had just gone bust, sympathetic irony was feeling like a crock. Jack was making a racket banging a spoon against a saucer, and a table of three gray-haired women was giving us sour looks.

There was a knot of misery sitting in my stomach, but I was refusing to pay attention to it and so instead I just felt blank.

I squinted and stirred my coffee, speared a bite of pastry into my mouth like I was fulfilling a grim obligation.

"Dah dah dah dah dah," said Jack, banging away happily.

I put my hand on his to still the banging, but the look he gave me back was so confused I didn't have the heart and so released him. Let him bang. It was either this or fuss. I had a ridiculous urge to explain my reasoning to the three older women judging me over their heaping salad bowls.

"Dah dah dah dah," Jack said again, insistent.

He was staring at a dog tied by its leash to a bike rack past the café's rope barrier.

"Dog?" I asked. "Are you saying 'dog'?"

But he just banged away. I slid the saucer inward from the edge of the small round metal table.

The dog, now that I'd noticed it, was hard to look away from. A small dog with wiry yellow fur, it was mourning the temporary absence of its owner by running in yappy circles. As it ran around the bike rack, the leash was tangling around its skinny, fuzz-pocked legs. The smaller the dog's circumference shrank, the more frantically it circled.

Keeping one eye on Jack, I stood and walked over to the small dog, now yelping at the strap wound around its legs. I put a hand on its trembling back. Gently unwound the leash. Scratched the wiry belly for a few seconds. Then returned to my seat to discover that I'd eaten the entire galette without noticing. What a waste. It had probably been delicious.

Jack was somehow still occupied with banging the spoon against the saucer, and this was as good a babysitter as I was likely to come across anytime soon, so I forced myself to slide the computer from my bag. I forced myself to open the document in which I kept the scattered, incoherent notes for my new book, and forced myself to stare at this incoherence as though there were some sense to be made from it.

I had to make some sense from it. Dr. Goodman and Adam were both certain that my problems could be solved, at least in part, by my getting back to work. I didn't disagree. I also missed that part of who I was, the part I would have formerly just called myself. And there was also the issue of money. This book was due to my publisher, who had shelled out a decent sum for it, in less than seven months.

I had written four chapters before Jack was born and not a word since. It didn't help that the book was my first attempt at a speculative romance, an old-fashioned love story set in a distant future.

I'd hatched the idea during the hormone hazy bliss of pregnancy. For nine months I walked around narrating the world to the child inside my belly, feeling as though, through the fetus growing inside of me, I was connected to every human being who had ever lived, each one of us once carried in a mother. I had never felt un-alone like this before. It was like being on MDMA 24/7. I was no longer holding lightly to all desires. I was deeply invested in this baby. And this should have been terrifying, but it wasn't. The combination of the club-drug pregnancy hormones, my growing anticipation, and Adam being as invested in each kick and hiccup as I was, had me so loopy with love that I never worried. Adam was the one who worried about things like how much coffee it was OK for me to drink, researched the risks of obstetrical interventions, came up with our birth plan. I spent my days taking long walks, eating pastries, and writing a sentimental book about the possibilities of transformative connection, a love letter to my husband.

And now there was a publishing contract I was at risk of breaching. There were mediators, apparently, who would need paying as well. I really didn't want to have to sell the house. I needed to remember how to write.

I could play down the love story if I needed to. I could maybe even change the whole damn premise if I could come up with a better one. The real problem was my inner life had undergone a vast flattening with Jack's birth, become a universe in one plane.

As if to prove that point, Jack banged the spoon one final time and sent the saucer crashing to the ground. I'd failed to notice it sliding back toward the table's edge. Now it lay on the concrete in three sharp pieces. I gathered them up, sucking my finger where I pricked it, and looked around for someone I could prevail on to watch Jack for a second while I ran the shards inside.

The three older women, triumphant in their vindication, were not good candidates. Four preteen boys in ball caps seemed unlikely to oblige. Then my eyes landed on two men who had just taken the table behind mine. One of them, in particular—an older Asian man with a chin-strap beard, face alight with intelligence and kindness. Although he'd traded in his Tilley hat and binoculars for a T-shirt tucked into pleated jeans, the face was unmistakable. Berkeley Birder of a Certain Age, male of the species.

"Akio," I said out loud, not meaning to.

He looked up, smiling. His eyes crinkled fondly, but without recognition.

"I'm sorry." His smile wavered. "I've forgotten how we know each other."

A strong Brooklyn accent. Just like I remembered, although I couldn't possibly remember this.

"I've forgotten, too. But it is—Akio? Is it?"

"Akio, that's right. And this is Freddy." The younger man sitting across from him held out his hand with a courtly flourish. I took it. "And, Freddy, this is—"

"Hannah."

"Was it through Grace, perhaps?" Akio asked.

"Yes, that's right," I said, "through Grace," but now I was fumbling, gathering my belongings as quickly as I could.

Jacket. Bag. Laptop. Child. I got Jack strapped into his stroller, but other than that, made no attempt to put things in their proper places. I tossed everything into the generous basket beneath Jack's seat, the ceramic shards as well, and lurched toward where the rope opened to the sidewalk. I was smiling broadly, even though I knew my smile had to look miserable and desperate and slightly ill. My face felt hot. A layer of sweat seemed to be slicking every surface of my body. The three older women were watching me with undisguised glee, at once confirmed of my incompetence and rid of me.

Jack started mewling. I seized on this as my excuse for fleeing, gesturing as though to say *So sorry, you know how it is with babies*. As though they couldn't see perfectly well that I'd started bolting before Jack started crying, that the causation was, if anything, the other way around. Child unnerved by mother's wild antics.

I wheeled him away quickly, cooing soothingly to prevent a full-on meltdown, but inside I was freaking out. I'd known Akio's name! I'd known his Brooklyn accent. I'd learned these things in a dream, asleep on my feet in my own kitchen, and dreams don't tell you facts about the real world.

It wasn't until I was halfway down the block, trying to beep the car door open, that it occurred to me that there was a perfectly reasonable explanation. I knew his name, knew his accent because I'm a pathological eavesdropper. I'd overheard the Berkeley Birders conversing on my street at some point. Driving with the windows down, I'd overheard them and forgotten. Was this plausible? Sort of. I had a condition that was like the opposite of face blindness. I remembered the strangest smallest details about everyone I met, the trivial things they told me, the way they pronounced their partner's name with an extra breathy exhale. This was from a childhood spent trying to deal with the practicalities of life as best I could for both myself and my sweet, distracted father. Without adult survival skills to guide us, I relied on careful observation. The habit now served me nicely as a writer.

I shoved the mess from the stroller into the trunk. With Jack strapped in, becalmed, I slid into the driver's seat, shut the door, and becalmed myself.

I smiled at Jack in the relay of reflections linking the rear-view mirror to the backward-facing car seat. He smiled back. He looked benevolent and wise, although he was also eating one of his own feet.

"Weird day, huh?" I said.

The sound of my own voice speaking to him steadied me.

Behind Jack in the rearview mirror, I could also see Akio and his friend really grooving on some point of disagreement. And the dog had just been reunited with its owner, a girl with long black braids. The dog was licking her hands in an ecstasy of relief, and she was laughing. I felt a surge of joy at the joy in this small scene, but underneath this, something dark still wobbled.

Akio. Saying that name aloud had felt urgent, painful to ignore, just like the impulse to wake Adam at night to talk about blue lips, a dangling arm. These bits of knowledge felt like clues, some awful scavenger hunt and the prize at the end was Jack safely delivered to adulthood.

I knew what Dr. Goodman would say to this. What she always said about my symptoms: That of course it felt that way, how could it not? I'd saved Jack's life during his birth by acting on my instincts, insisting on the cesarean against the advice of both Adam and the doctor. So of course each worry about my child felt like a clue I needed to unravel in order to protect him.

I knew she would say this and I knew it was sensible but also: I was certain, certain, certain, that I hadn't ever eavesdropped on those birders. I'd have remembered overhearing them because I always noticed them; they interested me because they had good faces and because of the way the woman always stared at me as though she knew me but didn't expect me to know her back.

Mommy brain be damned, I'd remember if I'd overheard them speaking. That wasn't how I knew his name.

"You are getting to be a sad, strange lady," I said out loud.

Jack squealed delightedly in answer.

Chapter Seven

"Mommy brain? Did you just seriously say that? That phrase makes me want to scream."

I was sitting with six other women in folding chairs arranged around a bright green rug ringed with jaunty ABCs. My moms group, a special one for cracked-up mothers: postpartum depression, anxiety, baby blues, that kind of thing. There were no entrance requirements. If you wanted in, you were in, provided you could pay ten dollars a session. The room we met in, in the basement of a lactation center, was windowless and small and smelled of burnt coffee, but someone had expended effort to make it seem homey. The wall décor was a little more thoughtfully chosen than it needed to be, woven tapestries instead of laminated informational posters. The lighting was a little more flattering. A devil's ivy hung from a hook near a low bookshelf.

The five other women shifted uncomfortably in their seats. This was meant to be "a safe and nonconfrontational space for interpersonal sharing," and Ash was not exactly not screaming. At me. I'd been the one to use the offending phrase.

"What gets called 'mommy brain' is really just selective attention," Ash went on, ignoring, as usual, the general unease she was creating among the other women in the group. "Which is actually, when you think about it, another name for intelligence. We are always selectively attending. Deciding what to filter out from our sensory data, from our cognitive data. If we didn't, we wouldn't be able to function at all. We'd be absolutely flooded with all the information coming in. Concentration? That's just good filtering. New mothers filter better than other people. But we filter for the safety of our offspring, which means filtering out things that aren't relevant to keeping our offspring safe. Mommy brain, if you insist on using the term, should be a compliment."

"That's an interesting point," our very young facilitator, Sarah, said from halfway inside her cowl-neck collar. "I might even borrow it, if it's all right with you. But perhaps we should hear from Hannah, who I think was still checking in?"

I looked down at Jack eating a piece of lint he'd picked off the letter R, the jauntiest in the rug's alphabet ring. I couldn't decide whether I wanted to reclaim my time. So far the sum total of what I'd said was "I'm having a very weird day. You know the phrase 'mommy brain'?" There was more I'd meant to say, but I wasn't sorry when Ash cut me off. Actually, Ash's angry speech was probably the highlight of my day so far. She had been warned several times in recent weeks about this tendency to make speeches and thereby eat up other people's check-ins, but personally I found her speeches both informative and relaxing. And, anyway, I couldn't say what I hoped to accomplish by telling these near strangers my problems. I'd been so pleased when I remembered, right after finally picking up my lorazepam prescription from CVS, that I had my mothers group coming up at four P.M. Driving down Telegraph, feeling the whole evening yawning open, just me and Jack, and then: A place to go! A place with other people, people who could speak. But being here was only making me feel lonelier.

"I didn't mean to co-opt your check-in," Ash said, fury still gliding beneath her words. "Go ahead."

"Actually, I'm good," I said.

"I can go," said Kate. "My mother-in-law is still doing that thing."

I was getting sympathetic looks from Charmaine and Sola. I didn't want their sympathy, even if it was just for losing my chance to do a check-in, so I kept my eyes down on the babies. Jack had rolled onto his stomach and was reaching out to try to grab Kate's daughter by the toes. Charmaine's daughter, the early walker in the bunch, was toddling unsteadily toward the rug's outer edge, and I wasn't sure if I should stop her, but then she tripped over Ash's son, landed happily on her butt, and started clapping. I easily could have watched the babies all day.

"And she said she couldn't." Kate was rounding out an anecdote I'd failed to follow. "That she needed to go to Marshalls to buy shorts. But for who?" She asked this accusingly, as though this were the rub, some secret shorts receiver in her family's mix. I admired her outrage, although I had no notion what had caused it.

I admired each of these women for their ability to share so fully of themselves in group. They seemed to just open their mouths and let whatever was inside come spilling out. Adam said that this was normal. I didn't doubt him, but it still amazed me. When I shared in group, it had to be the version I'd already crafted in my head. Like a PDF without editing permissions. Sometimes even Dr. Goodman got that version of the PDF. I had only ever trusted Adam enough to consistently give a less protected version, and look where that had gotten me.

"Can you imagine having helpful grandparents living close?"

Charmaine was saying. "I seriously cannot fully wrap my head around it when I meet someone who says, like, oh we just leave them with their grandparents on Wednesdays. It's like meeting royalty, or someone who won the lottery. Someone whose luck is just beyond."

Charmaine was meeting everyone's eyes except for mine as she said this. Probably because I'd avoided her sympathetic glance before. Both she and Sola had made a big effort to befriend me when I first joined the group. They'd both read *The Cinders* in their book clubs. I felt uneasy being associated with that book in here. It was a retelling of Cinderella in which Cinderella slowly allows herself to acknowledge that her mother never died; her mother had always been the sadistic woman she called her evil stepmother, and Cinderella had invented the dead good mother in her loneliness and despair.

It was not a book that screamed *This woman should have a baby* and so I was self-conscious about the fact that Charmaine and Sola had read it; I imagined them listening to my check-ins and thinking, "Well, *yeah*." It was probably why I'd panicked at their campaign of friendliness and avoided them for a while and now everything was awkward. We kept replaying the same dynamic but with them making smaller and smaller overtures, and I never got it right.

This, too, was unlike me. Just one more way I wasn't myself since Jack. I had always been good at forming quick and easy friendships, a skill that came in handy during my childhood because of how often my father and I moved. Maybe not *deep* friendships—it was clearly weird that I'd told not a single friend that motherhood was anything other than sheer bliss for me—but fond, pleasant, uncomplicated. I was a good listener. I knew the right things to do and say in social situations. No longer.

I'd lost the thread again.

For some reason Ash was saying, "Can I just say? Data on the correlation between maternal mental illness and lack of support at home is pretty decisive. It's not about blaming anyone. I'm not saying Jody is an asshole. I don't know her. I'm just saying these are facts, and sometimes the non-birthing partner needs some psychoeducation around this. Dan gets it. He's totally on board and I really think it's helping me. To me, Jody sounds like someone who would get it, too. And maybe some of this is your own shit in not wanting to tell her."

Even Sarah, our very young facilitator, who always spoke with her mouth halfway inside the collar of her shirt, even she probably would have told the rest of us if her husband had left her this morning. Normal people told other people things like this, especially if those people were an actual fucking support group.

Chairs were scraping back. Group was ending.

I felt someone beside me and turned to find Ash smoldering beneath her short red hair. Ash was tall, a good foot taller than me. I tended to forget how small I was when I was sitting.

"That was really interesting what you said about mommy brain and selective attention," I offered as I hitched Jack onto my hip.

"Oh. You thought so?"

Ash said this in a way that indicated she thought less of me for it.

I'd never before noticed that Ash's face was covered in an intricate lattice of pale freckles that made the skin look like the kind of fancy paper you saw in stationery stores and wished you had a reason to buy.

"You know what I realized the other day?" Ash went on. "Your husband is Adam."

"Ah," I said. Everyone in the world seemed to know Adam and love him, and usually this made me proud, but today, for obvious reasons, pride was not my first reaction. "Do you know him?"

"My postdoc is in Dino's lab."

"Small world!" I offered weakly. Dino was a college friend of Adam's who had called me by the name of one of Adam's exes for three years. I wasn't sure why he disliked me, but at least this was one upshot of my chickening out of check-in. Dino wouldn't learn from Ash that now I really was an ex of Adam's.

"Yeah. I didn't put it together until I saw him pick you up from group last week. You just don't expect women to share a last name with their husband anymore, or I might have put it together sooner."

"I guess that's right. Being conventional is the new unconventional."

Ash went on as though I hadn't spoken. "But what I realized is that if you're Adam's wife, then I've read your book."

"*The Cinders*?"

"No, the good one. The one about possible worlds."

"Oh. *Probability Lanes.*" It always surprised me when someone had read this book, but it was becoming more common since the uncanny success of *The Cinders* and the steady sales of the three I'd published since. Before this boost from four more appealing siblings, so few people had read my first novel that it had been a downright miracle that Adam was among them. Adam, who just happened to make a point of inviting writers to his AP physics class as a way to get the kids excited about the many uses that science could be put to. I had always considered this the best luck of my life and—well, it still was. Here was Jack in my arms, after all. I smelled his head. It did not smell fresh. We would not be skipping his bath tonight.

Ash had hefted her son up as well. She held him facing outward, one arm slung around his middle as though he were a bag of groceries. He looked perfectly happy with the arrangement, placidly watching a dust mote float between us. Jack would have had no patience for that way of being held.

Ash said, "The revenge story I could take or leave"—the entire book was a revenge story, about a husband chasing his wife's attempted killer across the multiverse and of course, in the end, it turns out that the husband's cosmic spree of vengeance leads to his wife's attempted murder no longer falling into the category of attempted; you can see the twist a mile away—"but I liked your solution to the problem of causal interaction between the Everett branches. Your nonlinear modification to the Schrödinger equation was legitimately smart."

I shifted to my other foot, hoping she wasn't going to ask a question. I did not really understand this solution of mine. I wasn't a sci-fi writer; I was a suspense writer who liked to play with science. Probably, if I were analyzing myself, I'd say I did this as a way to try to reach my unreachable parents, who had both been theoretical physicists. Probably to reach my mom especially, since most of what I knew about her, other than that she'd gone crazy when I was a year old and then disappeared when I was six, was that she'd been a brilliant scientist, working on the many-worlds interpretation of quantum mechanics, which claims to solve a whole lot of confusing questions about fundamental physics by positing that our world is just one among many, each existing simultaneously. It wasn't just my father who said my mother was brilliant—it was anyone I ever met from their old life. In fact, the first thing these people usually said to me was "Your mother was the smartest person I ever met." They always said it as though it would be comforting. As though this knowledge could read me stories at night or rub my back when I was frightened, teach me how to use a tampon.

Unlike my parents, I had no aptitude for science. But my own brain was sometimes much smarter than I was. That cobbled-together fix—no more grounded in reality than the warp drive, traversable wormholes, or tesseracts that allow every space opera to work around the inconvenient fact of the speed of light—had turned out to be the thing that excited and impressed people like Adam and Ash.

Jack had started climbing me like a baby monkey. He was trying to mount my shoulder. I wondered why Ash was not letting me go and why I felt I required her permission.

Ash said, "So anyway I think we should be friends."

The saddest, strangest thing yet about this day: I said, "I'd like that," and I meant it.

That was how alone I was without Adam.

Chapter Eight

In the kitchen, the windows streamed with late-day sun, soaking the white tiles golden.

Jack was on the floor in his ducky bath, a yellow inflatable thing with a big, bobbling head and orange beak.

It had to be in the kitchen, for some reason. If you tried to bathe Jack in one of the bathrooms he went nuts. Adam refused to accept this arrangement on principle. In the name of normalcy, he had been insisting lately on bathing Jack in the claw-foot tub in the second bathroom with predictably loud results. Tears, shrieks, what was the point? But Adam was adamant, so I just let him.

Jack was laughing and splashing, kicking his little legs, smacking the water with flat palms. The towels I had laid out on the floor to catch the overflow were sopping, as they always were at this point in the process.

Jack shot his hand toward my mouth. I kissed his palm. He laughed, and shot his hand again, but this time misjudged the distance and clocked me on the chin. I dabbed a sudsy dollop onto his head. I'd propped the warped square of a mirror from his jungle-themed activity mat against the ducky bath's squat neck because Jack liked to babble to the other baby he saw reflected there. In the colorful plastic mirror, Jack saw the soapy dollop on the soggy baby's head then reached to touch it on his own.

"That's right," I said. "That baby's you."

This would be the moment when Adam would say something like: "He can't know that's him. Self-recognition comes online around eighteen months." And I would say, "Breaking: Jewish mother thinks her firstborn son precocious," then hold my breath waiting to see if Adam was too annoyed with me to laugh.

I grabbed one of Jack's toes. He squealed and kicked it loose, then presented it to me again. We played this game for several minutes. The light flooding the room was turning lavender. Through the windowed wall the lush green world of our backyard was darkening to shadows.

I pumped pink baby shampoo into my hand and lathered up Jack's mop of curls to mild protest. As I rinsed out the shampoo, pouring a thin stream of water from a measuring cup, Jack's protests grew less mild. I felt rushed by the falling dark. I was spilling water on his head too quickly, getting it in his eyes, and he was not pleased. I would have liked to turn the lights on. But the switch was across the room, and I regarded with utmost seriousness the warning on the bottom of the ducky bath: *Babies have drowned while using infant bathtubs. Stay* in arm's reach *of your baby.*

Jack started grabbing at my breasts, pawing like an entitled date, asking to be comforted from the water torture I was inflicting. Somehow, he seemed to have more lather in his hair than ever.

To distract him, I presented him with the jungle mat mirror again. I was curious to see if he would repeat his trick, notice that the soggy baby in the shiny square was also being put through water torture. But instead, Jack batted angrily against its puffed border. Pow pow pow with an open palm against the blue, orange, and brown polka dots on a white background. It fell into the bath. When I fished it out, the water streaming over the cheap mirrored plastic gave the reflective surface a funhouse effect. Jack's angry little face was stretched and deformed, his jowls swollen, his temples pincered. He looked like a furious little demon. The effect was only heightened because he was clawing at my breasts again.

I laughed. Jack wailed louder in protest, and then I screamed.

The reflection in the mirror was perfect, vivid, crisp. There was no mistaking what was looking back at me, even in the thickening shadows: the bluish skin, the purple lips, the glassy staring eyes.

As I stared at it, my throat going raw, the room fell into darkness.

Chapter Nine

He was very still against me. I didn't remember lifting him out of the bath, but here he was, curled into my shoulder. Soaking through my shirt and jeans. Dripping on the floor. I could feel his breath shuddering in and out. His slippery back beneath my palm was trembling. He was terrified. I'd terrified him. I'd terrified us both.

The mirror was on the ground, faceup, reflecting nothing but the ceiling fan. Glint, dark, glint, dark, as it spun. Like an animal's eye, blinking. Watching.

I wrapped Jack in his towel, pale blue with a smiling whale stitched on its pointy hood, then went to flip the light switch near the windows. The room burst into brightness. Jack buried his face into my neck. The world outside the glass had disappeared, replaced only by us. A tiny woman clutching a trembling, sky-blue bundle.

"Jack?" I whispered.

His skin felt cold where it met the bare flesh of my sternum. Because the air was cold, the fan still whirring. He'd spent a long time in the bath. In the falling dark, the water cooling.

The air was cold, and also there was a smell hanging in it,

sweet and fetid. I looked around. Sitting on the counter just a couple of feet away the metal lid was off the compost. From the pale green plastic fringes of the liner rose a bounty of decomposing strawberries and bananas, all cut by Adam into bite-sized pieces.

Closing my eyes against the memory of that nightmarish reflection, I hustled Jack up the narrow stairway, murmuring reassurances in his ear: "You're OK. Mommy got scared, but there's nothing scary. You're OK. We're having fun. You warm, my love? You cozy?"

I couldn't stop speaking. I wished I would shut up; my own voice, straining so audibly for calm, was only making me more anxious.

In the nursery, I turned on all the lights, flooding the room with color. Way-too-many colors was the room's design scheme, basically. One wall was dominated by vivid orange shelving, repurposed from my office. On the abutting wall, an iridescent butterfly was pinned in flight inside its frame. And on the wall opposite was a large decal from Adam's mother, J-A-C-K spelled out as pastel building blocks, pink, blue, yellow, blue. The walls themselves were a deeper blue, the color of sunny skies in kids' cartoons.

The overall effect did not look good, exactly, but it did look cheerful. And right now, that was great.

I laid Jack on his changing table. His lips really did look kind of purplish. I kept the towel around his torso for warmth as my fingers went searching in the wicker basket stuffed with changing-related odds and ends for the thermometer. I braced for his cry as I inserted the cold tip between his butt cheeks. But for the first time ever he didn't protest. Not a peep as he stared up at me. He was tracking my every movement the way he used to in the early months, back when it seemed like he didn't trust this world outside the womb. Already intuiting it wasn't everything it should be.

"I'm sorry about the world," I said over the thermometer's beep.

I started at the number: 95.4.

I slid the tip back in again. Obviously the reading was a fluke.

"Mommy left you in the bath too long. Mommy let you get too cold. Mommy is a bad mommy."

95.5 this time. So, not a fluke. At least it was heading in the right direction.

That stupid fan, why had I left it on? I hated that I'd done that. But actually his low temperature, in a way, was reassuring.

It meant that he had gotten really, really cold. His lips were still a little purple, so in the bath they must have been dramatic. Surely it was the sight of them that had conjured up an awful association so that I'd thought I'd seen . . . that.

"Mommy was being absentminded, not broken-minded," I cooed at him as I tugged his warmest pajamas, the rainbow-striped ones, over his damp sausage arms. I thought of Ash's theory of mommy brain, and tried on this far more generous interpretation: I had been attending to nothing but my baby, filtering out all other data.

By the time I got Adam on the phone, I'd taken Jack's temperature twice more: 95.6 both times. I was still angry at myself for letting him get so cold, but he didn't seem any worse for it, or for the fright I'd given him. He was busy with a box of tissues in the corner, pulling them out one by one, examining each as though it were some splendid artifact from an alien civilization.

"Well, does he feel cold to you?" he asked.

"It's hard to tell. He feels damp, like a baby who just took a bath."

I was sitting on the royal blue glider, keeping an eye on Jack while also scrolling through alarming information on my laptop about the causes and effects of mild hypothermia in babies. The number one cause did seem to be bathing in insufficiently heated rooms. The number one effect seemed to be freaking out on message boards.

"Hannah." His tone was neutral, but still a warning.

"But his temperature really is 95.6. That's a number, not my opinion. So what do you think it means?"

It could mean a lot of things according to the message boards, the ones I always swore I would avoid, then always found myself returning to. A chronic low temperature could indicate a nutritional deficiency, for instance, such as might be caused by a mother who sometimes forgot to feed her child the cut-up fruit and vitamin-rich smoothies her husband prepared so lovingly; it could mean anemia, hypothyroidism, some dread neurological disorder. Although seventeen minutes probably didn't qualify as "chronic."

"I think it means that the thermometer is a piece of junk unless you bathed him in actual ice."

I hadn't thought of this. It mollified me somewhat. But not entirely, because his lips *had* been purple, I'd seen that with my own eyes. I went to get the thermometer from my medicine cabinet, a normal adult one, and coaxed Jack to keep it in his mouth long enough to get a reading: 97.8. I closed my eyes and let out a ragged breath, exhausted by relief. This day was throttling me. But Jack was fine, the baby thermometer *was* a piece of junk, and now at least I could put him in the crib and close the door, have some time to myself, and hope that tomorrow would be just a little better.

↔

Down in the kitchen, Jack at last asleep, I navigated around the bath mess and headed straight for the high chair where I ate his leftovers standing up. After that, there was really no excuse not to clean up other than that the prospect frightened me. I emptied the ducky tub into the sink first, spilling only a little water on the floor as I shimmied it across. Then I gathered all the soaking towels in a pile and dried the tiles with a microfiber cloth. I picked up the mirror last. Its fabric frame was still bloated with bathwater, and I squeezed it in the sink, trying not to think about the vivid image I'd seemed to see in the warped reflective plastic.

A line came to me: A disease of too much seeing.

What was it from? A poem? A fairy tale? Then I remembered. The disease Adam had diagnosed me with this morning. *Your imagination has become a liability and maybe it's because you aren't writing. It's like you have a disease, a disease of too much seeing.*

My fingers dug onto the granite counter, and I shook the thought away.

Then I reached into the far back of the junk drawer, deep in a tangle of rubber bands and mystery brackets, until I felt a battered pack of Pall Malls and a lighter. With my other hand, I picked up the wad of wet bath towels and stepped through the sliding doors. The air was warm out here, almost breath-like. The towels were clammy against my skin. I hung them over the railing quickly, eager to be done with them. Then I leaned over a bare portion of the railing and lit a cigarette. Inhaling deeply, I felt the pleasure tingle through my heels and elbows. You couldn't have paid me enough to risk a cigarette on the deck yesterday, but there were some advantages to being at home without Adam, and goddamn if I wasn't going to avail myself of each and every one of them.

I dragged over a chair and positioned it so I could put my feet up on the railing. Night had fully fallen, and the moon was a sliver glowing dully through the clouds. The orange end of my cigarette was like the last lit window before the end of settled territory. Beyond, it was only black. But I could feel the backyard waiting there: the thirsty succulents, twisting blueberry, towering redwood. I stared out at the dark green blur, feeling it press close. Almost breathing back at me. A vast unknown. Alive with possible dangers, all manner of dangerous possibilities, crowding around my defenseless offspring. I shuddered.

There was no denying it: My worry was getting out of control. A panic attack in Dr. Goodman's stairwell, a vivid nightmare while standing in my kitchen, and then whatever the fuck that had just been with the ducky bath. My mind was playing tricks on me today, and maybe there was something to what Dr. Goodman had said, that my brain was working hard to scare an audience of one. But *why*? Why was my brain working so hard to scare me?

I took a long breath in and pushed away the thought that my brain was trying to scare me because it was trying to help me see something that I wasn't yet managing to see. Something about Jack. Something I was missing.

But, no. This was the same fear speaking. Dr. Goodman was right: My maternal instincts were caught in a vicious feedback loop, scaring me silly.

Still, I wanted to ask Adam, genuinely ask him: What did he think parenthood was, the vigilance required, the immense responsibility, if not a condition of too much seeing?

↔

A rap on the glass behind me made me jump.

I turned and watched a face resolve in the glass in a kind of stop-frame motion: eyes, mouth, face, face I recognized. Adam. Adam staring at me through the sliding glass as though he were observing a perp through a two-way mirror. And like some two-bit crook, I had the instinct to stash my cigarette, hiding evidence already logged against me.

Instead, I threw my legs over the chair's arm and stubbed the cigarette on the wood, realizing too late that this would leave a mark. Well, let him scold me. Let him tell me it wasn't normal for a mother to smoke a cigarette within a thousand feet of where her child lay sleeping. This whole fucking day wasn't normal.

He slid the glass so it was no longer between us.

"Hey," he said. "What the heck? Why aren't you taking my calls?"

I could see him only by the dim light filtering through from the front hallway. The hall light was a bare Edison bulb in a clear glass globe, and it backlit him just slightly, making him look insubstantial as he slouched in the doorway. Nearly six two to my five nothing, and just now it looked like I could lift him.

"What are you doing here?" I asked.

"I texted like twenty times. I started worrying after we hung up that maybe something was actually wrong with him. And then you weren't responding to my texts. You didn't answer when I called. What happened to keeping me in the loop?"

I felt around me for my phone. It wasn't here.

"I must have left my phone in Jack's room. He's fine, though. You were right about the thermometer. It's a piece of junk. He had a normal temperature on ours. I'm sorry I didn't let you know."

Adam leaned against the doorjamb, arms crossed. A couple of dark curls tumbled over his forehead, and he brushed them back. It was an annoyingly sexy gesture.

"Fuck, Hannah. I was terrified."

I stood up suddenly, sliding over the deck chair's arm, and hugged him around the middle. My head came to just below his armpit. He wrapped one arm loosely around me, more accommodation than embrace.

As I followed him into the kitchen I said, "I'm so sorry. I wasn't thinking straight. I wasn't thinking at all. To be honest, I've felt all day like I was maybe losing it."

"Hannah." He was using his science teacher voice. His I-am-a-man-who-trucks-in-facts voice. Usually this voice made me feel protective of him. You didn't pull a voice like that unless something inside you was flailing. This time it didn't make me feel protective, but it did make me feel like I could trust him. Things might have soured between us, but he was still Adam after all.

I flipped on a few of the overheads. I wanted to see him properly. The light was pinkish and made him appear less scolding than I knew he really looked.

"Please don't lecture me or say that it's not normal. I'm trying to tell you something important."

"OK," he said.

Standing in the middle of the kitchen, he listened as I told him about all the strange things that had happened to me since the morning. Only the slightest distaste showed on his face. He was clearly making an effort.

"Well, what does Dr. Goodman say about it?"

"A panic attack in the stairwell, but she doesn't know about the other two."

"Maybe you should call her."

His voice was as loving as a tax audit, but he gathered me against him, kissed the tip-top of my head. He smelled like Irish Spring and Tide. I could hear his heart beating against my cheek. I was dreading the moment when he pulled away, which I knew was coming any second.

"I'm really sorry you've had such a lousy day," he said into my hair. "I'm sorry for all of this. Us. And this—this trouble you've been having. I know this isn't you. You're not this woman."

I was the one to pull away.

"Then who is she?"

And then a cry. Weak and desperate.

We both went running.

In the nursery, which I flooded now with light, there was nothing in the crib but the cow-faced lovey.

PART TWO

I believe, and so do you, that things could have been different in countless ways. But what does this mean? Ordinary language permits the paraphrase: there are many ways things could have been besides the way they actually are. . . . I believe that things could have been different in countless ways; I believe permissible paraphrases of what I believe; taking the paraphrase at its face value, I therefore believe in the existence of entities that might be called "ways things could have been." I prefer to call them "possible worlds."

DAVID LEWIS,
Counterfactuals

Chapter Ten

"OK, and exactly what time was this?"

Two detectives in the kitchen, both female.

"My wife just said. A little after eight."

"And how long before that would you say you heard him cry?"

"No time at all. Maybe a few seconds."

"You didn't call dispatch until closer to eight-fifteen. Could you walk me through those missing minutes?"

"Our son is gone. He's out there somewhere right now. Why are you questioning us like this?"

"Adam, they're trying to help."

"We thought he must have climbed out of the crib. We were looking all over for him. It was a few minutes before we let it hit us. That he wasn't here. I guess that's when we called. I don't really remember. Is someone out there looking? This feels like wasting time."

"We have a whole team out there looking. You asked if you should offer to make them coffee. Do you remember?"

A noncommittal nod. Flashlights bobbing in the dark on the slope behind our house like swollen fireflies.

"I promise you we're doing everything we can, including getting clear on all these details. The feed from the baby monitor. You watched that, too, before you called."

"The Nest cam. Yes. Because it didn't make sense. The windows and doors were all still locked. We'd just heard him, we heard him the whole time we were running up the stairs. It doesn't make sense—you saw the monitor. No one comes through the windows, no one comes through the door. He's there, crying, then the feed goes out for a fraction of a second, and then he's gone."

"So at that point you called."

"Yes. How is this helpful?"

"We're just trying to understand. Like you said, it's hard to make sense of that footage. What you're calling the feed going out, I'd call that skitter-scatter, that's the word we used to use when our TV set did that back when I was a kid. But I've never seen it on a phone."

"OK. Sure. Call it skitter-scatter. But what's your point?"

"Adam, they're just trying to understand the same way we are."

"I know. I'm sorry. I'm really sorry. I'm sorry."

"This is a hell of a night for you. For both of you."

"Please just find him. Please. I can't make it make sense. Where is he?"

There was no answer.

Chapter Eleven

In a daze, I walked outside to watch the two detectives move down our long driveway. In a daze, I swiveled on the gravel to head back in and gazed up at my house. The same white stucco, the same blue tile of the entryway rippling in the headlights. But now it looked like a house people crossed the street to avoid. Like a house where something bad had happened.

Just like I'd feared, just like I'd imagined, but now that something bad had actually happened, it felt impossible. It felt unreal.

Like I was watching from the outside as I moved back through the hallway and the living room, into the light of the sunken kitchen. I stopped on the second step, looking in. Adam was sitting at the table with a drink that was not likely to be water from the way he sipped it. He was staring out at the darkened wall of windows, the slope still alive with flashlights searching. I didn't let myself imagine all they might be searching for.

The way Adam's shoulders slumped, the way his back rounded protectively around himself, like something vital might escape—he looked like the Adam in my dream, the grieving Adam on the fire trail. But this Adam was real. As real as the counter I was gripping. As real as the two detectives who'd just sat here with their questions, as the men and women swarming in our backyard, as the nightmare now enveloping our family.

I said, "What should we be doing now?" My voice sounded distant to me, muffled, like I'd tuned in to some foreign frequency and, by strangest chance, heard my own voice being broadcast over the waves.

Adam didn't turn to face me.

"Nothing," he answered, his voice also sounding distant. "This. There's a whole team out there, trained to do exactly what they're doing."

"We can't do nothing." I came up behind him, but it didn't feel right wrapping my arms around him the way I wanted to, so I turned and went back to the counter.

"I agree," he said. "But what else can we do?"

"Form a search party. Talk to neighbors. Drive the streets. Put up posters?"

From within my muffled distance, I watched Adam dig his thumbnail into a divot in the raw wood of the table, made by a roast chicken–carving accident (mine) the first weekend we had the piece of furniture in our possession.

From within my muffled distance I heard him say, "Hannah, please let the professionals do their jobs. You'll just get in the way. Anyway, we need to be here in case someone tries to reach us."

For some reason this broke my trancelike stupor, let the world come rushing in.

As Adam continued to work his thumb into the divot I'd made in my carelessness, I said, "You don't think there's any way they'll think this has to do with custody, do you? Once they discover you've called mediators?"

He swiveled around to face me. He didn't look angry. Just stunned. Or maybe that was me, it was hard to tell, I was back somewhere far away again, miles or maybe decades separating me from this moment, which also felt as though it had never not been happening.

Without saying a word, Adam turned back to his drink, took another swig. I watched the rise and fall of his sharp shoulder blades beneath his thin T-shirt. From my great distance, I was considering. Whether it was possible: Adam. Custody. These things did happen. I was considering whether I knew this person at all. He put the glass down, turned to me again, and the doubt went whooshing out.

Maybe I knew Adam, maybe I didn't. But I knew the oceanic helplessness that slowed his every movement, even the way his eyes rose up to meet mine. We were drowned in it together, this Jacklessness, black and swallowing, immense. He couldn't fake that. He wouldn't know how. You couldn't imagine this place until you sank into its depths.

"I hadn't even considered that," he said. "If they decide it was one of us, that he's not in danger—"

"That was an awful thing for me to say," I said. "And stupid. Of course they wouldn't think that. And even if they did, they'd keep on looking. Come on, let's go and help. I can't just wait here. I really can't."

I seemed to be crying. Adam seemed to be standing, coming toward me at the counter.

It seemed to take him hours while I stood there with my arms outstretched, or maybe it was instantaneous, a blink, but the hug was quick, and then he reached behind me for the jewel-green bottle. The ice cubes clinking in his glass sounded like a wind chime, and the prettiness was jarring enough to pull me back again into this moment. Just long enough that I felt him clap a hand onto my shoulder, like a dad whose son struck out at bat. I heard him say, "I know it takes an extra-human effort to sit still when Jack is out there. I feel that, too. But right now we need to exert that extra-human effort."

"Why? How?"

I had no memory of our moving apart, but he was already at the table again, back turned to me.

"Because that's how the world works."

Because you're the goy from Ottawa, I wanted to say, but didn't. He expected the world to work. He really believed this: If you followed the rules, if you did what you were supposed to, the world would oblige. Whereas I, the Jew from Nowhere, knew that the world was hostile with no cause.

"The world doesn't work that way for me," I said, and went to grab my jacket from the hall.

Outside, I was struck again with the unreality of the scene. The commotion of it, the tragedy of it—cops everywhere, dogs sniffing—again brought the world rushing in. I turned left, toward the Neimann-Rosenfelds', and the numb set in again, made my eyes blurry, movements pillowy, a whirring in my ears.

Adam was right of course about the cops doing their jobs. They had been to the Neimann-Rosenfelds' already. And to the Krafts', and to the Nguyens', and to every other house up and down our block. Of course they had been, I knew they would have been, but still I kept knocking, asking, because how could you not. How could he not. Even if we were power-less, we had to register our protest, tell the world that we were keeping tabs: *You can't get away with this, I won't let you.* This was the conversation I was carrying on with the universe through my gestures.

The conversations I was carrying on with my neighbors, in contrast, were impossible to follow, shards of words sticking out of silence: *Have you?* and *If you do* and *Of course we will* and *Can't even imagine.* I had the sense that I was rallying them to our cause, although that couldn't have been right since they'd already formed a search party, a group of them already calling Jack's name up and down the slopes of their backyards before I got there. Others were already offering the cops water, coffee, snacks. And Adam, last I'd seen him, was still sitting at our kitchen table, staring vacantly, waiting for the world to conform again to his idea of normal. And here I was, apparently still going about the business of drawing breaths and pumping blood and replicating cells despite not knowing where my child was.

At some point I had gotten into the car. I became aware of this somewhat later than I ought to have, noticing that I was driving when I was already a quarter mile from our house. Slowly, up and down the switchback roads, looking, looking, I didn't know for what. Stopping back at home just in case there was news that hadn't reached me, then out again, back in the car, and it struck me, vaguely, distantly, that I ought to be in Dr. Goodman's stairwell. As though Jack were caught there, like how mist catches on mountain passes, suspended in fine particles. That if I went there, I could catch and coalesce my child.

I was parked outside our house when I had this thought.

A non sequitur about the stairwell, a misfire of a mind in shock, but it cut through the unreality like nothing else had. Cut through the shock, finally dispersed it, and left me only with: *My fault.*

I let my head collapse against the steering wheel, let a sob escape me, a sound like a dying animal, not really human, because no human being could withstand a thing like this, a child gone missing. Jack, in his rainbow-striped pajamas, somewhere, but not here.

This was my fault. My fault that this was happening.

In the kitchen I'd tried to blame Adam, tried to imply that somehow his leaving me, his calling mediators, had put our son in greater peril. I'd even considered, briefly, that he had taken Jack himself. But, actually, it was me who was responsible.

All day my brain had been misfiring. In the stairwell, in the kitchen, in the ducky bath. Showing me a world that had no Jack.

And it wasn't just today. For eight months I'd been obsessing over that memory, blue lips and a dangling arm, eight months of dreams and fears and trying not to bring it up with Adam. But I'd known, I'd known, I'd *known* that something was being asked of me. Something I had to do in order to keep him safe.

I was aware it made no sense. I was aware, even as I banged my forehead against the steering wheel, even as I sank my teeth into the satisfying give of its rubber coating, that there couldn't possibly be any connection between my missing child and what my insurance reimbursement claims called adjustment disorder with postpartum onset and Adam called Jewish Mother Overdrive and I called the car-swerve feeling. As if the awful way things could have gone during Jack's birth had come too close and now—now this was happening.

But still. Now this was happening.

Chapter Twelve

"Hannah! It's late. Are you OK?"

I hadn't expected Dr. Goodman to answer. It was after three A.M. I was in my bedroom, staring out the window at the flashlights. Downstairs, Adam had passed out sitting upright on the couch.

I'd expected to leave a message, but Dr. Goodman answered on the first ring.

"I'm not OK." I said it quickly before I could have second thoughts about proceeding with this phone call.

I pictured Dr. Goodman serene in silk pajamas, her hair falling in that glossy auburn wave. I had her in an empty room walled entirely in black slate, as though she lived inside the feeling she gave off: cold rock against hot cheek, unyielding and relieving.

I filled her in on the last seven hours, starting with Jack's empty crib. She listened without speaking until finally I said, "Adam was right, of course. Right now there's nothing to do but wait."

"My God." She let out a long exhale. "I can't even— Hannah, I'm so sorry. Truly sorry. I'm glad that you've reached out."

"There's also something else," I said. "I think I might be losing my grip a little. Losing my grip on what's really happening."

I could hear Dr. Goodman shift in a leather chair. It sounded like she might be reaching for a notepad. I didn't care why she was up at three A.M. I didn't know what I expected from her in this moment, what I was looking for in calling. But for some reason I was glad she had a notepad.

"The car-swerve feeling," she said.

"No. Not exactly. I'm not sure how to explain it. I don't really have the language."

"I imagine that in this moment it must feel almost as though you never left the delivery room."

"Yes. Yes, it does feel like that a bit. But it's more than that. I have this feeling like— Dr. Goodman, I think this is my fault."

"That's only natural. It doesn't make it true."

"No, of course, of course it's only natural. But today, I—" I hadn't thought out in advance what I was going to say, and now I came up short. *Today, I what? Lost track of Jack when he was right in front of me? Dreamed that he was dead and that Adam still liked me? Freaked out when his lips went purple in the shadows?* "What if today it all felt like too much? What if today *was* too much for me and I failed? What if some part of me wanted Adam back, myself back?"

"What if a tiny part of you felt some ambivalence about parenting is what I think you're asking."

"Yes."

"What if you did?"

"It's monstrous. I failed him. He's gone because of me."

"You believe you made this happen."

"Yes. No, of course I didn't. But I—I failed him. I didn't rise to the task set to me. I—I know that I'm not making sense."

"I think you're making sense."

"I am?"

"You felt there was a task set by that memory you couldn't have really had. By the car-swerve feeling. But you were never able to find out what that task was."

"Yes."

"And now he's gone."

"Yes."

"And so you failed him."

"Did I?"

"No. Because there never was a task set. The symptoms were a defense, just like we always spoke about. It was more tolerable to believe you had a concrete task, even if it was a mysterious and terrible puzzle involving an impossible memory, than to be subject again to the outrageous cruelty of chance. The memory and the dreams, the terrible puzzle, gave you the illusion of control in the face of the intolerably uncontrollable."

"So this sense I have now, that there's something else I can be doing, should be doing—" I squeezed my head with both my hands. Here it was again, what had been gripping me on and off. It was an urgent feeling, a strange sensation that came in waves, almost like contractions. Like a muscle memory of the mind: *There's something you can do, and you need to do it.* "That feeling is just more of the same? I just ignore it?"

"I think a better question is whether it's helping."

"Helping Jack?"

"Helping you. To believe that you did have some special control, a special task set to you, and that you failed him. Is it making things better or worse for you in this moment? I can only imagine what you're going through. I'm loath to take away anything that's going to get you through. But I have the sense that this feeling you're describing isn't serving you. I have the sense it's making you feel worse. Am I right? I think that's what you communicated at the beginning of this phone call, isn't it? That there's nothing now to do but wait? If you want my permission to let go of the puzzle, the guilt, the whole of it, and embrace the absolute terror of this reality, I'm happy to oblige. Hannah, there is nothing to do but wait."

Through the bare windows, moonlight was illuminating the dark outline of a puddle on the carpet from where Jack had sent an arcing stream of pee when I was changing him on the bed his second night home. Dr. Goodman was right: This was intolerable. She was also right that this was what I'd called her for: to tether me to this intolerable reality.

But she was wrong that knowing this felt better. That muscle memory of the mind, like an invitation to *do* something: It didn't feel brave to ignore it. It didn't even feel sane.

Dr. Goodman was saying she needed to get off now. Dr. Goodman was saying she'd call me in the morning. And I was thanking her and saying, yes, I'd try to get some sleep and, yes, I did manage to pick up the prescription.

My words all reasonable, normal, but it was taking all of me to withstand another wave as it washed over me, that strange sensation, a tugging outward. So much like contractions, that sense of me and not me, a demand that I let go.

She'd hung up. I pressed my forehead against the cushion of the window seat just to stop the feeling that I might give up, give in.

The little amber vial was still in the diaper bag, the lorazepam to help me slip out of this day without unraveling any further. I went rooting for it in the side pocket, then reached my hand into the layer of loose Cheerios, and this was beyond what I could take, as though I were feeling Jack, feeling my life with him, right here against my fingertips. Cheerios between my fingers, and where was he? Where was he? My fingers found the plastic cylinder. I put the white pill on my tongue and waited for relief.

Chapter Thirteen

I woke two hours later sitting upright on the couch. Adam was curled beside me, drooling against the black microfiber. Dandruff flaked in his dark curls. I grabbed my phone to see if there was any word, but there was nothing. Just the two detectives' business cards fluttering off the screen. I reached to grab them from the carpet and shoved them in the back pocket of my jeans.

I circled my neck left, then right, hearing cracks, feeling a twinge of pain.

On the street outside, all was quiet. They'd still been out there searching when I passed out in Adam's warmth a little after 4:00. Now, at 6:21, it was mostly light, better for searching I would think, but they seemed to have packed up and left. I shouldn't have gone to sleep.

I touched a hand to Adam's wrist. He twitched and grimaced. No point in waking him. My breasts were sore and swollen. Jack usually fed at 5:00.

The pump was in his room. I slipped upstairs, dreading having to face his empty crib, but at least I had something to do. Something for Jack.

In the nursery, morning sun was filtering through the picture window. Dancing off the garish orange bookshelves. Hitting the iridescent wings of the framed butterfly so that it seemed to be in flight. The room looked cheerful. Terribly decorated. Normal. The bad juju of the house, which I'd expected to be thickest here, seemed not to touch the room at all. Aside from the few items that the cops had bagged as evidence—the Nest cam, the cow-faced lovey—nothing had changed.

I went to the crib and closed my hands around the white lacquered slats.

Yesterday I'd stood just here and thought I was having a terrible morning. When in fact I'd been in the midst of a close to perfect day because Jack was in his crib and staring back at me. Safe. Maybe as close to perfect a morning as I'd ever have again in my life. I pushed that thought away.

They were going to find him. He was OK. He was going to be OK. The locked windows, the Nest cam's feed showing no one entering—these details buttressed my hope because the normal dark imaginings—some masked figure stealing in, a parent's worst nightmare—couldn't get a purchase. The feed from the monitor all but proved it wasn't possible. But then what? *What?*

The sense that had gripped me last night returned, but weakly. Some other thing I needed to do.

Last night I had almost convinced myself that this feeling was real and made sense, but now the sheen of sense dissolved like soapsuds. In the light of day, it was easy to see the truth of what Dr. Goodman had been saying: just a defense against the terror.

Of course, a defense because this was beyond what I could stand, this not knowing, this helplessness. Beyond what any person could stand. But what I needed to do was stand it. Keep it together. Be whole and sane and strong for Jack when he returned to me.

Down in the kitchen I set the pump up on the table, cleaned the flanges; they'd been sitting in the closet now for months, since I was always with Jack to nurse him. I settled down to milk myself, but nothing came. Even though my breasts were hard and ached with the pressure building up in them, I couldn't get a drop. I sat there crying, not producing. Because where was Jack, where was he, he needed to nurse, and how was a person supposed to stand this? No one was even out there searching after telling us that we were only meant to wait.

It was after seven o'clock now. Late enough that I could call the detectives and ask them for an update. I chose the top card, the older detective, the one who seemed like she could maybe be a mother herself.

"Detective Rodriguez speaking."

"I'm sorry for calling so early. I hope I didn't wake you. This is Hannah Bennett. Are there any—" What was the word? Words seemed beside the point. "Leads?"

"I'm sorry, what is this regarding?"

"Regarding—regarding Jack. My son. My missing son."

"You've reported him missing?"

"Yes. What? I—is there some extra step I need to take? I don't think you mentioned that last night, unless I maybe— I'm sorry, maybe I misunderstood. Is that why no one's out there now, why they've stopped looking?"

"What you need to do is call your local dispatch and file a missing persons report. How old is Jack? If he's over eighteen, they might not send a detective out to you for twenty-four or forty-eight hours, depending. Most missing people return within forty-eight hours of their own accord. That's the good news."

"But I did all that. And they sent you. You were here. You were in my house."

"OK. I need you to calm down. I can tell you're feeling

frustrated and frightened. I get it. I would be, too, if I didn't know where my kid was. But it's seven A.M. and I'm playing some catch-up here. You say you spoke to me about your son. Jack?"

"Yes, last night. You were here. And your—the other detective." I reached for the other card but it fluttered to the floor beneath the table. "He's eight months old? You took our Nest cam? You sat right here, right where I'm sitting."

I was trying to picture Detective Rodriguez, to match that image to this voice. A tall woman with lively gray eyes, a tight bun, a kind and competent demeanor, which was probably why they sent her out on calls to frantic parents on the worst nights of their lives. Was that not this woman? Was that not this voice? Could there be two Detective Rodriguezes, and somehow they had gotten their cards mixed up? A farcical mishap at the printer so that now I was trying to get information out of the wrong person?

"I'm sorry. I don't mean to be brusque, but I was not at your house last night. Can you tell me how you got this number?"

"From you! Or someone, someone with your name, I—I'm sorry, I'm sorry I'm not being calm, but Jack is only eight months old. He's missing. My husband and I called last night and someone came out to see us, two detectives, and there were other people, people looking in the yard and on our street. I thought—I was under the impression we'd done all that we were supposed to, and now you're telling me that— I don't know what you're telling me."

"Did someone say they'd opened a file?"

"Yes! Absolutely. Footage from the baby monitor, and, and all sorts of questions and— You took the whole camera, actually, the Nest cam. You took his, his lovey, it has a cow face. You asked all sorts of questions. Someone did. I thought it was you."

"Well then, we're A-OK. We're going to get this sorted. All right? It'll be in the system. I'm going to go look into this and get up to speed and call you back. Yeah? OK? Hannah, you said your name was? And the child is Jack? Surname?"

"OK, yes, please do. Please do call me back as soon as you can. Bennett, our name is Bennett. Hannah and Adam, our son is eight months old, Jack, he went missing last night, just after eight P.M."

I was still sitting there trying to make sense of the call when Adam shuffled in.

"There must be two detectives by that name," he said when I described the conversation.

He had taken the chair across from me and was holding my hands across the table. His hair was flattened on one side, and he had a crusty line of dried saliva on his chin.

"That was my first thought, too. But I just—I don't know. I had the sense that they were going to stay out there looking. If that's not true, then what's anyone doing?"

"Last night was surreal. We were in shock." Adam gave my hands a squeeze. "Now it's more real."

My hands hurt when he squeezed them. That sting across the palms, as though they should be raw and red, scored with cuts from my fall up on the fire trail. I yanked them back and turned the palms up. No cuts, of course.

Adam reached for my wrists, concern across his face, but I ducked beneath the table to retrieve the fallen card. The younger detective, Detective Palmer, squat and blond and skeptical.

It went straight to voicemail. I left a message. As soon as I put the phone down it started ringing.

Adam reached to answer, and I let him.

"No, this is her husband, this is Adam. Right, Jack."

"Rodriguez," he mouthed at me.

He looked so pale, I was almost surprised I couldn't see through him. I wasn't sure he wasn't still in shock. I wasn't sure I wasn't myself. But he was using his I-am-a-man-who-trucks-in-facts voice, and just now I was grateful for it. For his practical approach to life, for being the sort of person who could get this sorted promptly.

"We did. No, we did. I don't understand. That's impossible. You sat here at this table. I am looking at a glass you drank from. It's still sitting here, half-full of water. Well, is there another Detective Denise Rodriguez? No. I'm really asking. That's not what I— I am as calm as a person could possibly be expected to be in this situation. What— How am I supposed to— No, don't do that. No, I do not consent to your hanging up, I'll wait while you talk to— Hello?"

The look on his face as he placed the phone into my palm: as if the facts had turned around and trucked right over him.

"She says they have no record of our reporting a child missing."

↔

Adam was pacing.

He pulled his science teacher voice tight around him as he thought out loud.

"But is this level of incompetence even possible?" he was saying. "I sincerely don't know. Is it? Is this some kind of— some kind of corruption? Should we be contacting a lawyer?"

This sounded unhinged to me, but I had nothing else to offer.

I realized he was waiting for my answer. I said, "I don't think a lawyer's a good idea. We don't want to make them angry. Let's just go down to the station and deal with it in person. Report him missing again if we have to, answer all the same questions. It's all some strange mistake."

"She said they have no record. How can that be a mistake?"

I closed my eyes and tried to think. The strange feeling was starting up again, that sense of urgency, that pulling outward. I needed to control it.

"I don't know how it can be a mistake, but it has to be one," I said. "There has to be some reasonable explanation."

But now this was the thought whose sheen of sense dissolved like soapsuds even as I said it.

The pulling outward, the waves like contractions, were getting stronger.

And when Adam said, "I'm going to call Julian. He'll know the names of lawyers who specialize in policing the police," I didn't object, because as crazy as this seemed to me as a next step, I had no better sense of what to do.

As soon as Adam went upstairs to make his call, I dialed Dr. Goodman. I hoped it wasn't too early. It was just before eight, and she'd had a late night of it. But again, she answered on the first ring. Did this woman ever sleep?

"Hannah! I was just about to call you. Did you rest?"

"Something strange is happening." I was speaking quietly, hunched down beside the fridge. "OK, this is going to sound nuts, but I keep having this thought—*there's something I can do if I let go*. And part of me feels like I actually should."

"I think there's a lot of truth to that," Dr. Goodman said.

"To what?"

"To what we've been talking about all these months."

"Is this what we've been talking about?"

"Isn't it? Allowing trust for your own instincts without letting them control you?"

I squeezed my head with both my hands. The feeling was so urgent.

"I think maybe I'm not conveying how strange this feels."

"What comes to mind around that? The strangeness."

Another wave of urgency rolled over me, tugging me, I didn't know toward what.

"It's almost like contractions."

"What's almost like contractions?"

"What I'm feeling right now. A sensation that asks me to let go. Fighting it seems unnatural and wrong."

"Like fighting contractions."

"Yes. That's true."

"So let go, Hannah."

"How?"

"I don't think I can tell you that."

A man's voice, muffled, in the background.

"Hannah, I'm so sorry, but I need to get off now. I'm going to call you again when I get to my office, is that all right?"

She'd hung up.

Upstairs I could hear Adam speaking. His voice was raised but also measured. I felt a swell of gratitude to him for being himself. If there was something practical to be done, then Adam was already doing it. And maybe calling Julian, maybe getting a lawyer, was the right thing to do. It didn't seem like the right thing, but maybe it was.

I pressed my forehead against the cool metal of the fridge. The waves of urgency were coming on more frequently. The effort of resisting them was exhausting. I wanted to take Dr. Goodman's advice, even though it was clear we'd been talking past each other. Even if she didn't have a clue what I'd actually been describing, I felt that she was right. To let go was brave. To keep resisting was the opposite.

All yesterday, my mind had been trying to scare me, and my mind had been dead right. Jack had been in danger.

So I let go.

Just for an instant.

The whole room fell away.

It wasn't like the last time. I was still crouched next to the refrigerator, its hum steady against my cheek. I could still smell the coffee Adam had put up to percolate before he rushed upstairs, and beneath it the compost, sweet and fetid. Behind the fridge, a bundle of extension cords was fuzzed with dust. I put my hand to my phone, and it was still warm from my cheek.

But also. Almost as though if I just turned my head. Like peripheral vision.

Also, I was lying in the dark beneath the slanting eaves of my bedroom. Adam's backside was pressed against my hip, his head turned away from me, his snoring light. An acidic churning in my stomach meant that sometime in the last twelve hours I'd drunk too much red wine.

I was here. I was there. It was as though I could direct my attention to either one, and then that's where I was. Like looking at two sides of a room. What did it mean?

But the pain was starting now, the pressing down from all directions. The Jacklessness of the bedroom. This time it didn't sock me in the gut the way it had the last two times. As though it were an atmosphere I was slowly getting used to.

And NO—

I thought it hard. I felt it all through my body, a command. And then it was as though reality hadn't just split before my eyes. As though I hadn't just somehow seen the feeds from two different sources playing at once. Now I was fully back in a world where Jack existed, my world. Jacklessness no longer pressing in on me. This gave me confidence that he was out there somewhere. Terrified, surely, but he was somewhere, unlike in that other place, where he was not.

I put my fingers to my nostrils and they came away pink with blood.

I had made that split happen. And then I had made it stop. I could do it again, I was fairly certain. Go over there. A different place. A place where my terrible memory from Jack's birth made sense, and nothing else did.

But nothing made sense here either.

↔

"Hannah! Come up here!"

I found Adam in Jack's room, staring at the empty spot on the orange bookshelf that used to hold the Nest cam.

"Yeah, they took it," I said.

"Right. I know. And now they have no record of having taken it. It's lost somewhere in an evidence locker most likely." He was fiddling with his phone. "I was trying to gather what we'll need in order to get a lawyer up to speed, and I went to get the camera's history on my phone."

He held it up for me to see.

"What am I looking at?"

"It's not there. None of this camera's history. The histories from the two outdoor cameras are still there, but not the one that was in here."

"It must have uninstalled somehow. Something the cops did when they were copying the recording."

"Check yours."

I held my phone out for him so he could do it for me.

His head still down, he said, "Nothing. No history of this camera on either of our phones."

"What does it mean?"

"It means we have nothing to show the lawyer. And it lends some credence to what Julian was saying."

"What did Julian say?"

I asked it warily. Julian was a lovely person, a prison abolition activist in Oakland who devoted his every waking hour to his cause. But Adam was forever lamenting that Julian was a thirty-eight-year-old child with all-or-nothing thinking around good and evil.

"That there are rings, actual kidnapping rings, they take kids and sell them for adoption. There are documented cases of cops being in on it, paid off."

"Adam, that can't be what's happening, that's conspiracy theory bullshit. Julian's gone so far to the left he's ended up in QAnon. Jack needs us to think clearly."

I bit my lip, surprised at my own tone. What right did I have to speak this way? Even as we were having this conversation, I was trying to swing my view wide again, to see that other world sitting beside ours. But the urgent feeling had gone away now that I'd given in to it, and without the waves pulling me outward I wasn't sure how to make it happen.

Adam's face was pleading. "I know. I know how it sounds. It sounds that way to me, too. But how do you explain it? How do we proceed?"

I could say it. Tell Adam, *Here is what I think is happening: Reality is not stable. Something is wildly off in what we've always taken for granted in the world around us.*

If he believed me, if he was willing to try, we could figure it out together. With his methodical, focused mind at my disposal, we'd have a great advantage. But there was no way he'd believe me. I wouldn't believe me, either, and Adam—well, human nature was what it was. If he hadn't been able to tolerate my vivid worries when all was well, if that had freaked him out, then now, when he was genuinely frightened and with good reason, he'd hate me for it. Truly hate me.

He'd look at me and see nothing but my mother. Not normal.

Given my history, my mother losing her mind in the midst of a child-related emergency, it was possible I should have been more concerned than I was about what was happening to me. But I wasn't. I felt entirely sane. More sane, more in control, than at any moment since I'd faced Jack's empty crib.

I was aware that none of this made sense. But I was feeling my way toward figuring it out. Not as well as Adam might have, not as methodically, but in the only way I knew; the way I figured out the fictional worlds of my books, where the things we take for granted were always going haywire, replacing the classical world of cause and effect with a quantum universe of strange angles, curious corners, unexpected doors between realities. People with the ability to step sideways through what was, into what could be.

Just then a phone rang.

Adam grabbed for his, but it was mine. It was Dr. Goodman.

"Hey," I said. "Can I call you back? This isn't a good time."

"Hannah! You need to come!" She sounded breathless, nothing like herself. "He's here! Jack, he's here! I saw him!"

Chapter Fourteen

We were clattering down the stairs, toward the door. Adam backtracked for his wallet and I followed him, catching him up on all that Dr. Goodman had just told me.

"She was parking her car, and she saw him through the glass of the sliding doors. She tried to get to him as fast as she could, but she passed behind a pole, blocking her view for like a second, and when she came around the pole again, he was gone."

Adam fished his wallet from between two couch cushions and stuck it in his pocket. We raced back out the door again.

"But it can't have been him." His voice was loud with hope. "Can it?"

"She says it was. She says she's almost sure of it. His face, his smile, that one curl that always goes the other way. She met him yesterday. She'd know."

What I didn't say: the details that had actually convinced me. That the baby she'd seen through the sliding doors as she drove past had been parked in front of the broken elevator in a silver and blue stroller that sounded like the one sitting in our portico. I touched it now as we rushed past, half expecting my fingers to pass through the metal of the handlebars. (They didn't.)

Also: that the baby in this stroller had been just beneath the sign—"We're working on it!"—taped to the chrome at a slapdash angle. And the canopy of this stroller was draped with a white muslin blanket with pale blue and gray stars, pulled back so that it didn't obscure the child's face—perhaps because someone had decided at the last minute that they shouldn't block his view, knowing he liked to take the world in.

I'd grilled her on these details while Adam bugged his eyes at me impatiently, desperate to be filled in on whatever was eliciting this impassioned interrogation.

Every detail had been just right, just exactly like I'd left him yesterday before he disappeared on me the first time, and she couldn't possibly know these details. I hadn't told her.

"Who are you calling?" Adam asked as he took a switch-back turn too quickly.

In the back seat, Jack's car seat rattled like a dark hunched ghost.

"The police. So they can meet us there."

"Don't call them."

"What? Why?"

"Because what if Julian's right?"

"Adam, Jesus, no. Think that through a second."

I stared at him. The phone held to my ear was ringing. He didn't object again, and I took that as consent.

"Yes, hello, this is Hannah Bennett. I've reported a child missing and he's been sighted."

"You've located a child you previously reported missing?"

"No, no, I haven't found him, but he's been sighted. We need someone to come and meet us at the location."

"The name of the missing child?"

Clacking from the other end. Bored breathing. As though I were trying to change a flight.

"Jack Bennett. But do you need to—there's something funny with his file. Can you just send someone out?"

"There's no missing child by that name. Could it be under another?"

"Right, I know. His file is missing. There's something wrong with it, someone made a mistake, but I am telling you that my son, my baby son, has in fact been missing since last night and someone saw him and now we need some help."

"Do you want to report a child missing?"

"Yes, sure, I want to report a child missing, Jack Bennett, who I also reported missing last night, now please send someone to come meet us at the medical building on—"

I turned to Adam in disbelief. He'd grabbed the phone from me and hung it up one-handed, while he steered us onward at warp speed.

"Try Rodriguez instead," he said, holding it out to me. "That wasn't going to work."

The low-rise medical building was looming up ahead of us. Grayish concrete, squat industrial design. I had never seen a sight so beautiful, because inside those charmless walls there might be Jack.

I dialed Rodriguez. It went to voicemail.

"Hi, yes, this is Hannah Bennett calling again. I know there's been some confusion, but my son really is missing, has been missing, Jack, and now someone has sighted him and I really need you to come meet us, please. Please." I left the address and hung up.

We were parked now. We were here. On the top level of the open structure.

I turned to Adam. He was still gripping the wheel, staring straight ahead, obviously not really seeing the sight in front of him, dark clouds rolling off the hills. Although even if he had seen it, it wouldn't have meant what it did to me. I'd stood exactly here just yesterday, watching the fog, longing for a cigarette, longing for one luxurious moment of doing something for absolutely no reason other than that I wanted to, while Jack fiddled with his ear, the most urgent of his Tired Signs. Those had been the last seconds before I discovered I'd left the car key in Dr. Goodman's office. The last seconds before my world went haywire.

I jumped at a loud rap behind me and turned to see Dr. Goodman peering in the window.

I opened the door.

"You waited," I said.

She was dressed in a white shirt and black satin pants. Her auburn hair fell in its perfect glossy wave. But she didn't look the way she usually looked, remote, serene. She looked like a person who gave a shit, which was actually not reassuring. I wanted something, anything, to be the same.

"I've just canceled my nine A.M." She licked her lips. "I've never canceled on a patient in my life except for illness. But it seemed called for."

She looked away. Was I allowed to hug her? Did I want to?

But she was already clacking across the pavement in her sling-back heels. Adam and I hustled behind her toward the sliding doors.

"Right here." She'd stopped. Just inside the doors, below the sign—"We're working on it!"—taped at a slapdash angle on the brushed chrome of the door to the broken elevator. "Right here is where I saw him."

The right spot. That's what I'd thought when I parked him here yesterday morning. The right spot: impossible to see from the outside, shielded from the sun. Although I'd been wrong that it was impossible to see from the outside. From a certain angle, which Dr. Goodman had briefly occupied before her car passed behind a pole, apparently you could.

"I've been up and down every floor," she said. "I've gone

into every open office. There's no sign of him. When are the police arriving? I'm not sure what else we'll manage to do without assistance."

Adam opened the door to the stairwell. Just as I had yesterday, unsure whether it was OK to leave Jack here without me, stepping in, then whirling out, Jack laughing because he thought I was playing with him. *Peekaboo!* And he was gone.

Adam said, "We'll keep looking until they show up. Is there a basement?"

"Yes." Dr. Goodman slipped past him, into the stale air of the stairwell. I stepped in, too. My heart was pounding like it wanted out of my chest. "I'd forgotten about the basement."

My muscles carried me down the steps, just a little faster, lighter than was normal. My lungs seemed to fill with extra oxygen with every breath. Adam and Dr. Goodman trailed behind me, their footsteps sounding plodding, because I glided, I vibrated, because the atmosphere was different. An atmosphere with Jack. A Jackfulness to match the Jacklessness I'd felt here yesterday as I raced up and down, panic edging in my vision.

Now the air was thick with him. Like in the middle of the night when I slipped into the cool, whooshing dark of his nursery for a feeding, and the whole space would be alive with his bready sleep smell, loamy and delicious.

There was no smell here except damp and concrete, but the space was alive with him just the same. Even my body knew it. The front of my shirt was wet. My breasts were leaking.

He was close. I could feel him, and this made me sick with hope. He was here.

Except he wasn't.

An hour later, we'd been over every inch of the building we could access, and we had nothing. No Jack. No further evidence he'd ever been here.

We'd been in thirteen offices, spoken to more than twice as many people, and every person that we spoke to wanted to help, but not a single person had seen a child matching our description.

There were still plenty of spaces left to check. Offices not yet open for the day. A locked room in the basement. There was also a roof we didn't have a way to access without a key. But without the police, we were at a standstill.

No way to reach him, and yet I'd felt him.

Just yesterday I'd stood here and pressed the heels of my palms against my eyes, as though I could reboot the scene, and when I opened my eyes again, I was staring at Jack's face screwed red and tight. Jack in his stroller, wailing. And I'd been able to grab him to me, breathe in his salty smell, his animal heat, small pounding heart against mine.

Dr. Goodman said, "I don't understand why the police haven't showed up yet. Is time not of the essence?"

I pressed the heels of my palms against my eyes. When I took them away nothing was different. Adam was still leaning against the door to the stairwell. Dr. Goodman was still sitting on the bottom step of the rising set, sling-back heels dangling from one finger, runs on the feet of both her stockings. She had stuck with us through it all. She had canceled her ten A.M. She looked defeated.

But maybe she had already given us what we needed to find Jack. I thought back to yesterday, to what I had been feeling just before Jack disappeared the first time. Like Dr. Goodman had said this morning: ambivalence. Some part of me wanted Adam back, wanted my old pre-mother self back, some hidden part maybe even wanted Jack not to exist. And then he hadn't. The same had been true in the kitchen, with Adam impatient in my ear and Jack crying from upstairs, and all I'd wanted in all the world was just the space, for just one moment, to feel, to think. Maybe the same had been true last night when he'd gone missing, although it was hard now to remember what I'd been feeling just before Jack's piercing screams at eight P.M., since the silence afterward had been so catastrophic.

I closed my eyes again. I tried to conjure yesterday's ambivalence because maybe that feeling was a door, and on the other side would be Jack waiting. Just like yesterday in the stairwell: right there, exactly where he hadn't been. But it was useless. Impossible to feel ambivalence about my child when every cell in me was yearning to lay eyes on him.

"Seriously, where are the police?" Dr. Goodman asked again.

Adam shook his head. Held up his phone screen-out for me to see. "Julian's lawyer friend called. I'm going to call him back."

As I watched him lope through the sliding doors out to the parking structure, phone to his ear, Dr. Goodman said, "Do I just watch too many crime shows? In the shows they actually turn up when you need them."

"The situation is complicated," I said absently.

I was touching the elevator. The chrome smudged with fingerprints.

"The sign is gone," I said.

"What sign?"

"The one that was here. 'We're working on it.'"

"Working on what?" Dr. Goodman was massaging her feet.

"The broken elevator."

She frowned. "But the elevator's fine."

Just then my phone rang.

"Detective Rodriguez. Thank you so much for calling back."

I was running my fingers along the smudged metal. No

sticky residue, no evidence a sign had just been hanging here, just like yesterday. I pushed the "up" button and it glowed yellow.

"I'm sorry it took me a minute to get back to you." The detective's voice was kinder than it had been this morning. More like the woman I remembered from last night. The woman who put a hand on mine when I was trembling too badly to get the water in her glass.

"Are you on your way?" I asked.

"Ms. Bennett, I don't think that's going to be possible."

The elevator doors dinged open. Then closed again when no one exited or entered.

"But you have to. Jack was here. He was in this building. We have an eyewitness who saw him."

A long exhale over the line.

"Ms. Bennett. Hannah. I'm going to say something that I think is going to be difficult to hear, and I want you to know that I wish I didn't have to say it. I really do. I want you to get the help you need. But I'm not it. Do you understand?"

"Do I understand what?"

I pictured her. This woman who last night sat at my kitchen table and asked detailed questions about Jack. Gray eyes, black hair scraped back into a bun. Professional and competent, only a little gruff. She was talking to me in a tone I'd only ever use to talk to a small child. And only a very sad or scared one.

"Your son is not missing. I looked into it, into him. I take it very seriously when someone says we're not doing our jobs, and the idea that you had filed a missing persons report that was not showing up in the computer system, that upset me. I wanted to get to the bottom of it. And I did. Your son isn't missing."

I braced, somehow knowing what she was about to say.

"Your son is dead. Your son died eight minutes after he was born."

"That isn't true. It isn't true."

The way one tiny arm trailed like a doll's would. The clipped, efficient sorrow of the quiet that descended.

"I'm sorry. I'm really genuinely sorry to have to say this to you. I'm a mother myself. I—I can only imagine."

"But you don't have to imagine. What you're saying simply isn't true. I'm not—I'm not what you're thinking."

Dr. Goodman, still sitting on the concrete step, had her head cocked in curiosity. Her feet were back in their patent leather sheaths.

"What am I thinking?" asked the detective.

"That I'm delusional. Grief-stricken and delusional and draining public resources in my inability to face reality."

Dr. Goodman quirked an eyebrow. I turned my back to her.

The voice on the line said, "It's interesting that you heard all that in what I told you."

"It was a straightforward implication. But we don't have to debate this. I'm standing here with my therapist. A board-certified psychiatrist. And she happens to be the one who saw my son. My son who is very much alive and who is missing and who was sighted in this building just before nine A.M., which is why I need you to take me seriously when I tell you that you are making a mistake. Can I put her on?"

I didn't wait for her to answer. I held the phone out to Dr. Goodman. She looked nonplussed as she teetered over to accept it, but, bless her, she put it to her ear.

"Hello? Yes. Dr. Zora Goodman. No, with a Z." She smiled at me reassuringly.

The elevator dinged open again, and this time three people got off. Dr. Goodman and I parted to make way for them. They were speaking loudly. She put a hand over her free ear.

"I did. Yes, a little before nine A.M. That's correct. Yes, 2999 Regent Street in Berkeley. That's correct. I'm sorry, confidentiality forbids me from disclosing that information. Mm-hmm. I'm sorry, I don't understand. Are you actually saying—"

The people had surged past us, through the sliding doors, and now Dr. Goodman leaned a hip against the wall. She locked eyes with me, then looked away. She seemed too thin, her clothes a mess of expensive fabric draped over her bones.

"Right. Yes, but I can't disclose that information without a written waiver signed by a patient. I see. Right, of course. Yes, in the abstract that's correct but as regards this particular individual— Correct. Well, yes, that's of course public information but I'm not saying— Yes. I appreciate that. You as well."

She handed the phone back to me. I was surprised to see that she'd hung up.

"She's coming?" I asked.

"Hannah." She straightened up to her full height, and I could almost see, almost hear her pulling something deep within herself together. Like a complicated puzzle clicking into place. Her outer self looked pulled together, too. Her hair once again falling in a perfect wave over one eye. Her black satin pencil pants once more creased to a knife-edge point, and her white blouse so crisp I could imagine biting into it like an apple. Even the way she was standing, as though her feet no longer ached. "I know how hard this is."

I already knew the answer, but I had to ask.

"Is she not coming?"

"This is worrying. I'm worried. You're going backward rather than forward." Her tone wasn't that different from the detective's. She'd never spoken to me this way.

"Toward what?"

"Toward resolving your grief."

"I'm not in grief."

"And that's the problem. There's no way out but through."

"Through what?"

"Jack's death."

I had to grab the wall for balance. That feeling in my stomach. The bottom falling out.

"Dr. Goodman, don't. Don't say that."

I steadied my voice. "You saw him this morning. You called me. Why do you think you called me? What do you think we're doing here in this hallway?"

I could see a flicker of confusion pass over her face. I watched it move like a shadow, darkening her features. Then it resolved. Her features bright again with certainty.

"Do you really not remember?" she asked gently.

"Do you?"

She pursed her lips. "I'd prefer to discuss this in my office. For the sake of confidentiality. Will you come?"

"No. Tell me now. Why do you think we're here? I'm not going anywhere with you until you answer me."

"OK. OK. We're here right now for the same reason I want you to come upstairs. Because I didn't want to speak with the police until I had a chance to check with you in person. It's serious, Hannah, making false reports. There could be real repercussions for you."

Was it possible? These past eight months. Every memory. Was it possible that none of these were real? That I had dreamed up my child's whole existence?

The thought knocked the breath right out of me, knocked the decades out of me, and I felt like a small child again, standing in a yellow, sun-drenched room that smelled of bleach working overtime. These were my sole memories of my mother, the three times we'd visited the place that was meant to keep and contain her, and somehow hadn't. Her: mute, eyes empty, body always rocking back and forth as though there were some music only she could hear. Me: clutching at my father's hand, feeling woozy, holding my breath against the smell of bleach and the notes of urine underneath it.

I'd been afraid to breathe. To call attention to myself. To draw my rocking mother's hollow eyes in my direction. Because I knew that if she turned to me, if we locked eyes, then I might see that this was really her. The same mother who, back then, I still dimly remembered as something other than a mute and rocking cipher. In that sun-drenched room she'd seemed more animal than human, and so did I: a hot, shameful trickle running down my leg because I'd wet myself in fear of my own mother.

I almost never thought about that room. I thought instead about the photograph, the laughing woman holding me. I split off what I couldn't tolerate, tried not to remember. So maybe I'd done the same again: split off and denied that my child had died in birth.

My mother had had a severe mental illness that first appeared postpartum. Maybe I did, too.

On the other side of the glass, Adam was staring at his phone.

"Will you come upstairs?" Dr. Goodman asked again.

But the velvet whorl of Jack's ear. The way he ate peas, double-fisted.

I pulled myself up taller so that I was closer to eye to eye with Dr. Goodman.

"What you're saying isn't true. My son is alive. Just yesterday you held him on your lap."

"Hannah, I never met your child. I couldn't have. Your child died at four-thirteen A.M. on the same day he was born. Remember? Remember the way you described the sudden silence in the operating theater? Like nothing from something. Such a powerful description."

She had a hand resting on my arm. I looked down at her

slender fingers, the perfectly polished nails in palest pink, and I didn't know. I didn't know.

Minutes ago, it had been clear to me that the world was insane, not me, but now—now that it was Dr. Goodman, so relieving in her cold way, I didn't know for certain.

"Hannah," her voice so smooth, so wonderfully unyielding. "You know what I'm saying is true. You're searching for a child who doesn't exist."

I could see Adam approaching through the glass. It had started raining, and dark patches of wet had blossomed on his jeans and the flannel he wore open over his T-shirt. Droplets catching on his eyelashes and nose, but he didn't seem to notice. He had his phone gripped by his side like a last-ditch weapon, and his face was slack with a very particular agony, the agony of desperate hope deflated. Because Dr. Goodman had called us here, she had, she'd called and said she'd seen our son and we'd come and hadn't found him. She'd called and now she had forgotten. Just like Detective Rodriguez had sat at our table last night and then erased the memory from her mind.

Adam walked through the sliding doors, dripping on the industrial gray carpet, and I had no doubt. I wasn't crazy.

I said, "Say it again, Dr. Goodman. Say it to both of us."

Her voice so calm, so certain: "You aren't going to find your child because your child died at birth."

I watched Adam's face as she said these words, the twitch of horror in his sane brown eyes, the fury bleeding his mouth shapeless.

"Lady," he said, his upper lip pulled tight now with disgust. "I don't know what you're playing at, but you saw our son here in this building just this morning. You called us because you saw our child, who very much exists, and you damn well know it." His hand closed tight around my arm. "And now we're leaving."

Chapter Fifteen

We left, but we didn't get far. We dodged through the down-pour to our car and then we sat there, soaked and stunned, not speaking for several minutes. Rain was coming hard against the windows, making a moving Rorschach of the world be-yond the glass. The view of the Oakland Hills was a watery blur.

Eventually, Adam said, "Hannah, what is happening?" He was speaking without looking at me, staring at the windshield. "I'm starting to think—I'm starting to think there are bigger forces at play here than we've imagined. That this thing is big, whatever we've been caught in."

I shifted in my seat to face him, jeans squelching wetly against the plastic seat. I wanted to tell him. Was aching to tell him. Yes, this thing is big. We have been caught in something big since the moment Jack was born, and I have been trying for eight months to tell you.

He looked, just now, like maybe he could hear it. Sodden, scared, split open by confusion. *Normal* now some distant memory for him the same as it always was for me.

I opened my mouth to speak, to try at least, but he was

pulling closed again. My goy from Ottawa, for whom the world had always made such seamless sense.

"This lawyer, Reichenbach." He swiped his palm over his face. He looked exhausted. "He has some theories, nothing firm. He thought you might be right about your custody concern. If they think this is one of us trying to pull a fast one on the other, they might be feigning incompetence just to catch out the bad actor. It would be criminal if true, but Reichenbach says the police are nothing if not the worst-run criminal organization in the country. And if we can prove they're sabotaging an investigation, which we can, a judge will change the jurisdiction so we don't have to worry about retaliation. His retainer is insane, but he's giving us good terms because he says he's rarely seen a case so open and shut. I was starting to feel we were finally getting somewhere when I was on the phone with him. But now—how does this keep getting stranger? What bullshit was that with your therapist?"

I looked at the rain obscuring the world beyond the windshield. I was trying to think of how I could begin.

Adam said, "I'm leaning back towards Julian's theory, honestly. The adoption ring. I mean, if your shrink is in on it, too. Which she obviously is, right?"

I swallowed. Ventured, "If she were in on something, why would she call us in the first place?"

"To throw us off the scent."

"What scent? We have no scent." I'd raised my voice. I sounded angry. I wasn't angry, not at him, but I wanted him to see we'd reached the end of logical explanation. I wanted to take him with me, out past normal. So that I didn't have to be here on my own.

"But we do." Adam was speaking softly, reassuring. "We know the cops are lying, and now your shrink is lying as well. We know someone erased things off our phones. The Nest cam feed for one. And Reichenbach asked for photos. Look at this."

He held his phone out to me, opened to his photo app. Adam logged hours every week on this app, arranging and rearranging every documented moment of Jack's existence, making it maximally searchable, Jack grinning through all his stages. Now he scrolled through, showing me: nothing.

He held out his hand for my phone, but I held on to it, thumbed the app open. The most recent photo was a very pregnant selfie taken in our bedroom mirror a few days before I went into labor. Since then, just some blurry shots that looked accidental.

I stared at the final blurry photo, just a close-up of my finger. On the surface, this was possibly the least strange thing that had happened over the past twenty-four hours, a bunch of photos disappearing. But now I understood, now it seemed so obvious what was happening: Jack was being erased. Slowly, mind by mind, device by device, and eventually it would be as though my child had never lived past the first eight minutes of his life. A whole world without his imprint, except inside my mind. Mine and Adam's.

My vision was swimming. I steadied my gaze on Adam, my husband believing absolutely in a half-cocked conspiracy theory because he had to trust in something.

Because otherwise it was too much to withstand.

My world began to wobble. The waves were starting again, the pulling outward like contractions.

I'd found it: the hidden door between realities. Ambivalence, yes, but not the sort I'd seized on earlier, not a broadstrokes love-hate of the all-consuming role of being a mom. No, something more specific: the ambivalence at being subjected to this much fear. The agonizing need to keep this someone safe, a need as bodily and insistent as hunger, thirst. But impossible to satisfy because, deep down, you knew that you were powerless: against accidents, disease, an active shooter. Against your baby disappearing from his crib without a trace. Surely every parent felt this. It was too much, the hugeness of what we'd opened ourselves up to. A child was too much to have at stake.

I swung the car door wide, letting in the driving rain.

"What are you doing?" Adam shouted. The rain was pounding on the pavement.

"I'm staying. I can't leave. It's the last place Jack was seen."

The air had been thick with Jack in there. Outside that elevator, which worked and didn't work, where a sign both hung at a lunatic angle and didn't hang at all. He was still here, not gone yet, not totally, and I could do this. Make him reappear the same way I had yesterday. I could save him. Keep him. I could do this.

Adam looked bewildered.

"But she was lying," he shouted. "Either then or now, she was lying. We can't trust anything she said."

I had climbed out of the car already; I was getting soaked. I stuck my head back in. "It's still the last place anyone claimed to see him. And she might not have been lying."

"But I can't just leave you here." His eyes were huge. They looked so much like Jack's. It felt cruel to abandon him alone in his lunatic theory, but what else could I do? His lunatic theory was wrong and mine was right. Jack was in that building. "How will you get back? How long are you planning to stay?"

I said, "I can't leave yet. I can't. Does that make sense?"

My hand was still on the car door. I could see that he was also itching to get on with it, to pursue his own loony theory, his mistaken path to Jack.

He blinked and then: "OK. Yeah. Fine. No, that does make sense. It does. Call me when you need me."

He reached to squeeze my hand, but the real reassurance

was the feel of the rain hitting my skin as I raced back toward the building.

The real relief was the glass doors sliding open, letting me back in.

I touched my fingers to the smudged chrome of the elevator. I let it overtake me. What I'd felt yesterday, but so much stronger. Ambivalence at what I'd opened myself up to. The fear of this much love.

And I was in my kitchen.

Chapter Sixteen

In my hand, the electric kettle, steam billowing from its spout. Against the wall of windows, the day's same driving rain.

I was here, I was there. Still in the hallway of the low-rise medical building, someone's abandoned black scrunchie gathering dust in the corner behind a fern. But also in my kitchen.

In the kitchen, the Jacklessness was pressing in from all directions.

I had to put the kettle down to catch my breath. This level of pain required careful calibration of every muscle twitch, every inhale. Like learning to live at a high altitude.

This isn't what I'd imagined. I'd imagined I would see my child, just like yesterday, exactly where he hadn't been. I'd imagined I was about to get him back.

Stepping purposely through a hidden door between realities wasn't nothing. But it was a far cry from the payoff I'd expected. I couldn't get derailed by disappointment.

I looked around. There were two blue lacquered mugs on the white granite countertop, both with tea bags in them. Through the arch to the dining room came the sound of a pen scratching against paper. Probably Adam grading blue books. The exam he'd given yesterday in tenth-grade chem.

I glanced in, wondering why he wasn't at work. He looked pale, peaked. I was making tea for both of us. Maybe we were hungover. That acid, red wine churning in this body's gut this morning. It wasn't like Adam to drink to excess, much less on a school night, and it wasn't like him to miss class no matter how rotten he felt. But this hardly seemed the mystery to focus on at the moment.

I moved quickly, quietly away from the arched doorway, through the kitchen, through the living room. Up the narrow front staircase that led to the two bedrooms. I winced as my foot made a creak against the third step from the top.

The other Hannah had been making tea. Just like yesterday, the other Hannah had been taking a hike on the fire trail. And now she was gone, and I was here instead, creeping up my own stairs and down my own hallway like a burglar.

I was in front of Jack's bedroom. I reached for the door-knob. I closed my eyes. A stupid instinct. I forced them open and felt a burn of bile in my throat.

The walls were still the vibrant blue we'd painted them to-gether, laughing over our gendered conception of babyhood even as we succumbed to it. But other than that, there was no sign this had ever been a nursery. It was just an empty blue-walled room. Even the stickable art Adam's mother had given us—"Jack" spelled out in colorful blocks—had been scraped imperfectly off the wall; there was still the corner of a J.

I jumped as two strong hands closed over my shoulders.

It was Adam. Of course, it was Adam.

He had no reason to be surprised to see me, but something in my face must have alarmed him, because he took a few steps back.

"Oh," he said. "It's really happening."

"What's really happening?" I asked.

"Exactly what you said would happen. Well, not you. Or not exactly."

I looked over his shoulder, down the stairs, and tried to think.

It felt as though, at last, there was some right thing to say to Adam, something that would get me past whatever had been in our way these last eight months. Something that would make this man into the partner that I needed. The partner who could help me get to Jack.

He was waiting for me to speak. He was watching me so closely.

But I was too afraid to think clearly enough to find the words to reach him. And it was strange, because fear was my oldest friend, constant companion, the basis for my livelihood. I was a suspense writer for goodness' sake. Fear was my mother tongue. But this level of fear right now, these past eight months, every second since the moment Jack was born. This level of fear was something altogether different, something that broke open the rules of how the world worked.

I opened my mouth to speak, still unsure what might come out.

"I'm so afraid," I finally said.

Adam took one step closer.

"I know you are. That's always when you start to ride the possibilities."

Chapter Seventeen

.

I watched him watching me. Focusing in on my eyes, then my mouth, then my eyes again. As if each were a separate clue. It seemed that he was searching me for signs that I was not myself. It seemed as though he really did know what was happening.

I wanted to ask everything, but didn't know where everything began.

"Did you just say—"

He cut me off.

"I'll tell you what I know," he said. "I want to be of any help I can. Anything for Jack. But let's not stand here any longer."

He reached around me and shut the door, then started walking down the hallway toward our bedroom. I found him standing in the middle of the wall-to-wall cream carpet, waiting. My eyes went immediately past him, to the spot on the carpet where Jack had sent an arcing stream of pee his second night home. There was no dark outline of a puddle. But otherwise the room was correct in every detail. Uncanny and bewildering. It smelled of Febreze. The Linen and Sky scent because here, too, apparently, they'd been out of the Bamboo scent at the Safeway.

Adam was still observing me in that careful, piecemeal way. On the bedside table, atop a teetering pile of books, were the pad and pen I used to keep beside me while I slept, in case I woke with inspiration in the night. I grabbed them, and also grabbed a book to use as a hard surface, then went to sit on the wall-long window seat. Adam came and sat beside me, but at the furthest corner of the cushion, which was a good ten feet away. He looked uncomfortable. Shy, and embarrassed at being shy. I held my pen poised above my notepad, ready for an explanation.

He said, "You must know more than I do at this point. I mean, you're here. You got yourself here. Three times now, right? At least? That's what you—that's what my Hannah said."

I pressed my legs into the firm give of the striped cushion beneath me. Getting this cushion made to fit the ten-foot seat had taken up an astounding portion of my third trimester, and then I'd hated the pattern I'd chosen as soon as it was done. All of that had happened here as well. This world and mine had been the same until they weren't.

"But how does she—" I was finding it hard to form full sentences; every question seemed to bud off twenty more. "How does she know that? She can tell when I'm here? What does it feel like? Where is she now? And why are you talking about this like it's—like it's normal? Wait—don't answer any of that. None of that's important."

"No, not when your son is missing."

"How did you know he's missing?"

"Because that seems to be what happens."

I leaned against the window. Beyond the glass, the rain was coming hard. The redwood just outside the glass, that made a tree house of our bedroom, was thrashing its thick branches like tentacles. But at least I was finally talking to someone who knew things. Someone who could help me.

"So tell me what to do. How do I get him back?"

Adam winced. "I wish I knew."

Or, no: I was talking to her husband.

"What *do* you know?" I asked, my pen at the hopeful ready.

"I know that until yesterday she thought it was her fault."

"That what was?"

"That the Jacks kept disappearing."

The Jacks? "Why would she think that?"

Adam put his hands flat on his thighs and leaned forward the way he did when he was feeling at a loss.

He said, "Is it OK if I tell this in my own way? I'm still having trouble wrapping my head around it. I only learned about the situation yesterday, and I wasn't even sure that I believed it until five minutes ago."

I wondered again what had happened to the Hannah who belonged here. If I was here, then where was she? I wished there were some way of cutting out the middleman, talking to her directly.

"What happened five minutes ago?" I asked.

He looked surprised.

"You showed up."

He was waiting for something to click for me. When it didn't, he continued, "Well, it was clear to me the second you turned around. As clear as if you'd had a stranger's face. You're not my wife."

As the rain battered the glass behind me, I let my eyes roam over his face and tried to guess whether I'd know he wasn't my husband if the situation were reversed. I could see how I maybe would. Not that he looked different in any concrete detail. The way the stubble thinned on the left side of his chin, the way the muscle in his jaw twitched while he watched for my reaction, the way the tendons on his neck rose from the collar of his worn gray T-shirt—every individual detail was correct. But the sum total of them wasn't. When you added them up, they were someone different. Sweeter and more vulnerable, more like pre-Jack Adam. But, unlike pre-Jack Adam, this Adam had a gravity to him. The same handsome features, but they didn't look boyish.

"Hannah1," I said. "Can we call yours Hannah1? I'd say Hannah2, but that seems presumptuous."

Adam smiled, which seemed to me a strange reaction to any aspect of this conversation.

"What? What did I say?" I asked.

"She calls herself Hannah42. So as not to be presumptuous."

I wasn't about to smile, but it occurred to me that I really liked her. I mean, we certainly got each other's references. Forty-two, the meaning of life according to *The Hitchhiker's Guide to the Galaxy*. But my liking her was broader than the trivial fact that we shared a sensibility pretty exactly. It was the way she seemed to have things under control here. The way she was taking care of some very strange business as if it were no big deal. She was my kind of woman. The kind of woman I'd been before becoming a mother: cool, collected. I admired her. In fact, it was possible that I was jealous of her. Not only was she who I used to be, she had a husband who, when given the chance to decide between the world or his wife being normal, had decided to put his money on his wife.

If only I could talk to her, this Hannah42, I might be getting somewhere, closer to finding Jack. But Adam42 was all I had for now. Adam42, who was staring out the window at the world-erasing rain.

Without turning to look at me he said, "Our son didn't

make it. He died. It was . . . well, losing Jack was the worst experience of my life, as I'm sure you can imagine. I was—" He shook his head. "But Hannah. She was magnificent. She got me through. She really did. She was sane and even-keeled. She handled everything. Kept us fed and paid the bills and let the relevant people know that things had not gone as we'd planned, to please not send more tiny clothes or stuffed animals or books. That was the worst part, getting those packages in the mail from people who somehow hadn't gotten the memo; it went on for longer than you'd believe. And God knows what else she handled while I was basically one step better than comatose for what had to have been weeks. Without her, I'd have been—well, what am I now? I don't know. But I'd be worse."

He took a long breath in and out. He closed his eyes. When he went on speaking, his voice was softer. I'd never heard this voice of his before. It sounded nothing like the Adam of the past eight months, tight with certainty. But also nothing like pre-Jack Adam, who even in his most serious moments had a playful sparkle always skittering underneath, a little boy desperate to charm the world in order to keep it functioning. This voice was sad and strong and unafraid.

"The thing was, she had this memory. It made no sense. It hadn't happened. She told me about it once, and I asked her not to bring it up again. I'd lost my son that day, and hearing her insist on this false memory, hearing her describe the way—it was too awful."

"What was the memory?"

He looked at me.

"He cried."

"Cried?"

"She swore she heard his voice, his first cry, loud and piercing. But I was there, too, and he never made a sound."

On my notepad I wrote down *Common factors: jangling memory, birth, life and death.* My hand was shaking, so the words were barely legible, but this didn't seem like information I was likely to forget.

He went on. "I thought she'd taken my words to heart, realized it wasn't possible. Just a strange effect of all those drugs, the trauma of his death, the whole terrible experience. But she hadn't let it go. She—she used it. She rode it. That memory, it was like a door, she said. Another way things might have been, another way that came so close, and it brought her into a world where the memory made sense. A world where Jack had lived."

"My world?"

"Not your world."

"How do you know?"

"Because the Jack in that world is gone. He disappeared six months ago. He disappeared from his crib one night, just— poof. And then that whole world seemed to forget that he had ever lived at all. That world was almost worse than ours for Hannah. That possibility. For two months she'd gotten to watch our child thrive, grow, experience joy and misery and frustration. She saw his first smile. He existed and she could visit him. At first, the visits happened by accident, she'd be here, wracked with grief, and then suddenly she was there, holding a bouncing baby. Eventually, she figured out how to control her movement, and she started going over there more often, almost constantly in fact. I thought she was depressed. She'd lie in bed all day, unmoving, but I didn't think too much of it, it was her turn to fall apart. My turn to take care of us. I wonder now—if he hadn't disappeared, might there have come a point when she just stopped coming back to me? I might have done that in her position."

He looked away again. I jotted down a few more notes: *My*

body when I'm traveling = looks asleep? But my hand was trembling badly. I put my other hand on top to settle it.

"Anyway," he said, "when that Jack disappeared, she somehow found her way to another world where he was living. Watched him grow and thrive again. She saw him roll over. Sit up. Then that Jack also disappeared, two months ago. That was when she stopped riding the possibilities. Because she decided it was her fault. That she was making them disappear by going where she wasn't meant to be. And then she decided it had never really happened at all. She found a therapist who helped her to make sense of it. They concluded together that this had all been in her head, a kind of extended metaphor, her own way of grieving, and that now she was ready to accept what her mind had been trying to teach her in its own way all along: that there was no escaping reality. Our child had died and that was all that could ever be, because that's what, in fact, had been."

"Was her name Dr. Goodman by any chance?" I asked, rubbing my twitching right hand with my left.

"That's right. She really helped. You, too?"

"She's had her moments. Sorry to interrupt. Keep going."

"Well, that was it. Until yesterday. Right after a session with Dr. Goodman, actually."

I licked my lips. My mouth had gone all tingly. His words had brought me back to yesterday morning, running up and down the stairs outside Dr. Goodman's office, searching for Jack, who was there and then not and then there again. Maybe he hadn't actually disappeared that time. Maybe I'd slipped through to here, to Hannah42's world. My consciousness, but in Hannah42's body. Running up and down those stairs, her heart pounding, drenched in sweat, legs buckling, frantic with the sense of having lost something that was everything. And that would mean that Hannah42 had been in this body, too.

We both had. What must that have felt like to her? Running, frantic, but with no sense of why.

"She knew it was me making her run up and down the stairs?" I asked.

My hand was jerking around the page now, almost like it had a mind of its own. Leaving pen marks in its wake. Fear driving my body bonkers. Adam was now staring openly. I covered my right hand with my left again, trying to still it. Adam gently reached and took my left hand off. The right kept moving.

The marks were almost like letters. The marks were letters. The letters spelled *wallte*.

"Wallet," Adam said.

He had shimmied closer to me to get a better view.

"Hi, Hannahbelle." *His* Hannahbelle. He was touching the paper, tracing the pen marks. His touch was so tender I felt a different kind of in the way. Then, to me, "She thought she'd lost her wallet. That it had fallen out somewhere in the stairwell. Eventually, she found it in her bag." I must have looked perplexed because he added, "She told me this yesterday. I didn't figure all that out from 'wallte.'"

My right hand was still moving. Slowly, unsteadily, but it was movement, deliberate movement, and I was not its author.

Pst c jusfctin

"Post-hoc justification," Adam said.

First your body moves, then your mind starts scrambling for a story that says why.

Splt brn

"Split brain," he said.

I nodded. "I know the feeling."

Sharing Hannah42's body *was* a little like being a split-brain patient. Like the quantumly doomed wife in my—in our—first book, *Probability Lanes*. Her character was one of a cohort of severe epileptics who had been treated by a severing of the corpus callosum, the bundle of neurons that connects the two hemispheres of the brain. The crazy thing about split-brain patients is that the left and right sides of their brains can't communicate at all. So the left hand might be doing something—say, trying to put on a pair of pants—while the right hand is simultaneously undoing it, taking the pants off.

Now my hand was moving with more fluid strokes, but the strokes were not quite letters. It was hard for Hannah42 to make this hand move, difficult for us to share intention in this body. I wondered why today I seemed so much more in control than she was. Yesterday on the fire trail, we had seemed to trade intention back and forth, one speaking then another, battling it out; it had been so hard for me just to kick a rock. But maybe that was because we didn't yet understand that we were sharing a space only meant for one. I tried to relax my claim to this body, drain all intention from my mind, but this was easier said than done.

fr tral

"Fire trail," I said, for some reason eager to beat Adam to it. "When it happened again on the fire trail, that's when you started to suspect something abnormal was afoot."

Dr. Goodman had convinced her that she hadn't ridden the possibilities, that it was all inside her head, an extended metaphor to get her through the enormity of her grief. But all those times, when she'd gone over to those other worlds, she'd probably wondered the same thing I had been wondering as I climbed the stairs up to Jack's bedroom: Where did the other Hannahs go? Up there on the fire trail, she finally had an answer: This was what it must have felt like to be those other Hannahs, the ones whose bodies she had borrowed when she rode the possibilities.

I continued, "That's when you realized Dr. Goodman was

wrong. That it had all really happened. You had ridden the possibilities, and someone else was riding them, too."

yesss

Adam let out a long exhale. I glanced up. He looked queasy.

"You OK?" *He's reached his limit of not normal,* I thought, and my disappointment was surprisingly keen. *E tu,* Adam42?

He licked his lips, raked the curls off his forehead, that annoyingly sexy gesture. "Yeah. Yeah. No, it's just . . . this is feeling like something from a ghost story. Like she's—"

He left the thought unfinished, but it didn't matter. I'd been wrong. His discomfort wasn't about not normal. It was about loss. This Adam had been through so much loss already.

"But she's not a ghost," I said. I was feeling relief, pity, a pang of jealousy. "She's very much alive, and I promise you you'll have her back."

My hand was writing again. A weird tingling had started spreading from my fingertips to my forearm. As though the hand were plump with something precious. Twice the intentionality, twice the consciousness as ought to be in one physical form, a vibrant abundance.

if another Hannah riding, another Jack in trouble

Adam had moved even closer to me, as though he wanted to crawl inside my skin, get to his wife. His breath was warm against my neck. I was finding it hard to ignore. The way this Adam felt was so familiar and so alien—how could I not wonder how else it might feel different to be with him?

I shifted my body ever so slightly away from Adam's and said, "So you reasoned that if another version of you was riding the possibilities, then another Jack had probably disappeared. Because why else would I ride to a world without him. Is that it?"

+ stairs fear wallet

"Got it."

"I don't," said Adam.

"The fear she'd felt in Dr. Goodman's stairwell was all out of proportion when attached to a wallet. But not when attached to a child."

yes yes

I glanced back up at Adam to see how he was faring. He met my gaze and gave a reassuring nod. How had he become this game and grounded version of himself? Maybe grief had done this to him. Was that the only way?

"And she told you all this," I said. "When? Why?"

"Yesterday, up on the fire trail. She told me the whole story then, starting with riding the possibilities. In case you came back. In case you needed help. You. Your Jack."

My Jack. Who seemed to have disappeared just like those other two. My child in his rainbow-striped pajamas floating in some existential limbo. What could that be like for him? Was he afraid? Confused? In pain? I started to imagine, but that kind of thinking wasn't smart. It brought with it an abject terror that, left to fester, would derail me; I wouldn't be able to stand it. I shut the question down.

I said, "And you believed her."

Adam looked away. He seemed to really be considering.

"No. I wouldn't say that," he finally said. "She wasn't even sure whether she believed herself. She said it might all be nonsense, backsliding, another round of what Dr. Goodman called her manic denial of grief. But if there's any chance it's true, that another Jack is disappearing, then what's worth more? Her being right or his existence? She's willing to risk seeming crazy to herself just for the slimmest chance of helping. I can't think of anything braver. What else can I do but try as well?"

"That's why you're home today," I said.

"Yeah. Of course."

It was puzzling, the things he thought would be obvious to

me in this situation, but I touched his wrist in thanks, then quickly drew my hand back.

I said, "So once this process starts, this disappearing. It takes—how long? How long do I have before my whole world thinks Jack died eight minutes after his birth?"

My right hand was moving again. It only took one try this time to form the letters.

varies

"By how much? How long did it take for those other two Jacks?"

24 + 27

"Hours? Days?"

hrs

Fuck. If that was my timeline, I might only have ten hours left. If it wasn't, I might have less.

"But do you understand it? What's actually happening? Why do the Jacks keep disappearing?"

My hand lay still.

Adam said, "She doesn't know. Neither of us can figure that part out. Maybe worlds that briefly split in two then start collapsing? Turning back into the same world? That was the best we could come up with last night."

"Like a quantum collapse kind of thing? Two possible ways things might have gone during the birth, child living, child dying, both equally true, both equally real, but only for a time because reality can't stay"—I searched for the right word, was pleased when it presented itself—"probabilistic? It has to be determinate?"

"Yeah, kind of."

"But that's not how it works at all. It's only subatomic particles that act like that, not the things that they make up. You're not talking about Everett branches and many-worlds, you're talking about a single world acting like an electron in the two-slit experiment." I knew this because I'd been hearing bits and pieces of it all my life from my father, and because I used it in *Probability Lanes*. Adam knew it because he knew stuff like this, taught it.

"No, I know. I'm sorry. I wish we had something more helpful to tell you."

I pictured dozens, millions, an infinity of Jacks winking out of existence one by one like dying stars. And an infinity of Hannahs tumbling through the hidden doors and crooked angles of the universe, trying to save them. I'd battle anything for Jack, do anything, obviously, he was my child, but if it was me against the laws of physics, I didn't stand a chance.

"It's hopeless, isn't it? I'm not up to it."

My hand was moving again. The words came quickly this time. Urgently.

Youre, here.

I looked up at Adam, confused. He gave an encouraging smile.

"She has a point," he said. "I imagine you never thought you could step between realities, and yet here you are. Who knows what you're capable of?"

I forced a smile back, trying to find this bizarro version of an inspirational poster reassuring: *You can do it! You defy the laws of physics!* What I really wanted was to climb into this Adam's arms, have him hold me, love me, soothe me while the other, better Hannah saved my son.

"So what do I do next?" I asked.

The pen dropped from my fingers. Fair enough. I needed to figure it out myself. For a second, I wondered if Hannah42 could read my thoughts, knew I wanted her to save my ass while I took comfort in her better version of my husband. But then my body rose to standing. Began to stagger toward the bed, then past it toward the bedside table. Now that I saw where she was aiming, I helped to smooth the motions, reached for the teetering pile of books, none of which I owned in my world, because I had no time to buy books, much less read them. The first two on the pile I set aside. They were novels I'd never heard of. The third one looked like an academic book, something about the brain. I'd have laid this one aside as well, except that my hands were now flipping it open to the back jacket flap.

A familiar face gazed up at me from the author photo. Sharp features, rather birdlike, and an intelligent mouth that was tilting into a conspiratorial grin beneath a profusion of frizzy gray hair. Berkeley Birder of a Certain Age, female of the species. Whom I often saw outside my home, and then saw on the fire trail, and whose partner I'd run into at Baker and Commons where I discovered to my horror that I knew his name when I shouldn't.

According to the bio beneath the picture, she was Grace Reggio-Watanabe, a neurologist and neurobiologist at the Weill Institute for Neurosciences at the University of California, San Francisco. She lived with her husband, the string theorist Akio Reggio-Watanabe, and their cat, Schrödinger, in the Berkeley Hills.

These two must have popped up all over the place for Hannah42, same as they did for me. That's why she'd bought the book. Trying to solve the puzzle before Dr. Goodman convinced her there was nothing to be curious about except her own strange mind.

Grace and Akio Reggio-Watanabe. It wasn't much. But it was something. A lead.

I was itching to go, now that I had a clue to follow, but from across the room, Adam was watching me carefully again, expectantly. I could tell he had something he wanted to say, and that it was hard to say it. So I held on, waiting.

"What's he like?" he finally asked, his voice unsteady. "What's he like at eight months old? Can I ask that? Is that all right?"

I swallowed my urge to decline this question. What if it put Jack in further jeopardy, my sharing details about him with someone who had already lost him? But I didn't see how it could. This Adam, who was not my husband, would never get the chance to know his son. Because of him and Hannah42, I stood a chance to keep on knowing mine.

So I said, "He's wonderful. He's perfect. He eats peas double-fisted and his hair has the most delicious smell when he wakes up every morning, like fresh-baked bread. He likes to take the world in. He's exuberant and willful and never took a bottle and is impossible to sleep train. He rarely sleeps through the night."

Adam was crying. I hoped he didn't regret asking. I didn't regret telling him.

"Go find him," he said. "Go."

Chapter Eighteen

Back in the stairwell in my own world, I was sitting on a concrete step. My nose was bleeding again. I tilted back my head
and found a tissue in my back pocket, applied firm pressure to
my nostrils, and the bleeding slowed, then stopped.

As I dabbed at the last rivulet, I thought of Hannah42, of
her Jack, who'd died. A spasm of grief shuddered through me,
for him, for her. She'd lived out my worst fear. And now, in
some sense, I was living hers. Because she, too, had learned to
ride the possibilities, and when she did, Jacks disappeared. I
needed to figure out what was disappearing them. I needed to
figure it out quickly. I didn't know exactly how long I had before Jack fully disappeared, ten hours more or less, but time
was not my friend here. And all I had to go on were two names:
Grace and Akio Reggio-Watanabe.

I stuffed the sodden tissue back into my pocket, then took
out my phone and looked up Grace. It wasn't clear to me
which one of them Hannah42 was suggesting I approach,
Grace or Akio. Akio made more surface sense because string
theory seemed more relevant than brain science to my situation. But Grace was the one who always looked at me as

though she knew my face. Whereas her husband, when I'd accosted him at Baker and Commons, had stared at me without a flicker of recognition.

This was a shame, because Akio's office was less than a mile away, on the campus of UC Berkeley. Grace's lab was in Mission Bay, across the bridge in San Francisco. Traffic there and back across the bridge could eat up ninety minutes when time seemed of the essence.

If I went to Grace, she might not be there. If she was there, she might not be willing to speak to me, a total stranger showing up uninvited. But all my instincts were saying she was the right one to approach, and I was trying to trust my instincts.

As I pushed up off the step and toward the sliding doors, a group of people surged out of the elevator and gave me a wide berth. I looked down at my milk-and-blood-stained T-shirt and realized my appearance was a problem. No driver was going to pick me up like this. Nor was this a look likely to win me the confidence of Grace Reggio-Watanabe. I veered off toward a restroom, where I dabbed at my clothes with a series of disintegrating paper towels, my breasts so full and aching now that the friction made me flinch. The results of my cleanup were not great, but at least I no longer looked like biohazard. Plus, I was a woman nearing forty with the soft paunch of a childbearing stomach, so I was basically invisible anyway. It at least seemed safe to summon a Lyft.

Outside, the weather had done a full one-eighty. The sun was shining, the clouds were thin puffs in a pale blue sky, kids shouted gleefully from the sand park across the cul-de-sac as their nannies stared down at their phones. As though this were just a normal day. In fact, a better than normal day because it had rained this morning, which we badly needed, which we always badly needed in California. No bite in the air of imminent world collapse.

As I waited for my car to show, the minutes ticking frighteningly down, I watched people go about their lives and allowed myself to envy them. The toddler girl in Peppa Pig–themed boots staring at me through the rails of the park's metal fence with the affectless intensity of a hit man. The handsome man walking through the glass doors of the low-rise medical building, impeccably dressed and trailing toilet paper from his left heel. All the many people in their cars stuck at the traffic light on Ashby.

All of them conceiving of things the way they'd always conceived of them, as I had always conceived of them. With reality being sometimes remarkably shitty, but still the sort of thing you could depend on. Unitary and consistent. One past, one present, one future.

I stood there and I envied them and maybe I even hated them a little.

But I couldn't sustain this feeling. And when my Lyft driver, Ionut, pulled up in his silver Fiat and asked me if I minded the eastern European rap music he had blasting at ear-splitting decibels, then peeled off without checking his blind spot, I almost burst out crying for love of this twentysomething idiot. Or, rather for his mother, wherever she was, for how much she must love this child of hers who had had the great good fortune to grow into a man.

As we drove past the CVS on Telegraph, I had the sense that I was retracing yesterday's steps. But soon we were crossing the majestic white expanse of the new Bay Bridge, high above the glittering turquoise water, and this at least was different, this felt like progress.

Adam had been sending me texts almost since the moment that we parted just over an hour earlier, and as Ionut hurtled me over the bay toward Grace Reggio-Watanabe, I took the opportunity to read through the expanding thread of them.

They were mostly updates on his research. Adam had discovered the story of a woman named Georgia Tann who had run a widespread kidnapping ring that hit its peak in the 1950s, stealing the children of the (mostly) poor to sell to the rich through adoption. The police had turned a blind eye to her enterprise in return for generous kickbacks. There had been a *60 Minutes* segment on this, which Adam had now watched in its entirety, live texting me throughout. Georgia Tann's kidnapping ring had been responsible for supplying Joan Crawford with the two kids she'd abused throughout *Mommy Dearest*. It was all very disturbing, if irrelevant.

Interspersed with this history lesson, Adam had also sent along communications from the lawyer, our lawyer now apparently, named Reichenbach. These would have been alarming for their degree of buy-in on Adam's ravings, if only I thought that any of this had the least bit to do with our saving Jack. Thank fuck-all it didn't. The thinnest of silver linings.

He had sent me 179 texts so far. I would be desperate to hear from him if the roles were reversed. But there was no way to explain why I was heading into San Francisco at this moment, so I just texted back *Amazing*.

It felt like such a waste. We might be helping each other through this ordeal, but here we were again, unable to team up in the effort. We were as bad at losing Jack together as at having him. I stared at my single-word response at the end of his text message treatise and knew that what was happening between us now was a reprise of the past eight months: Adam busy researching, thinking he could find the rules to tame the chaos. Me inside the chaos, flailing on my own.

I felt a hot wash of shame spill over me, thinking of Adam42. *What's he like at eight months old?* He'd also lived my nightmare.

I'd been so busy feeling baffled and betrayed by my husband's pre-to-post Jack transformation, I'd never considered why such a loving man would turn into a rigid, rule-bound version of himself. I'd never considered that he was every bit as terrified as I was. Just like me, he'd watched our child hanging between life and death, those first ten minutes when he took no breath, made no sound, the room filling up with urgent, worried people dressed in scrubs. "Normal" was a word Adam wrapped around himself like a blanket, because the world was random and chaotic and infinitely cruel in its indifference and he couldn't stand being helpless against that when it came to his own child any more than I could. That much terror, who could stand it, but Adam had found a way: He defended against it with his baby-sleep rules, baby-feeding rules, baby-bathing rules, rules for every interaction with this fragile little being as though *normal* would protect us against *tragic*. And now that the experts' rules had given out, he was searching for the hidden ones.

Whereas what had I ever found to help me through the terror? An impossible solution. To protect Jack with my perfect love and presence at all times. An idealized mother, constant and unreal. No one could live up to that. I had failed to contain my terror, and it had turned into an ambivalence so unwieldy that reality couldn't contain it either. Just like Hannah42's uncontainable grief. So big and so unthinkable they yanked us out past thought, out past reality.

So maybe Adam had been right all along about me as a mother. Maybe this was all my fault. Because why else would the children disappear? It had to be the mothers. When the mothers rode the possibilities, maybe the children rode them, too. A mother's unthinkable thoughts, uncontainable feelings, destabilized her child's very existence. Maybe. If it *was* true, then Jack would be safe in my arms right now if I'd only been better at managing my worry.

My thumbs moved quickly over the keypad, replying still to Adam: *I love you. We're going to find Jack. It's going to be OK.*

I deleted all but the first sentence and sent it off.

↔

Grace Reggio-Watanabe's lab was not what I expected.

She was a big deal, clearly, some kind of funding goddess. Her lab was on the eighteenth floor of what looked like a brand-new building. Her lab *was* the eighteenth floor, the size of an airplane hangar, with soaring ceilings, floors of sealed concrete, young people rushing around importantly. It looked as though someone had been tasked to design a set that could double as both "lab of the future" and "chic hotel."

As I lingered in the doorway, faced with this impressive show of status, it occurred to me that I had formed no strategy or plan. What was I going to say to Grace? If she had knowledge that was relevant to finding Jack, how was I going to elicit it? Did she even *know* she had whatever knowledge this might be? And this was assuming she had any connection at all to my situation, which was a pretty big assumption.

I was losing faith, and this wasn't good, so I ran my fingers through the tangles of my hair, probably making matters worse, then stopped a young man rushing past me with a clipboard.

"Excuse me, I'm looking for Dr. Reggio-Watanabe."

The young man, round-faced and barely out of adolescence, looked at me skeptically over tortoiseshell glasses.

"Is Dr. R expecting you?" he asked.

I shifted my left arm so that it partially obscured the largest pinked-out bloodstain on my T-shirt. Just this slightest pressure against my breasts was painful.

"Not exactly. But she'll want to see me."

I stated this with so much confidence that I almost believed me. The young man shrugged. He didn't believe me, and he didn't disbelieve me. He didn't need to settle on either, because he didn't care. It was no skin off his tortoiseshell either way. He pointed to a clump of people next to a stand of machines that looked like, but surely wasn't, stereo equipment. Just a little above the other heads, gray frizz was spilling upward.

I made my way with purpose toward this upward spill of hair.

When I said her name, she turned to me, but this time there was no flicker of recognition. It gave me another moment of doubt, but this one was short-lived. Because, in fact, this was a good sign, wasn't it? Every other time I'd seen this woman she'd looked at me as though she knew my face. So now she had to be pretending not to know me. Which meant she really knew me. If anything, this was extremely promising.

The younger people around her were all peeling off.

I was now facing Grace Reggio-Watanabe, big-deal neuro-scientist, alone. She was waiting.

"I'm Hannah," I said.

"I'm Grace."

"Do you know me?" I asked.

She quirked an eyebrow. "Should I?"

"I think maybe you should."

"You'll have to help me then."

It occurred to me that this was a very kind woman I was speaking to. It occurred to me that this was such a kind woman I could risk saying almost anything. At worst, she'd quirk her eyebrow as she steered me toward the exit.

"My son is in terrible danger."

She knit her brows. Her faced clouded with pity and confusion. I kept on speaking.

"I thought maybe you knew—"

She stared at me. Tender, confused. Just another variation on Detective Rodriguez and Dr. Goodman. Writing me off, compassionately. Which meant I had to go all in. Either it would work or it wouldn't. Either I'd be escorted out or something good would happen.

I said, dead serious, "Maybe it's in another world we met?"

It was like I'd said the secret pass code. Her whole face changed.

"OK," she said. "Give me a second."

She went and whispered into the ear of the round-faced boy who went and spoke to someone else who went and spoke to someone else and they ricocheted like billiard balls, each telling something to another, until, one by one, they were clearing out. The whole vast space was emptying.

As this strange dance of an exit was happening, Grace was standing next to a piece of the stereo-looking machinery, fiddling with knobs, ignoring me. Maybe she was actually such a kind person that she was clearing all potential witnesses before calling security. Would that in fact be kind?

But once the echoing space was empty, silent except for the low competing hums of the machinery, she looked up at me and smiled.

"Hannah," she said. "I'm so incredibly glad to meet you. Come into my office?"

Chapter Nineteen

Off the hangar-sized space were several smaller rooms, and one of these was where Grace Reggio-Watanabe led me now. She shut the door and locked it behind us, which seemed excessive given the echoing emptiness of the eighteenth floor. But then again, I had no idea what was normal for these circumstances or what these circumstances even were.

Her office was cramped and cozy. The view was a high-end real-estate eyeful of the San Francisco Bay. But otherwise, this space bore no thematic relation to the larger one we'd left. The room was overstuffed with cheap mismatched furniture and books and art and tchotchkes, like someone's grandmother had moved into their dorm room. Grace Reggio-Watanabe was almost certainly someone's grandmother. A lot of someones actually, or else some very prolific someones. Every inch of wall left bare of bookcases was covered over in paintings quite obviously made by tiny hands.

I lowered myself onto a purple sofa. The clock on the wall said it was 11:47 A.M. If it was true that I'd had ten hours left after leaving Hannah42's world, I now had a little over eight before Jack fully disappeared.

Grace was puttering at a long, low row of cabinets.

"Can I get you something?" she asked, turning to smile at me. "We just got a Keurig as a gift from one of our donors who apparently is unaware of the environmental impact of the pods. Just having it here is making me insane, so I'm trying to get through these as quickly as I can so that I can toss the whole contraption. I realize it makes no sense, I could toss it regardless, but honestly? The coffee isn't bad."

Grace seemed easier in here. She held herself differently. Now every glance and gesture seemed to speak of familiarity. Of familiarity with me.

"Thank you," I said, "but I'm in sort of a time crunch."

She was already handing me a terribly misshapen ceramic mug, painted in highly glossed splotches of red and pink.

"You want me to tell you what I know," she said, settling onto a floral-printed armchair. "About yourself, the many worlds, your son. Why people are forgetting him."

"Yes. Exactly," I said, amazed and grateful that this was turning out to be so easy.

"Well, let's start with this," she said, watching me above her own misshapen coffee mug. "I know your mother."

"My mother," I repeated.

The words sat strangely in my mouth. I rubbed my fingers over the hot, mottled surface of my mug, considering the likelihood that Grace had mistaken me for someone else. Admittedly, it didn't seem likely.

Then she said, "Eva Aisch," and removed any last lingering doubt.

"You know my mother," I finally managed to say.

"To the extent that anyone can."

"You mean before she—?" My mind turned over the options. My mother had been a scientist. So was Grace. Had they been colleagues? Friends? Grace was a neurologist. "Was she a patient?"

"She was at first. Then something closer to a collaborator. Now perhaps a teacher? I think it's safe to say your mother is the most extraordinary person I've ever met. That is, if it's even safe to say I've met her."

I took a sip of coffee. I couldn't taste it, but the burn felt good going down. Something to focus me on the real task at hand, which was getting the necessary information out of Grace and ignoring all things extraneous.

"*My* mother," I confirmed. "You're speaking of her in the present."

"I suspect there's a lot you don't know about your mother."

I took another sip of coffee, using the excuse to slide my eyes away. I was feeling jangly, unable to make the grooves fit. This all felt wrong. Like I was going backward rather than forward.

"I can't argue with you there," I said. "I haven't seen or heard from my mother since December 19, 1986. I was six years old. Until this moment I had no idea whether she lived or died after that date. I take it that she lived?"

I closed my eyes and saw my father's face, his walrus mustache, his deep-set hazel eyes that crinkled in the corners as though at some point they had laughed a lot, although I'd never seen it, not even once. All he wanted to do for all my childhood was bury himself in work and grief. All I'd wanted for all my childhood was not to feel alone.

I opened my eyes to see Grace with her fingers tented before her pursing lips.

"No, of course you wouldn't know that, would you," she said when I met her gaze. "That was thoughtless of me not to consider. I'm trying to think of where I should begin."

I said, "Maybe you could start with where she's been for over three decades?"

She nodded, began several times to speak, then stopped herself before saying a word.

Finally she said, "I'm not dodging your question. But it's a less straightforward one than you might imagine. Or maybe you can imagine. Given what you seem to know. You can do it, too, I take it? Walk astride the possibilities?"

I was struck by how similar this phrasing was to Hannah42's language of "ride the possibilities." I wondered whether this meant that Hannah42 had pursued her lead past buying Grace's book, had also had some version of this conversation, in which case I was only recovering old ground. Or whether instead the similar phrasing was a signal that we were converging on actual fact. Possibilities. Possible worlds. I chose the latter option, convergence on the truth, because I needed to believe that I was getting somewhere.

"Yes, I can do something . . . something very strange," I said.

Outside the window, three birds lifted off a ledge at once and joined a sudden burst of others that exploded above the bay.

Grace said, "That's a relief. I didn't break our pact. Akio and I swore to each other we wouldn't tell you anything unless you also had the capability. It seemed too cruel. Why know you're losing your child if there's no way you can stop it?"

I had to will my mouth to speak slowly enough that the words didn't slur together. "So there is a way to stop it? You know how?"

"There are some relevant things I know. I'm just trying to think how best to say them." She paused, considered. "OK, let's start here. Birth is a rather unique event, would you agree?"

"I'm not entirely sure I understand the question."

"Let me try that another way. I've never actually tried to speak about this to someone new. Ah, how about this? In one sense, giving birth is a purely biological event. A body emerging from another body. Yes?"

"Sure."

"But it's more than purely biological as well, right? Something more metaphysical, you might say."

"Something from nothing, you mean," I said. "A life where there wasn't one. Is that it?"

Grace nodded, looking relieved.

"That's it exactly. The moment of birth is deeply metaphysical: the coming into existence of a new person, a new mind, a new consciousness, a new self, a new subjective world. Let's put aside the old acorn of when life begins, and just stipulate that it's at birth. For the sake of what we're talking about, that seems to be the case. At birth, it's as though the universe hives off a new universe, one that contains a self—or soul or mind or person or consciousness or subjectivity—that the preceding one did not. What I mean to say is, birth and possible worlds are not an arbitrary or random juxtaposition. When a child is born, a whole new infinity of possibilities also winks into existence, a whole new infinity that is the new soul, new subjectivity, new life. Are you with me so far?"

"Yes, I actually think I am."

I had an image in my head as she spoke, of a cluster of tiny soap bubbles forming on the surface of a larger bubble.

"OK. Very good. This is going better than I'd hoped. You're a quick student, which I suppose I ought to have predicted. I think I don't need to explain to you that it's not just at birth that choice points spawn off possible worlds. That's happening to us at every moment, as we're sitting here, just now, just now, just now. I think you know this. I've read your books. They're very good, by the way. Very unnerving. But at birth it is a *profligacy,* an immense proliferation. A whole new infinity of possibilities instead of just a relentless branching of the actual. Now comes the crucial step. At birth, the boundaries between possible worlds are not yet fully formed. Normally, of course, there's no causal interaction at all between possible worlds. But these newborn clusters, they're strange. Wonky. The boundaries between them act funny."

I pictured the filmy, iridescent surfaces of my bubbles where they met, skins joined to share a common wall.

I said, "The wonky boundaries—that's true for everyone? For every birth?"

"Every last one of us. But some mothers can actually see other possibilities at their child's birth, a glimpse of another way things might have gone. I suspect you were likely one of them."

"A condition of too much seeing," I offered. Just what Adam had accused me of yesterday morning when he told me he was leaving.

"Ooh. It's fun to talk this over with a writer. You put things so much better than we scientists."

I decided not to let her know she could chalk that one up to a high school science teacher and said instead, "So you might have memories, then, that make no sense. Is that it? Like you might remember seeing a nurse carrying your stillborn child even though he lived, or you might remember hearing his first cry even though he never took a living breath."

"Yes. That's it. I take it those aren't hypothetical examples."

I had somehow sunk deep into the bowels of the purple sofa and was trying to shimmy forward. My post-baby stomach muscles were no match for the mushy cushions, and I ended up slipping deeper in.

I said, "I saw Jack die. My son. I saw him dead. He wasn't dead, but I saw it. Are you telling me that's why—are you telling me it's because I saw what I wasn't supposed to see that Jack has disappeared now?"

Here it was. Confirmation of what I'd already begun to know on my way over. My fault. Not because I'd failed to get a better handle on my worries, as I'd been thinking, but simply because of who I was: a person who saw what I wasn't meant to see. At least this was one way the world was still predictable: You never could go too far wrong by blaming the mother.

But Grace looked aghast. "Oh God, no. No. Jack's disappearance has nothing to do with you at all. Let me try again. Forget your condition of 'too much seeing' as you called it, although I'd like to quibble with the 'too much.' For now, let's focus on the children. I've told you about the wonky boundaries at birth. The next crucial step to know is this: the boundaries are funniest at birth, but it takes them quite a while to firm up fully, to start to act the way that we expect them to, each reality impermeable and nonnegotiable, established fact. It's gradual, the process. We're not talking materially, of course. I don't mean to say there's some substance that forms boundaries around possible worlds and that the substance changes its properties as the infant ages. What we're talking about really only makes sense as mathematics. The metaphors and images we try to substitute just aren't up to snuff. Are you your mother's daughter mathematically speaking, by any chance?"

"Not even close. Math isn't my language."

"Ah, well. We'll make it work with metaphors. Just bear in mind that the translation won't be precise. Without the math, perhaps it's best if you *do* picture it as a substance."

"I'm picturing possible worlds as bubbles. Does that make sense?"

"If it's working for you, run with it. What I want to get across is that throughout infancy, there remains the chance of possibilities interacting. They shouldn't be able to, according to our current physical theories, and yet they do. As a result, a baby is always in special danger of moving from existence to nonexistence. Put another way, a baby is a very unstable state."

"I'm sorry, you're losing me a little. Are you not just stating the obvious? That babies are soft, small, vulnerable creatures? That they can die? Crib death, choking, a fall, a common cold, a blanket on the face, the room too hot, the room too cold. Who doesn't know this?"

She pursed her lips again and tapped her two long index fingers against them. She said, "Sometimes it's remembered as an infant death of the sort you're describing, that's true. Other times, the world forgets the child more completely. It all depends on the point of intersection. But death isn't the danger I'm speaking of, or not exactly. Rather, because of the strange openness to interaction between their possibilities, every infant is at every moment rather tenuously holding to their life because at any moment, the possible world they occupy might interact with a possible world in which they died. At that point, it's a simple numbers game, and I'm afraid your Jack has gotten unlucky."

Weirdly, this made a kind of terrible, intuitive sense to me. It echoed with what I'd felt ever since becoming a mother: the terrifying tenuousness of this new life in my care. Every time I ran to his crib in the middle of the night to put my ear near to his mouth because his breathing on the monitor sounded "different." Every time I watched his tiny chest cage rise and fall or felt the smallness of his body up against mine and wondered how a being so vulnerable was meant to stay alive, how this could possibly be working, his living, his thriving, my ensuring that he did.

But on a more concrete level, I was not at all sure I was following. Adam was the abstract thinker between the two of us. I thought in images, in narratives. I tried again to picture the filmy, iridescent surfaces of my bubbles where they met, skins joined to share a common wall. Now I tried to picture some of these filmy borders as incomplete. This made the bubbles unstable, so some were popping, and others merging, and a very few were hovering in the improbable configuration of two nearly perfect bubbles without a proper boundary. Eventually geometry demanded that these two bubbles merge or burst. Apparently so did the mathematical laws of whatever it was that Grace was describing.

I said, "You make it sound like this is common. How often does this happen? How unlucky is my son?"

"It's such a good question. But there's really no satisfying answer I can give you. Bear in mind we're speaking now of infinite possibility. Probabilities aren't very useful for carving up the infinite. And, anyway, once a world where a child existed becomes a world where the child no longer does, the world forgets the child. So how could we collect any data that speaks to this? There's no one to report it."

"But why does the bad way always win, the child gone, the world forgetting? Why can't the interaction go the other way?"

"Technically, it can. But you have to consider entropy. The laws of nature favor a move toward disorder; things fall apart. Or, actually, put it this way: the number of arrangements of atoms in a system that amount to any particular child existing is far outstripped by the number of arrangements that don't."

"But it *can* happen? Maybe Jack will be OK?"

"Well, no. If the interaction were going the other way, then he wouldn't have disappeared, and people wouldn't be forgetting him. Again, this would all make better sense if I could show you the math."

I wished Adam were here with me to understand the math for both of us. I was angry at him for not being here and angry at myself for needing him when I ought to have inherited this competence from my two physicist parents. I was mad at absolutely everyone, even Grace, because I was desperate with frustration. "But so where is Jack? Where is he right now, right this second?"

"Somewhere in the spread of possibilities."

"But *where*?"

"I'm not at all sure that there's an answer. At the moment, there's no fact of the matter about whether he is, much less where."

"But my therapist saw him earlier this morning. So he *was* somewhere, at least for a few seconds."

"Well, that's interesting. The coincidence of it, I mean. But, no, he wasn't somewhere even then. Or rather, he was, for those few seconds, but—would it make sense to you if I said he was flickering in and out of existence in our world? Like an electric grid on the fritz?"

This did make sense to me, and seemed like very good news. "But so I can catch him—when he flickers back, I can be there. And then I can . . ." I trailed off, not sure what I would do after that, how I would keep him from flickering back out, but certain that getting to him was a tremendous step in the right direction. "Should I go back to where she saw him? Should I be waiting there?"

"I wouldn't if I were you." She might have been advising against my ordering the grilled cheese at a restaurant. "The chances of him flickering into the exact same spot again are infinitesimal. So long as he's flickering between existing and not existing, he can flicker into being anywhere in this world. He's not bound by location in the way we are because he's not quite *of* this world at the moment. He doesn't belong to it, the way we do. What I mean is, there's no way to predict where he might be at any moment. You're not going to get to him like that."

I tried again to shimmy from the couch cushions. But it was useless.

I said, "If there's no way to get to him, and it's all just a numbers game, and my Jack drew the wrong number, why are you even telling me about this?"

"Well, because of you, of course. Your capability. There's nothing unusual about his situation—your child is subject to chance like any other. But there's something terribly unusual about you. You can walk astride the possibilities. You can save him."

Whatever words were next were the words I'd come here for, the crucial words, the ones that I could act on. I waited, but she seemed to be waiting for me as well.

"And how do I do that?" I finally asked.

"I wish I knew." She spread her hands wide, nearly toppling a framed photograph of five very cute small people who all shared certain features of her face.

"But you must know something about what works. If all the mothers with my capability have done this, you must know what they've tried. How many of us are there?"

Grace licked her lips.

"I've only ever known about two women who had this capability. You're the third. And you're only the second one I've had the honor to meet in person. The first, of course, was your mother."

"My mother."

I was somehow not expecting this even though it could not have been more obvious when I considered the conversation's arc. She'd as much as said it several times.

"But do you mean I disappeared?"

"When you were just shy of a year."

"But, no, I never—" I trailed off. I had gotten very sick just before my first birthday. This was the story as I knew it: I had gotten very sick, I'd almost died. Eventually I'd gotten better, but before I turned the corner my mother suffered her psychotic break and never recovered. My father had never mentioned anything about my disappearing. But he wouldn't remember that, would he, if what Grace was saying was true. A sick child was a way to make sense of something that otherwise didn't make sense, much like Dr. Goodman rewriting the history of our treatment outside the elevators this morning.

"But she did it," I said. "She saved me." I paused, realizing. "Saving me is what made her lose her mind."

Grace nodded, but said, "Your mother never lost her mind. She's—are you familiar with the concept of a superposition?"

"Kind of like if you play two musical notes at once?"

"Yes, but not with musical notes. With quantum states."

"Quantum states?"

"Right. If we extend the analogy again, your mother is in a kind of superposition with respect to possibilities. She's lost the ability to be in any single one. She exists in all of them simultaneously."

I was trying hard to be the quick study Grace had called me, but my mind felt at capacity. I pressed a thumb and forefinger against my eyelids and attempted to shape the content of this conversation into coherent understanding. Grace had told me that all possible worlds exist at every moment, never interacting, but that in infancy these intermingle strangely and sometimes, based on odds, this wipes the child from existence. Unless the mother could save them, as my own mother had saved me.

"So you're saying when my mother saved me it left her in a kind of cosmic statelessness, still alive but an exile from all possible worlds. That that's what made her act the way she did, mute, rocking, seeming blind and deaf to everything around her. She was like that because she can't exist in any single possibility. Do I have this right?"

Grace nodded. "You have it right exactly."

"That must mean there are other versions of my mother, infinite versions of her, that are normal, healthy. That are just my mom, whoever she might have been."

She was looking at me in a way that made me feel exposed.

"She never stopped loving you," Grace said. "She watches in her way. She worries in her way. She worried especially when you had a child. It was why she asked us to keep an eye."

"But how did she do it?" I asked. "How did she bring me back once I disappeared, how did she stop me from flickering before I flickered out once and for all?"

"Hannah, I don't know. I don't think she knows. If she knew, I don't think she'd be spread across the possibilities. She'd be here, being your mother."

"But, still, she did it, right? You're sure she saved me."

"Well, here you are, so, yes, I'm certain."

"So it is possible."

"Absolutely. Absolutely, Hannah, it's possible. I wouldn't have shared any of this if I didn't think it was possible. You have the capability. Same as your mother."

This was what I'd wanted to hear, that it was possible, but it was feeling more impossible than ever.

"But what is it, this capability? What actually is it that I can do?"

"Actually, that's a good idea," she said. "Let me show you something." She turned toward her computer and began typing quickly. "Ah, the MRI is booked for the next hour. Hold on a second."

She picked up a landline sitting on her desk.

"Hi, Meg, it's Grace. I have a favor to ask. You guessed it. Or even if I could just slip in for thirty minutes. Yes, right now. How about you offer her my three P.M. slot both today and tomorrow so she doesn't feel rushed. Perfect. Thank you so much. I appreciate it."

Grace hung up, smiling sheepishly.

"I hate to pull rank, but—" She shrugged. "It does happen to work."

She stood and offered me her hand so I could finally free

myself from the purple couch. She did it so naturally that it left no room for being embarrassed that I'd been unable to extract myself unassisted. I followed her back out into the larger lab space, still trying to muster the comfortable confidence she seemed to have in me. My mother had saved me. That was something at least. Better would have been if I had the faintest clue of how she'd done it. But there was a third woman Grace had mentioned.

Hurrying to keep up with her as we cut across her gleaming, empty lab, I said, "What about the last one? You said there were three women you knew of with this capability. Who was the third? Did she also save her child?"

Grace was walking purposely with her long strides, and she was several steps ahead of me. She said over her shoulder, "She did, and I married him. And, speak of the devil, here he is."

She had reached the large glass doors that led out of her lab just as Akio was approaching from the other side. With him was a girl of four or five, with an untamed halo of hair like Grace's, but blond. She was wearing a frilly blue party dress and a backpack larger than her torso. The backpack was shaped like a Tyrannosaurus rex.

"I see you got my message," Grace said, not slowing as she passed them. "This is Hannah. Eva's Hannah. Of course."

"Of course."

This time Akio looked at me as though he'd known me for years, an old friend of the family. The smile crinkling the corners of his eyes held just the slightest hint of mischief. If he was proud of the poker face he'd mustered at Baker and Commons—not to mention all the other times I'd run across them—I couldn't blame him.

"Hannah, this is Akio, my husband. But you've met."

He fell in step with me as we followed Grace down a wide hallway.

"I'm sorry about yesterday," he said. "In retrospect, I could have been a little more informative, but your son was with you, so I punted. It wasn't clear to me you'd actually turn out to need to know how strange the world is."

"And this is Lulu," Grace said, still not breaking stride. "Who has no school today."

"I'm four and eleven-twelfths," said Lulu matter-of-factly.

Several people passed us, and Grace greeted them warmly without slowing. We walked down two flights of stairs, down more hallways, and then we stopped. She rapped once at a shut door and it swung open to reveal a narrow, windowless room filled with electronics. The room was separated by glass from a smaller room. On the other side of the glass was the MRI, large and white and noisy. It was making a rhythmic humming like fluorescent lights, but louder. A woman about Grace's age looked up at us from one of the computers.

"That was fast," she said. "You want me to stay, or is this another subject you want to run yourself?"

Grace smiled. "Go take an extra-long lunch if you'd like. I won't tell if you won't." To me she said, "You ever been in one of these?"

I shook my head. The tech had gathered her purse and was slipping from the room. She waggled her fingers playfully at Lulu before shutting the door.

"No cochlear implants, pacemaker, other metal in you?"

I shook my head again.

Lulu had sat herself on the floor directly at my feet and was unpacking her backpack. A blue and white plastic tea set emerged first, followed by five dinosaur figurines.

"The predators will eat the herbivores unless they get some ice cream," she announced.

Akio said to no one in particular, "I think someone needs to learn a little patience."

Lulu looked up at us, amazed at this injustice.

Grace bent down to kiss the girl's head and said, "Hannah, I'm going to ask you to take off any metal you might have on your body or clothes. You can put them here in this plastic tub. And these earplugs are for you. Akio, while I get set up, maybe you could tell Hannah about the maze of mirrors?"

But Lulu had wrapped herself around Akio's leg and was saying the word "please" over and over.

"Sorry, one second." Akio leaned down and whispered something in Lulu's ear. She disengaged and began to slither across the linoleum floor like a snake.

"I'm sorry," he said, watching her go. "I tried to find someone to watch her when Grace let me know that you'd turned up, but Camp Grandpa was already our daughter's last resort."

I waved the apology away. The truth was, I was finding Lulu's presence grounding. The stolid reality of her felt like an antidote to the frightening abstraction of Grace's information.

"How did your mother do it?" I asked. "How did she save you?"

He was following Lulu with his eyes again. It might have been to avoid meeting mine.

"It would really help if I knew that, wouldn't it?" he said. "But I don't. I only know she lost herself in the process, same as your mother."

"How can no one know what our mothers did? How can no one know this?" I said it more petulantly than I meant to. But it was ridiculous that I was starting from square one when at least two mothers, including my own, had already figured out whatever it was I needed to do. Somehow there was no wisdom to pass down. Somehow I was on my own while doing exactly what other mothers, who knew how many, had already done for their own children. It occurred to me that all of mothering had felt like this, in fact—thrown into a demanding, high-stakes role without assistance or preparation. Only the stakes had never felt as high as this, nor the demands as thoroughly confusing.

Akio nodded. "It's a terrible shame there's been no cumulative knowledge built up. It is. But Grace asked me to tell you about the maze of mirrors. And I think she's right that it might be useful. Would you like to hear it?"

I licked my lips and looked away, so he wouldn't see the tears of frustration pooling in the corners of my eyes.

"Yes, I would like that," I said.

"OK then. Here we go. I've never told this story to anyone but Grace, so bear with me. This was an experience I had when I was thirteen years old. I was with my grandmother at a carnival. We were in the maze of mirrors and I briefly lost her. I probably lost her on purpose. I was thirteen, like I said. I remember I was looking at my own reflection. Reflection upon reflection of that same boy who happened to be me, and I felt this sense of *why* and *how* is that person reflected there *myself*? Why that person and not another? What connects that skinny boy with floppy hair to the sense I have at every moment of myself? I'm sure you've had thoughts like this. Most people have. That feeling of coming loose from yourself. I'd had similar thoughts plenty of times before with no repercussions beyond a brief, disorienting trippyness. But this time suddenly I remembered I could do something. Only remembered isn't really the right word. It was like a muscle memory of the mind. I felt for it, this muscle memory. And then, without warning, I was somewhere else entirely. Not anywhere very interesting. Just back at my grandparents' house in Astoria, in the front yard, and the screen door was opening and I felt the most extraordinary sense of anticipation, a feeling like falling through the looking glass into a pool of marshmallows and puppy dogs, a feeling like every good thing you've ever known rolled into one and covered over with malt balls, and then I was in Brighton Beach again, in the maze of mirrors, and my grandmother was coming toward me looking like she wanted to take me over her knee."

Akio's face, as he spoke, had assumed a distant look, but now he looked at me with warmth.

"I've been trying to explain that one experience to myself all my life. I was never again able to do what I did that day, and not for want of trying. But I knew from then on that the world was a more interesting place than I'd previously assumed. That reality was not as uniform, nor time as linear, as I'd believed. I found my way to confused and confusing ways of framing my discovery to myself. Leibniz's conception of possible worlds as ideas in the mind of God. The Buddhist teaching of *Kegon kyo,* a cosmos of infinite realms, each containing all the others, an infinity of Buddhas on a blade of grass. And then, eventually, when I was in graduate school, string theory. My whole career as a physicist has been about trying to figure out what happened to me that day."

"And has string theory helped you understand it?"

"No." Akio smiled. "I can't say that it has. Your mother has helped me, though. And Grace. And this." He gestured toward the machine, indicating that I should follow him around the glass, and so I did.

Lulu was slithering back toward us, her face deformed into an exaggerated snarl. Perhaps she was being an alligator or crocodile or prehistoric beast, and not a snake as I'd assumed. But she stopped at the glass partition. She seemed to know she wasn't allowed on the far side, where the giant magnet whirred.

I climbed up on the platform and Grace guided me down, placing a blanket over me, fitting foam pads around my shoulders. She laid a white cloth over my eyes. She maneuvered the earplugs into my ears more expertly than I'd placed them.

But I could still hear Akio's voice from the other room saying, "You need to be patient if you're going to earn the ice cream."

Then Grace's voice was in my ear, through a speaker in the machine.

"Lie perfectly still," Grace said. "Try not to speak unless you absolutely have to. You have this button here if you need to get out, but try not to use it. This shouldn't take more than twenty minutes."

The platform I lay supine on was moving backward into the machine, and the magnet had begun its loud, arrhythmic thumping. It was surprisingly unpleasant. The noise seemed to come from everywhere at once, and the tunnel was so dark that I felt set adrift in boundless space rather than pinned inside a narrow chamber. The situation filled me with a vague, disorienting apprehension, very different from the focused, motivating fear that had been driving me all day. Supine, I thought of what it must be like for Jack, whatever he was going through. Flickering, as Grace had put it. It was a terrifying thought. Almost too frightening to bear. Could it really be *anywhere* in the world that he flickered into being? I pictured Jack on a busy city street, in the middle of a desert, on the ocean floor. It was hard to imagine how a child appearing and disappearing in plain sight could fail to be big news. Maybe people filtered out the view of him the same way they filtered out his memory; maybe they needed to in order to maintain their sense of continuity. But for Jack, there would be no continuity, no sense to be made from one moment to the next. And no one there to soothe him, gather him, hold him together against the terrifying confusion.

I wanted out of the MRI. This had been a mistake. I needed

to be on the move, I needed to be *doing something* to help my son. Instead I was lying motionless in the dark, while time slid past me, thick, slippery, and muscled like an eel. And every passing minute was a minute fewer that Jack had left.

I tried to push my thumb down on the button. For some reason I couldn't. It wasn't just that dread was deadening my limbs, making me feel paralyzed. It was that, somehow, I was falling. Not really falling, not off the MRI, but my stomach was dropping as though I were tumbling into endless shapeless space. I'd forgotten this feeling. I'd had it often as a child, lying in my bed, alone in the dark, too terrified to fall asleep because it was right there in the phrase, *falling* asleep, it felt like this, like I was tumbling into blackness and my surface might disintegrate until I was just another undifferentiated part of the nothingness that I was falling into. For most of my childhood, I could only fall asleep by swaddling myself tightly in sheets and blankets. The linens were like a backup skin; they reassured me I'd cohere.

But here, now, there was nothing to wrap around me. There was only the terrifying sense of dissolution. Alone in the dark. Unable to move. And now I could hear crying. A child's desperate call.

I felt a sharp stabbing in my breasts. The gush of letdown. I was spurting milk, like when I heard Jack's hungry cry. It was his cry. I knew that sound as well as I knew anything.

I managed to smash the button with my thumb.

"Let me out! I need to get out!"

The platform was moving. I blinked into the fluorescent brightness of the room and sat up, gasping. The front of my shirt was soaked completely, blood and breast milk mingling. For some reason, my nose had resumed bleeding.

On the other side of the glass partition, Akio was rushing a screaming Lulu toward the door. Lulu, howling for her ice cream. It hadn't been Jack's cry. I could have sworn it was. I could have sworn that Jack was calling for me, that I'd heard his actual voice. And I began to sob. Thinking we had been in communication and then having this conviction stripped from me felt like losing him a second time.

Grace was standing over me, stroking my back with one hand, while her other held a handkerchief to my nose.

Very calmly she said, "Come. You want to see why you can save your son?"

Chapter Twenty

On the other side of the glass partition, she sat me before a monitor and leaned over my shoulder to adjust the screen. I was looking at an image of a brain; I assumed that it was mine. Normally I'd have found it interesting to see my brain. I never had before. But I was still so shaken by the mirage of Jack's scared cry. It was a struggle to pay attention to the image on the screen, which seemed abstract and hopelessly removed from what I wanted, which was just to hear his voice for real, to follow it to him.

Grace was saying, "Akio wanted me to apologize to you for leaving so abruptly. He said you should feel free to reach out any time. I'll give you his number before you go. Lulu, on the other hand, was utterly without apologies or regrets." She was clicking through images as she spoke, each one layered over the others. She pointed at the screen. "OK, yup, here we go. See that? Anterior insula." She pointed at another spot, indistinguishable, and then three more. "Anterior cingulate cortex. Amygdala. Ventral striatum. Substantia nigra/ventral tegmental area."

It was like looking at a photo of oatmeal and being told the names of particular oats.

But I squinted with purpose and asked, "What should I be seeing?"

"A surprising amount of gray matter throughout your salience network, especially in the right anterior insula. Your mother has this to an extreme degree. Akio only very slightly. Yours is like your mother's. You could say that this part of the brain controls the direction of the spotlight of attention. It's critical for enabling interaction between cognition, emotion, and action. Bilateral volume reduction in these areas has been detected in individuals with schizophrenia, and this reduction has been linked to the severity of reality distortion. It's possible that an abundance of gray matter, conversely, corresponds to an unusual receptiveness to reality. Maybe, maybe not. The direction of causality is difficult to determine. A left-handed pianist, after all, is going to have an unusually well-developed cortex in the region devoted to control of the left-hand fingers."

From behind the glass, the MRI still hummed insistently, and I tried to block it out. I associated the machine now with that awful frozen dread I'd felt inside it, the threat of impending disintegration. The alone-in-the-dark feeling I hadn't thought about since childhood. The memory made me feel small and powerless, unequal to my task. Which right now was to understand what Grace was telling me. She had taken the seat beside me, and I swiveled around to face her. This brought us very close so that our knees were almost touching, but instead of scooting back, as the laws of personal space demanded, I stayed exactly where I was. The closeness of another body made me reassuringly aware of where I ended and all that was not-me began.

I said, "But what does that even mean, an unusual receptiveness to reality? Do you mean, like, a vivid imagination?" My father had always said that what made my mother such a brilliant physicist was her scientific imagination. That my talent for invention was inherited from her. I liked believing this. It made me feel that we were linked to each other through my work.

Grace paused, considering, then said, "Imagination helps us access fictions as often as truths. Whereas this capacity is a means of accessing the actual, the real. Using this capacity to write your books is a bit like using a fire hose to fill a glass with water."

I stared at the screen, at my unusual gray matter.

"But, so, does this capacity only get triggered when you have a child? Because if I had this fire hose at my disposal, I'm pretty sure I never used it until yesterday. Unless maybe on the day that Jack was born."

Grace nodded. "Yes, that's right. I suspect that there have always been aspects of the way you process the world that are a little unusual because of these unusual features of your brain. But it does seem that the full capacity, the ability to walk astride the possibilities, is triggered by having a child. I suspect it might be the hormones."

"Or the emotions," I said.

Grace put a hand on mine. "True. There's nothing like those first months, is there? Nothing can prepare us. Not just for the immensity of the love and responsibility, but for the sheer physicality, the touch, the sounds, the smells. Hannah, I really do believe you're going to find him."

I was crying again, because my child was lost in a spread of possibilities, and I didn't share this woman's faith that I could find him. I was crying, too, because of the confessional kindness of Grace's tone, which made me feel, just for a moment, what it might be like to have a mother.

But also, it was that phrase of hers, *the touch, the sounds, the smells*. The words conjured up sensory details that clicked a thought very nearly into place: breast milk, spit-up, soiled diapers; shrieks of displeasure that felt like the world ending, that I myself would end if I couldn't soothe his fury and his pain; a little mouth sucking voraciously, skin against skin, wet and devouring, a confusing swirl of annihilation and contentment. All of it another form of communication, wordless, gestureless, conducted instead through intense sensory intimacy unlike any I had ever known, except, I supposed, when I was in the other role, the one of infant. And perhaps that was why this intimacy stirred up so many confusing emotions in me, emotions that seemed not new at all, but so old they predated my use of words, encoded instead in the mental equivalent of cuneiform. So that I didn't know, even now, how to speak about them. Like a whole lost civilization stirring to life inside me, untranslatable, and all of this happening while I was mostly on my own, trying to care 24/7 for a defenseless being in constant need. I was crying for all this, too, because, seriously, how did this not break everyone, it had been so hard, and also it had been so wonderful, and I'd lost it, lost him, where was he, but also there was something else, something so important and so close, something I needed to figure out, something about reaching Jack, whose voice I could have sworn I'd heard but hadn't, and if I could just figure it out—

But Grace's voice cut off my thought. "Oh, and the sleeplessness of course," she said. "I suspect the sleeplessness is crucial. It loosens one's typical grip on the senses. Makes you a little loopy, in exactly the right way."

I'd lost it now, the thought.

"Uncontainable feelings," I said instead. "That's how the capacity first gets triggered, right? The initial mechanism for travel?"

Grace looked surprised. "You're the one who's done it, so you tell me. Your mother's theory of the mechanism for moving between worlds is rather different, but to be honest I've never been able to make heads or tails of what she means by the things she says on this score. I'm inclined to place my bet on feelings, if you say so."

I thought back to that moment yesterday outside the elevators in Dr. Goodman's building. Until now I'd thought it was my ambivalence that tore reality in two for me. My passionate love and equally passionate hatred for the umbilical radius that tied me at all times to my child and therefore to my terror. A love that held me hostage to this paradox: Keep him alive, keep him well, but also know that you can't, that you have no control, not really.

But I'd misunderstood. My ambivalence had been inevitable and unremarkable. Faced with the broken elevator, the four flights of stairs, the heavy stroller, of course I'd wanted desperately to be free of Jack so that I could run easily up and down the steps to retrieve the car key. And of course my wanting to ditch him to get the key had hived off other fantasies of freedom: to hear my thoughts; to write my book; to sink into the grief of losing Adam; to not lose Adam.

Of course, in that moment, I'd wanted desperately to be free, and of course, in that moment, I'd wanted just as desperately not to be, because I loved my son. But I could only allow myself one half of this, the wanting to be with him, always with him.

I'd made ambivalence unthinkable.

So what was I supposed to do with the tremendous feeling of wanting to be away? Forbidden from thinking it, forbidden from feeling it, I must have cast around for some other way to handle it. And that was when I'd found another thing my mind could do. Beyond thinking, beyond feeling, beyond sensing.

Grace was watching me, waiting. It was clear she was curious to hear more about the mechanism of travel, and I felt I owed it to her to add to her knowledge given all she'd done for me.

Finally I said, "How could you discover your body has the capacity to fly if you never leave the ground?"

She nodded. "You have to need it to access it."

"Exactly. But I think now it'll be easier. Discovering it required desperation. Using it seems to require something less."

Even this morning, knowing nothing but that I'd done it twice before, all I'd had to do was feel into the ambivalence that seemed to be the door to Hannah42's world and it had opened. Maybe every world had a door like that. Each a longing, dreading, hoping, fearing for another way that things might be, another door that could heave me out of space and time with passionate confusion. What if I didn't have a child? What if Adam still loved me? What if I'd never met him, fell in love instead with someone else? What if I'd had a child years earlier? What if I had never become a writer?

What if my mother hadn't gone away?

"Where is she?" I was surprised I hadn't thought to ask it sooner. "If my mother can't exist in any possibility, then where actually is she?"

"I don't know where she is," Grace answered. "I wish I did. But I have a good feeling about you, Hannah. I had that feeling when I met your mother, too. I don't know how to account for it, really. What told me to take the things she muttered from time to time so seriously? I had an intuition, that here was someone who shared the experience that Akio had so often spoken to me about, never sure if he was describing fantasy or reality. Following that intuition was perhaps the best decision I've ever made. It gave me all of this, for one." She gestured at the MRI humming beyond the glass, but I knew what she meant. The glittering lab. The glittering career that went with it.

Someone rapped twice at the door, and then the man with the tortoiseshell glasses stuck his head inside.

"The folks from Berlin are waiting in the conference room," he said.

"Got it. Thanks."

This time he spared me the slightest glance of curiosity before he disappeared again.

Grace rubbed her hands together vigorously, then clasped them before her chest.

"I've told you everything I know now, I'm afraid. At least everything I know that seems like it could possibly be helpful. But if I think of anything else, I'll get in touch. Put your number in my phone?" She handed it to me. "I'll text you mine and Akio's. And if you have any more questions that you think we might be able to answer, please, reach out. Think of me as— well, think of me as Grace. Your mother's friend."

She gave my hand a squeeze, then pulled me toward her, folding me in an embrace. She smelled of cinnamon, rubbing alcohol, and coffee.

I had one last question I'd been planning to ask. It was the same question I'd been asking for the past eight months: Was I up to this? But, for the first time since Jack's birth, I found I had no need to put the question to someone else.

The information from this extra sense of mine was becoming unavoidable. The way sound demands to be heard, or light demands to be seen: another round of waves pulling me outward like contractions, but more weakly. I wasn't sure yet how to control it, use it. I'd have to learn. I'd teach myself to fling open the doors and stalk through distant worlds looking for my prize like some kind of ancient hero.

Of course I was up to this. Jack needed me to be.

Chapter Twenty-one

On my way out of Grace's building, I stopped in a first-floor bathroom to tend to my soaked shirt. The bathroom was fancy, like a five-star restaurant's. Tiny rocks studded the walls; there was an orchid on the counter. My shirt, in contrast, was a disaster. I tried blotting it with a paper towel, and then gave up and turned the shirt around. It was no more comfortable, but I looked better provided you only saw me from the front.

I considered trying to hand express in a sink, just to relieve some of the pounding fullness of my breasts, but this was beyond my skill level. Traversing parallel universes, yes. Hand expressing, no. I'd head home, use the pump, check on Adam. And then?

I wasn't sure yet. The weak contractions were still pulling at my mind, beckoning me toward new realities, new streams of information, but I didn't want to pick the wrong one and waste more precious time. It was 12:34 P.M. I needed to be deliberate, I needed to be smart. But the feel of these many worlds beckoning gave me hope; the sense, quite literally, of possibility.

Outside, the sun was sparkling on the blue water of the bay

and the tall white temples of science that made up this urban campus. My phone alerted me that I had eighty-seven new texts from Adam. I felt I ought to call him. What I really wanted, though, was to call my father. I didn't often have this urge. He'd been too absent in life to really warrant missing in death. I'd loved him for his gentleness and good intentions, I'd done my best to care for him and let him think that he was taking care of me, but his loss hadn't been so much a violent wrenching as a subtle final fade. Still, just now, I would have liked to call him. His diffuse presence, his smoke-filled cardigans, his confusing anecdotes about errands gone bizarrely wrong, all would be so reassuring in this moment. And maybe I could have helped him to remember something more about my mother and what she'd done to save me.

He'd died of a melanoma he'd ignored for far too long, just like he'd ignored all aspects of the present. And what if he hadn't? What if I'd prevailed on him to get that weird mole checked?

This was a door. I could tell just by its complicated texture, the way it bunched and snagged instead of yielding to my thoughts. Not all what-ifs were doors. You probably couldn't rip through reality with regret over your lunch order. I didn't know what made the difference, but I knew a door now when I felt one. This was a door made up of missing and remorse. I wanted to go through it. I let my mind move over the feeling, then gave in to the waves that started to heave me like contractions.

Then there I was. Standing on this street corner, but also in a checkout line at the Safeway. I was behind two frat boys with a cart filled entirely with Bacardi and beer. I took out my phone and called my father. My fingers trembled as I selected his name from my contacts. He didn't answer. As usual. He never used to answer, and it always took him days to call me back. I left a message telling him I loved him, then let the door swing closed. Just by ignoring the stream of information. It took concentration, like tuning out an interesting conversation at the next table in a restaurant, but it was no harder than that.

I wanted to try again with other doors. I wanted to see what I could do, test out my limits, but first I needed a plan. I couldn't just go opening doors to other realities willy-nilly and think that I'd find Jack. I needed to be methodical. Like Adam would have been.

I looked down at my phone again, at Adam's unread texts, now eighty-nine, then thumbed open the Lyft app.

"You following me?"

An electric blue sedan had pulled up next to me. In the rolled-down window, a face, familiar, mouth closing around a slice of pizza. Ash from my mothers group. With her teal fleece and orange bowl cut, her tall, sturdy frame and her delicate freckled skin, like fancy stationery.

"What are you doing here?" As soon as I asked it, I remembered. She'd told me yesterday that she was a postdoc in Dino's lab.

"I work here. What are you doing here?"

"Research," I said, not really lying.

I didn't want to tell her Jack was missing. I wasn't sure how the forgetting worked, but it seemed to be contagious. Dr. Goodman had forgotten him while talking to Rodriguez.

"Cool." She was staring openly at my breasts. I looked down and saw that I had leaked again, two wet circles now darkening the fresh side of my shirt.

"First full day of childcare, huh? If you're desperate—" She gestured with her chin toward the back, where, to my surprise, a wireless pump sat nestled in her son's car seat.

"You pump in here?"

"It's either this or the lab bathroom. Which is unisex, by the way. Nothing quite like sitting in a dirty stall milking yourself like a cow while two grad students talk about the girls they 'almost fucked' last weekend. Honestly, if you're interested, it's here, the pieces have all been washed, so, go ahead, knock yourself out."

I was tempted. The fullness of my breasts was bordering on agony. And her back seat was clean, surprisingly so given the pizza. Not even a Cheerio in sight.

"If you're headed back to Berkeley, I could drive you," she added. She took another bite without breaking eye contact.

"A ride would be great actually," I said.

Ash wiped her hands on her jeans and came around to show me how to settle myself between the front and back seats to shield myself from view. As soon as I positioned the flanges and turned on the machine, milk started flowing. The relief was instant.

"This is really kind of you," I said, as she climbed over the console to the driver's seat.

"Um, *yeah*. I'm kind." She popped the final bite of crust into her mouth and started the car. "So you finally agreed to a nanny share?" She didn't wait for my answer. "No offense, but I'm impressed. I had you pegged as one of those attachment parenting nap-when-the-baby-naps dodos. That fucking prelapsarian fantasy of mother-infant fusion."

I realized, several seconds too late, that she was expecting me to speak now.

I said, "Oh, no, you were right, that is absolutely my brand of dodo."

Ash made a sound that was a snort, but a somewhat sympathetic and approving one.

She said, "It's all a lose-lose anyway, isn't it? If you're not all gooey maternal devotion then you're a cold and unnatural bitch. And, if you are all gooey, then soon enough you'll be called out for your smothering failure to separate. Motherhood gets idealized, mothers get shit on. That's how it's always been and probably how it's always going to be. What's your address, I'm going to plug it into Waze."

Another text came in from Adam as I was telling her my address. I forced myself to look. A bar graph showing the number of unsolved kidnappings per year and the number reported in the media. This did not seem like information that required visual aids, but I texted back *Unbelievable,* struggling to move my thumbs over the keyboard without letting the flanges drop.

"Don't do that." Ash was glancing at me in the rearview mirror. "Hear that whistling sound? That means you broke the suction seal and you're no longer expressing."

I looked down and saw that she was right. My left nipple was squished against the conical plastic, and no more milk was coming. I readjusted it so that my nipple was back inside the tube, moving forward and back in rhythm with the pump's monotonous dirge, and the milk began to flow again. I stared at this blurred and bloated piece of me, half mesmerized and half horrified, finding it hard to connect what I was seeing to my own body. It occurred to me that I'd been overlooking an important clue. All day my breasts had been inconsistent, sometimes leaking and sometimes acting dried up. This morning it had been impossible to pump a drop from them, and now they were giving forth a bounty.

Under normal circumstances, weren't my breasts in constant communication with Jack? Producing more in response to his hunger, letting down whenever he cried out. Maybe, under these abnormal circumstances, my breasts were still connected to him. Maybe their inconsistency went in tandem with his flickering, so that they filled whenever he flickered into being and dried up when he flickered out. If so, this meant that right now he was *somewhere* instead of nowhere. Just knowing he was somewhere in the world didn't give me much to go on, it wasn't information I could act on, but it felt good. And even better was the possibility that we were still connected, engaged in some bodily form of communication that bypassed my mind entirely. Maybe this was how I was meant to reach him.

"Why do you think that is?" Ash asked, startling me out of my reverie.

"Why do I think the pump doesn't work when you break the suction?"

"No. Why do you think everyone's so invested in idealizing motherhood and shitting on actual mothers? Personally, I think it's because we're all so furious at our own moms. We all believe they robbed us of the perfect care that was our due. If we stop idealizing motherhood, we can't hold them accountable. And misogyny of course. You can't discount the pleasures of misogyny. Do you have a good relationship with your mother?"

I closed my eyes and wished Ash would stop speaking so I could think about what my next move ought to be.

"What about fear?" I said, more to myself than her. "Maybe we just want to believe in something perfect to protect us. Goodness without badness, safety without threat."

I was picturing Grace's spread of possibilities, infinitely branching, barbed with danger. Danger in each separate world and danger in their mixing. But of course there was hope, too, in the spread of what was possible. Everything was in there, and, for now at least, that included Jack. So long as people remembered him, so long as my breasts were still producing milk for him, he was part of the full spread of what was. I couldn't get to him in my world for the reason Grace had said—he could be anywhere, at any moment. But maybe, if I could access the full spread, I could use whatever still connected us to find him.

But how? How could I access it? I was still picturing the worlds as bubbles. Bubbles were easy to take in all at once, bubbles were small, discrete, so maybe this was my problem, a bad metaphor, an unhelpful image, because my mind was coming up with nothing.

There was no traffic on the bridge, at least. We were making good time. But the pressure to act, to *do something* was building up again to unsustainable levels. My son was out there, time was leaking, and I needed to be everywhere, seeing everything, so I could find him. Instead I was stuffed between the back seat and the front seat of a sedan, hooked up to a pump, unable to even use my hands for fear of dislodging the conical plastic flanges suctioning my nipples.

Ash was still speaking. She was on religion now. I wasn't sure how she'd gotten here, something about keeping good and evil separate—she was really grooving in that way she did. She didn't seem to want or need my input any longer, so I let myself feel for another door. It was becoming easy to detect the emotions that seemed to pull me outward. I could feel so many now. The question was which one was the right one. I let my mind move over variations of fear and dread, hope and desire, fury and regret, then stopped: a very specific longing, and so pure. Nothing but Jack Jack Jack Jack Jack. I opened myself up to it, I felt the waves. My view swung wide.

I was here, I was there.

In my world, I was pumping breast milk in Ash's car as we hurtled over the 580. In this other world, I was sitting on a folding chair directly over the R on the round alphabet rug in the basement of the lactation center where my mothers group met three times a week. There was the devil's ivy hanging over the bookshelf. There was the smell of stale coffee. And here, again, was Ash. But no face other than Ash's looked familiar.

A very tall woman was saying, "I realized today that I don't have anything that smells like Daisy anymore. I was hoarding all her onesies for a while. Only smelling them once a day. But now I've wasted all the smells. Now I have nothing left."

The Ash in this other world looked like Ash always looked in group. Like it was taking everything she had not to stand up and make a speech. She didn't look like she'd been through something grueling. Although she must have been, if she was here, in the noon group: stillborns, infant deaths, and third trimester losses.

This wasn't right. This wasn't where I wanted to be. Another Jackless world. It was possible that Ash's presence in the car was gumming up the works. Maybe it was my irritation at the relentlessness of her conversation, or else my guilt for ignoring it, or maybe the mechanism wasn't nearly as simple as I'd been imagining, no one-to-one correlation between emotions and realities. In fact, this last bit was almost surely true. If it were that simple—specific feelings opening doors to specific worlds—I'd have lost some respect for the laws of nature.

Still, for whatever reason, emotion seemed to work for me, if imprecisely, so I tried again. That longing. Pure. I zeroed in on it, I felt the waves, I let them take control, and another door now opened.

The tiny, fenced-in playground that Jack and I often visited in the afternoons.

I was in our local park. And so was Jack.

Chapter Twenty-two

He was in a baby swing. The one directly underneath the shadiest tree, our favorite. I was pushing him. He was laughing, kicking his legs delightedly. At any moment his laughter would start tilting in the direction of frightened hiccups the way it always did several minutes into swinging, but right now he was happy.

Although, of course, it wasn't him, or not exactly. But as I lifted him from the swing, as I clutched him tight against me, the difference seemed so trivial. I breathed in the smell of his sweaty curls. My hand pressed up against his diaper, felt how it had leaked a little through the cotton of his pants. This was Jack. Jack who gathered every strand of my attention so that it was hard sometimes to remember what it felt like just to be a person in the world. To remember or believe that I had ever been such a simple thing as *myself.*

"My love, my love," I whispered in the velvet whorl of his ear, and he began to scream. I told myself that he was screaming in relief. Because I'd found him.

I was fighting hard against my own relief, because it was overpowering. Jack here, Jack in my arms. Badly needing a diaper change. But safe, intact, mine.

Except he wasn't mine. This was a Jack who hadn't disappeared from his world. A luckier Jack or, anyway, one whose luck was holding. My Jack was still out there. I hadn't found him.

Of course I hadn't. How could I have thought that this would work, riding a possibility straight to him? My own Jack wasn't in another world. He was still in my world, flickering in and out like an electric grid on the fritz. So that Dr. Goodman had seen him, briefly, where moments later there was no sign of him. So that my breasts sometimes gushed and sometimes seemed dried up.

I needed to return to my own body. To my own world. Where my own Jack both was and wasn't, and where, when he was, he was scared, alone, in what had to be by now a terribly soggy diaper, soaking through his rainbow-striped pajamas.

I needed to go back. As easy as tuning out a conversation at the next table, but the problem was I didn't want to. I didn't want to leave this world where I held him. And why should I, if they were all equally real? It was asking too much. The way his hair smelled. And that distinctive splotch of red that spread across his neck when he was screaming, the shape of it so uncannily like a squid. I pressed my lips against it. His fat little fingers clenched my hair. I kissed the white moons of his nails.

I didn't want to. But my own Jack needed me. It felt insane to let the door close, but I did.

In my own world, Ash had fallen silent. She caught my eyes in the rearview mirror.

"You can keep napping if you want to. I don't mind."

I looked away, too stunned to speak. I'd held him. I'd let him go.

I forced myself to look at Ash's eyes again in the rearview, remembering that other Ash, the one in the noon group: stillborns, infant deaths, and third trimester losses. She didn't know about that shadow world lurking. But maybe she felt it. Every parent was held hostage to this brutal contingency.

I closed my eyes again. Other worlds weren't the answer. It was my own world Jack was flickering in and out of. The solution seemed so obvious: just find him when he flickered in. I even had the bat-signal of my breasts to tell me when that was. And yet, as Grace had pointed out, there was no way to anticipate the where and when specifically enough to reach him. This seemed like such a technicality, but I couldn't think my way around it.

I needed to bat ideas around with someone else. I wanted that someone to be my Adam, but I couldn't pose this problem to Adam, not in these terms or any like them, so I felt again, for another door, the door to Adam42's world.

Chapter Twenty-three

I was in my bedroom. The other Adam was on top of me, inside of me, his face gone slack with pleasure.

As I stared into his face, his eyes went wide. His body stopped moving against mine.

"Oh shit," said Adam42. "It's you."

He rolled onto the rumpled sheets.

"I'm so sorry. I hope I didn't—how long have you been here?"

I put a hand against his shoulder to reassure him. I wasn't not his Hannah. I'd once been her, up until eight months ago, when we diverged in the minutes after giving birth. Granted, this complicated issues of consent.

Adam42 flinched from my hand, sat up. He pulled the sheets around his waist. The sheets were damp. Tangled into ropy segments. I wondered whether it was me he was pulling away from or whether instead it was what I represented—a reminder of his son. On the fire trail he'd mentioned feeling conflicted over seeking joy in the months since losing Jack. I wanted to say something kind, to reassure him, but I was feeling too impatient. Time time time, time leaking second by second and my son leaking out alongside. It was 12:47 P.M.

I tugged an edge of sheet back for myself, covering my breasts. All the shades in the room were drawn, leaving it cool and shadowed.

He tossed a T-shirt at me and pulled on a pair of jeans. Then he handed me the pen and notepad I'd used this morning. The top page still bore the eerie scrawl of Hannah42.

Adam sat down on the bed again and said, "You want her help, right? That's why you're here?"

Instead of answering directly I spilled out all I'd learned in one unbroken rush.

Adam listened patiently. I could tell that Hannah42 was also with us, listening. That same sensation that had tingled in my writing hand the last time I was here now spread throughout my body. As though all my cells were plump with something precious.

I had adopted Grace's matter-of-fact tone without intending to. The tone helped keep my mind free of emotion so I could focus on providing a thorough explanation. But I couldn't keep the tears from coming when I finally reached the cruel taunt of the flickering. By then I'd also brought the narrative as far as my own reasoning could bring me. Adam was chewing on the inside of his cheek, the way he did whenever he was thinking hard. Because of the position of the bed, I could see myself reflected in the mirror above my dresser. Myself, but better rested, ten pounds lighter. Myself, but behind that face another mind was also working. It was uncanny to regard my own reflection and also be looking at someone else, and so I brought my gaze back onto Adam.

Who said, "OK, I'm just speaking aloud here for a second, but—well, where does he go when he flickers *out*?"

"Nowhere," I answered. "When he flickers out, he simply isn't. He doesn't exist."

I suppressed the *obviously,* but it was there in my tone. It wasn't fair of me to be impatient when he was playing catch-up, but I needed him to be a quicker study than I could ever be.

My irritation wasn't helped by the fact that I was also feeling dizzy. Badly dizzy. Weirdly dizzy. It took me a moment to realize that there was probably a reason, and that the reason was probably Hannah42. She was doing something, maybe trying to tell me something. Directly, mind to mind, instead of via writing. I tried to quiet my thoughts, to open myself up to her communication. This felt a lot like what I did when I was writing, but much more bodily. The vertigo was intense. Like trying to thread a needle while jumping on a trampoline. It seemed as if we were trying to get our internal vision aligned. And then: a memory. My own, and also hers. I was eight or nine and sitting on a swivel chair in my father's study, asking what the universe expanded into. It was a happy memory. I was feeling high on the rare drug of my dad's attention as he explained that the universe wasn't expanding into anything, because there could be nothing outside the universe. His answer made no sense to me, but that wasn't why I kept insisting he explain it in a dozen different ways. I just didn't want the moment to end. I kept insisting; if it was expanding, then there had to be another place outside it, a place of no-place, nothing.

"What's happening?" Adam asked. He was looking at me warily.

"She's talking to me," I said. "Your wife is. She's reminding me about the time I tried to force my father to admit there had to be something outside the universe if the universe was expanding."

"So she agrees with me," he said. "It does make sense to ask where he goes when he flickers out."

I was about to object—it was *me* she was backing up—but now my hand was writing *no-place no-place*.

I glanced up at the mirror as though I might lock eyes with her and get some clue from her expression. But of course it was just my own expression staring back at me: a look of blank confusion.

Adam said, "Is it so crazy, given the context? If your son is in some kind of a limbo state, a state between existing and not existing, then maybe there's some kind of limbo place to match."

"What, like an anteroom to all possible worlds?"

"Sure. You could call it that. A place that is not itself part of a world."

"What could that even mean? It sounds like a contradiction in terms."

But even as I was saying this, I was recalling what I'd felt inside the MRI. That annihilating dread, like falling into nothingness, the terrifying sense of dissolution. My nose had bled the way it did whenever I traveled. And I'd been sure I heard Jack's cry. Could that have been the anteroom, a place of no-place? The thought was terrible and now, as if in answer to my question, I felt again that I was falling. I was falling, and this time Jack's cry was everywhere. Not a sound so much as a knowledge all throughout me. Impossible to get a view, a sense of scope and sound and vista; this place was just coldness, terror. I needed to get out of here or I would not survive, and so I closed my mind against it. Just like that, and I was sitting on my white and beige bedspread in the shadowed room while Adam wrapped his arms around me. It seemed that I was sobbing.

"What just happened?" Adam asked. "Are you OK?"

He grabbed another discarded T-shirt from beside the bed and held it to my bleeding nose, but I batted it away. I was staring at the mirror. I was shaking too hard to speak: I'd felt Jack's cry, and I'd left anyway.

I managed to say to Adam, "You were right. There is a place. A limbo place. He's there." The thought was unendurable, because the place was.

"And you can get there?"

"I think so."

"But that's great! So go!"

"I can't."

I was struggling to put it into words. The wrongness of my going there was too basic for words to do it justice.

Eventually I said, "When I'm there I can't move. I can't think. I can't *be*. How can I possibly save him if I can't move or think or be?"

I'd brought us to another dead end. Adam was still chewing at the inside of his cheek, still working at the problem, but I could tell that he felt stumped, and so did I. But Hannah42 did not because I was getting dizzy. I felt a surge of hope, along with vertigo as we struggled to align our minds, then there it was, another memory she wanted me to see: I am very small, lying in bed, wrapped tightly in my blankets. I am intoning a kind of prayer, a single word. *Mommy mommy mommy mommy mommy.* The word was all I had because I'd lost her.

On Hannah42's bed, I was looking across the room at my reflection. But now I actually saw what had been staring me in the face. It was so obvious. I needed the person who had already done what I was trying to do, what seemed impossible.

I needed my mother.

Chapter Twenty-four

I opened my eyes to see Ash turned around fully in her seat, watching me without particular interest or concern, like she was scrolling on social media. That she was watching me and not the road alarmed me for a moment, but then I realized we were parked outside my house.

"Man, you were really out," Ash offered neutrally. "Are you guys co-sleeping or something?"

"It's been a rough few nights," I answered.

I was trying to unscrew the bottles from the flanges without spilling their contents. I'd filled the bottles to their brims. Over the brims, in fact. Ash watched all this without comment. I felt that I was moving awkwardly in a way that I could not define, and I was certain she could see this, too. I shimmied from the car, feeling I was rattling around inside my body.

"Just keep them," Ash said, gesturing at the bottles. She'd finally turned away from me. "I've got so many." She was looking out the windshield now, regarding my home with the same disinterested appraisal. "Jesus, your house is creepy. Is that, like, a branding thing?" My silence must have conveyed confusion because she added, "Because of your books."

I looked and saw that it was true. My house looked spooky. No one had pruned in weeks, possibly months, and the garden had tipped into that look it sometimes got when we grew lazy with the upkeep. Dense and high enough that for a thousand years someone might sleep behind the thick of it unnoticed. Forgotten.

"Thanks so much for the ride and the—" I gestured to the pump, which now sat under a dirty tangle of tubes. Did I need to offer to wash the parts? I didn't offer. It was 1:17 P.M.

"Anytime. Maybe I should set up shop. Mobile lactation unit. Can't be less lucrative than academia. I'll see you later at group?"

I made a noncommittal noise and waved as she backed down the driveway. Then I placed the bottles carefully on the gravel by my feet and pulled my phone out.

Stickily, I thumbed out a text to Grace: *How do you get in contact with my mother?*

Three dots immediately appeared, Grace already replying. God bless that busy woman. She hadn't been lying when she said she'd do whatever she could to help.

But then her reply came through: *I don't. I'm sorry.* Then: *She always reaches out to me.* Then: *Her messages tend to be electronic in nature. They show up as emails without addresses or text messages without associated cell numbers. Oh or error messages when I try to load a page.* Then: *Once she got a message to me from a readout on the MRI. That one stumped me I can tell you.* Then: *None of this is very helpful I realize I so wish I had more to pass along.*

The three dots appeared again, then disappeared, and there was nothing else.

I put my phone back in my pocket and wiped my hands on the backside of my jeans. I picked the bottles up too roughly, and more milk sloshed down the sides. All this power, but what was the point of it, if I couldn't do what was needed to save Jack by myself? I was still just a messed-up kid without a mom, and it seemed unfair that I needed her at all. Jack was my child, after all, only mine.

I stepped through the door and Adam called out, "Hannah?"

Well, mine and Adam's.

His voice was coming from upstairs. I kicked off my shoes, put the bottles in the fridge, rinsed my hands in the kitchen sink, then went to look for him. I found him in our bedroom. He was sprawled on his back across the bed, eyes closed, his phone balanced on his stomach.

I felt disoriented for a moment. I had just been in here. The window shades drawn, the sheets damp and tangled, Adam42 striking an open palm against his forehead when I told him what his wife and I had figured out, that I needed to find my mother. Offering to help in any way he could.

Here, the shades were open, sun was streaming over the tidy bed, over my own Adam. The brighter room looked lonelier, remote. Adam looked remote and I knew that I would, too, to him, if he even bothered looking. We'd abandoned each other, months ago. The fact that we'd both done it didn't soften the hurt at all.

It was 1:24 P.M. And I had no idea how to reach my mother. But I could maybe reach my husband. Together, we'd be so much better off.

I pulled my shirt over my head, put on a fresh one that stuck immediately to the layer of breast milk still coating my torso, and settled next to Adam. He didn't move to conform his body to mine, just let out a moan and without opening his eyes said, "I don't get it. I really don't get it. How did they get to Reichenbach?"

"Reichenbach, your lawyer?"

He opened his eyes and pulled his head back just enough that he could look me in the face.

"*Our* lawyer. Well, not anymore. Did you not see my texts?"

"Not all of them, not yet."

He didn't seem to hear me, or else he didn't seem to care.

"Honestly, we should sue him, too," he said.

"Sue him for what?" I asked, even though I already knew the general outlines of the answer: one more mind forgetting Jack, all trace of him disappearing.

"For malpractice. For—for defamation. For, I don't know, for emotional damage, gaslighting. The guy lied straight to my face. A child is missing, and he lied straight to my face. He swore we'd never spoken, he pretended to not even know my name. Less than forty-five minutes after I wire transferred the retainer. Which he claimed to have no record of."

He was six foot two and vibrating with rage, but he seemed so small compared to the other Adam. So young. Like a child, the child he might have been. His father leaving for another woman, his mother fixated on keeping up appearances. I pictured Adam, at five or six or seven, not understanding why but understanding urgently and clearly that this was what was asked of him: to take part in his mother's project to prove they weren't tragic, were just as good as anybody else. He would have been such a natural asset to this venture, with his sparkly charm, good grades, good looks.

I had no idea if any of this was true, but it was what I'd always imagined when Adam said his childhood was perfect. It was my only way to make sense of how someone so smart could believe something so stupid. It made sense if believing this was part of what he felt he owed his mother.

Now I pictured a grown-up Adam facing the terror of Jack's birth. I was only guessing, but I could imagine how, faced with the magnitude of that near-loss, feeling impotent, old habits had kicked in. He'd dealt with the helplessness he couldn't tolerate by denying it existed. As though by following the right rules he could make any threat of danger moot.

In that context, I must have seemed a terrifying threat. Doing exactly what I shouldn't. Focusing on my fear, on the car-swerve feeling, mocking rules and clinging tight to intuition.

I had no idea if any of this was right. Maybe I was focusing on the wrong parent. Maybe his behavior these past eight months was really about his father, who'd left the family for a younger woman and moved across the country, a man Adam claimed he couldn't even hate because he didn't feel strongly enough to warrant it, whose funeral ten years ago Adam hadn't bothered to attend. Maybe his leaving me was his fucked-up way of mourning a man he pretended hadn't hurt him. Or maybe it was both these explanations, or maybe it was neither, maybe he just disliked who I turned out to be, maybe we were incompatible as parents. I had no idea.

What I did know, though, was that Adam42 was different. Sad and strong and unafraid of feeling helpless. He knew that he was helpless. He knew the danger was something else.

"I'm so sorry," I said. "I really am."

"You couldn't have seen it coming." Adam was staring at the ceiling. "Who could have guessed that Reichenbach was in with your therapist, with those crooked cops, I just don't see how—"

I cut him off. "No, I mean I'm sorry I haven't been here." I rolled onto my elbow so I could see him better. I laid a hand on his chest; I was surprised to feel his heart was pounding. "I'm sorry we haven't figured out how to do this together. But I think we should. I think we can. I think we should try, at least." I searched his face for a sign that he was hearing me. "Don't you?"

He gave no evidence of hearing me.

"It's still me, you know," I said.

He sat up then, crossing his legs in front of him. I pulled myself up, too, so I was facing him. His eyes were moving piecemeal over my face, not unlike the way Adam42 had looked at me this morning. Like he was searching my face for clues, but this time for evidence that I really was myself. The woman he loved, the woman he'd married. *I know this isn't you,* he'd said last night. *You're not this woman.* It occurred to me I both wasn't and I was.

He seemed about to speak, but then he didn't. Instead he reached and tucked a strand of hair behind my ear. I grabbed for his hand before he could retract it and brought it to my mouth. I kissed his palm.

"Hannah," he said, and for a moment he looked like Adam42. Open, here. Just for a moment, and then his face was crumpling. He was sobbing.

"Hannah, please please please, just make it stop." His words were hard to parse, his voice was strangled. "Make him be back here. Hannah, he must be so scared."

There seemed to be no shape to him, the structure of him gone, a mound of clay. And it really did seem possible that I could tell him, that he would hear: Our child was disappearing. We had to save him. We needed my mother's help.

If he believed me, if he was willing to, we could do it together.

I was holding him with both my arms. His chin was pressed into my shoulder. I kissed his temple. I was trying to think how to begin. I knew it was possible because Adam42 believed his Hannah.

Adam was crying more softly now. We were lying down again, and I stroked his back and realized with some surprise that I was also crying. We were crying together and holding each other, and this made the gap seem bridgeable.

A phone was ringing.

It was Adam's phone, wedged between us.

It stopped ringing as it went to voicemail, then started up again seconds later. This time, Adam stirred himself enough to fish for it and put it to his ear.

"Yeah, this is Adam." His voice sounded sleepy, slurred.

He sat up suddenly.

"Do you mind telling me— OK, yes, yes, we can be there." He looked at me with eyebrows raised. I couldn't read his expression. "But can you not just tell me—? Yes, fine. Fine. Yeah, give us half an hour."

He hung up, still staring at me.

"That was Detective Rodriguez. They want us at the station."

Chapter Twenty-five

He was breathing audibly through his nostrils, which were flaring with the effort. I put a hand against his back. Beneath my palm he vibrated like a cornered kitten.

"What for?" I asked.

"I don't know. But it sounded kind of—good? She sounded different. That's all I know. She sounded, maybe, apologetic?" He stood and took my hand in his, pulling me off the bed and then, as if in afterthought, wrapping his arms around me to press me close to him. "You need anything before we go?"

I shook my head against his chest. He kissed my hair, directly on my part, the way he used to. It would have felt so good in any other context. But right now, I was too attuned to the way that hope was giving him his shape again, making him a stranger to the helplessness I needed him to feel. The timing of the call had been unfortunate, but actually maybe not. Whatever was waiting for us at the station, it wasn't going to be good news. Whatever it was, it was going to further undermine Adam's faith in our salvation through the rules. Eventually he'd have to stop bucking against it: He'd be like Adam42 then. I'd be able to reach him. I just needed to be patient.

Outside the car, he gripped me by both shoulders and kissed my head a second time, before he slipped into the driver's seat. And so he missed the Neimann-Rosenfelds walking their lab-radoodle, smiling, chatting. As they caught my eye, they gave a cheerful wave. No longer aware of a tragedy unfolding on their street.

I slammed the passenger door before they could strike up a conversation.

As Adam white-knuckled the steering wheel, I looked down at my phone again, wondering how to reach my mother. Electronic forms of communication, Grace had said, but the communication sounded like it only went one way.

It had been decades since I'd stopped allowing myself to wonder whether my mother was alive or dead, miserable or somehow happy in what I'd believed to be her blankness. It had been decades since I'd rooted out those kinds of thoughts, but I still searched for her in the faces of strangers. Even yesterday. That woman at the CVS whom I'd mistaken for a teen-age boy. And all that time she might have found a way to reach me, and she hadn't.

I looked over at Adam, who was chewing ruthlessly on his bottom lip as people surged around us. We were easing into the snarl of cars, pedestrians, and general chaos that always clogged the streets near Berkeley's campus. The crowd was always the same here, a mix of college students and down-and-outs, their lives on opposite trajectories in every way except that at the very same moment they were crossing the very same street. Just now, a man wearing a garbage bag like a cape and pushing a baby stroller full of empty cans nearly collided with a beautiful girl in short shorts, thigh-high boots, and a chic camel hair coat. For a moment, that man, that girl, were almost interchangeable, spatially speaking.

And was this any less strange, really, than the hidden doors

I'd been moving through today? This was a way I'd always known the world worked; that for some people reality was nightmarish while for others it was not, and that only chance, for the most part, accounted for the difference between the people in this crowd whose afternoons would be spent in learning, loving, practicing, perfecting, and those whose afternoons would be spent figuring out where it was safe to sleep. Between my laughing mother in the photo and that rocking woman with the mute stare.

Just now it seemed to me far harder to wrap my mind around this strangeness than that every possibility existed as a world. There was a sort of exhaustive, exhausting logic to the latter; to the former, there was none.

I turned my head, feeling suddenly overwhelmed by all these people, and rested my eyes on Adam. He must have felt my stare because he turned to look at me as well.

Only for a second before his gaze snapped back to the road, but then he said, "I love you, too." He was speaking extremely loudly, the way he always did when he was nervous. "Your text, from earlier? I love you, too. I can't decide if it's too obvious to say or whether you won't believe it."

"Both," I said. "And thank you."

I felt a flash of insight, and closed my eyes, trying to capture it before it faded. Something about how much I loved Adam, could feel his love through mine, which did make his saying the words seem redundant. Or maybe how much I resented him, could feel his intense frustration with me through my own, which also made his words somewhat difficult to take in. Was any of this it?

I studied Adam's profile, so familiar and so unknowable, and felt doors humming, a whole host of them, a multitude. Adam's doors were easily accessible, but they weren't the ones I needed.

I licked my lips and focused on my mother. The single photograph I had of her, eyes flirting with my father behind the camera. My memories of our visits, bleach and my own urine in my nostrils, afraid to catch her eye, afraid to know her, as though allowing in this version of her would utterly destroy the other, the mother from before, a safe and loving mother who, back then, I must have still remembered. This afternoon in Grace's office, learning she had saved me. Learning she was still alive.

I ticked through the feelings like a checklist.

Anger? Here was anger. That she had been out there all this time, existing, persisting, in whatever way she did. That she hadn't managed to just be here, just be my mother.

Fear? Fear of being so unprotected, as unprotected as I had felt my entire life, so that I held on to all things lightly, knowing how easily they slipped away. That is, until Adam came along and convinced me to hold tightly.

Sadness! Sadness over the loss of her, what I might have had, who I might have been, if I'd felt loved, protected, wanted. If I'd known I had a mother who loved me enough to save me, who'd lost herself to save me.

My mind moved freely through these feelings and many others. They were hallways, wide and smooth-walled. They weren't doors.

Adam was cursing beneath his breath. We were stalled in road construction now. The clock on the dashboard said 2:29 P.M. I felt time like a hand around my throat, cutting off my breath, because this wasn't working and my son was in that awful no-place, unendurable, and I had no way to reach him without first reaching her—when lacking her had been a state that defined my entire life. Step 1: Do the single thing that you've never been able to.

But now I did feel—something. Something painful, something insistent. A wanting, a greed, a desperation. For what, exactly? Sense impressions sliced so thin they had no start or finish, just my mother's arms and voice and smell. The world, and I am loved within it. The opposite of absence and, where was she? *Where?*

And, yes, something was happening. Feelings that were doors, but these feelings were so strong, so hungry, I was afraid to open them. To travel safely, I needed to hold on to my own world through a constant stream of information, and doing that required immense concentration. These feelings seemed unlikely to permit such concentration; keeping both streams of information open would be like trying to read a textbook at a heavy metal concert; already, just lightly touching them, it was becoming hard to hold on to reality. What if I went through, lost my hold, and then couldn't get back here? So I shut my mind against them. I *no no no no no*—

"Hannah?"

I was bent over my knees, gasping. Blood was seeping from both my nostrils.

"Oh my God, Hannah, are you OK? What's happening to you?"

Adam had his hands off the steering wheel, was leaning over me.

"I'm fine," but I could barely get the words out. I gestured through the windshield to indicate that traffic was finally moving.

Adam put one hand on the wheel but kept another on my leg. He was stealing glances at me as he drove. He looked so scared I almost felt that I could tell him everything right then.

Fuck patience. I needed not to be alone in this any longer. I needed something strong enough to hold me here, something that would keep me in this world as I opened myself to the dark and hungry feelings that connected me to my mother.

Only Adam could anchor me like that. There had to be some way to explain it all right here, right now, so he could hear it. There had to be.

"You ready?" he asked. He grabbed my hand.

We were parked outside the station.

Chapter Twenty-six

The room they led us to was nothing like what I pictured when I thought about police stations. It looked like a normal, dingy conference room. One wall was painted in a muddy green that wanted to be turquoise. There was a window. The space had decent light. The air felt hot.

I'd cleaned myself up in the bathroom when we first arrived, blotting blood off my face and clothes. You drew attention, it turned out, when you walked into a police station looking like an extra from a slasher film. "Nosebleed," Adam had explained to the receiving officer, then steered me proprietarily in the right direction.

I was getting to be good at cleaning myself off in public restrooms. The blood yielded readily to a wet paper towel, becoming almost undetectable. A smart move, choosing a black T-shirt when I'd changed. But even clean, I looked noticeably worse for wear. It was my face, I realized. It looked like the primal prototype, the face my face was based off. I didn't dislike it.

In the conference room, no one seemed to notice I looked off.

I took a seat next to Adam at the table. The two detectives, Rodriguez with her scraped-back hair and kind gray eyes, Palmer with her bouncing blond ponytail and bored expression, were sitting side by side at the table's head. Across from us sat an overweight man who was sweating profusely in a pilling sweater. He'd been introduced to us, but so quickly that I had not been able to register who he was.

The table was long, and with all of us hunched at one end, the configuration felt like a family gathering no one wanted to be at.

I could tell already that, whatever we were here for, it was going to be as ugly as anything I'd hoped for. I could tell that it was going to be harrowing for Adam. I looked into his handsome, sweating face, his brown eyes desperate, searching mine, clearly worried about me now in addition to all his other worries, clearly looking like he was one false move away from vomiting, and all I thought was *good*. Good. Bring us home, Detective Rodriguez. Do your worst, with your kind gray eyes and pitying voice. Bring us out past normal so I can find my son.

Rodriguez intertwined her hands in front of her on the table and said, "So."

She was not smiling, but even so she had a gentle look about her. "Carl got in touch with me. To appeal to my humanity, I guess you might say. Because we go way back, Carl and I, although I would not exactly call us friends." When neither of us responded, she said. "Reichenbach? Carl Reichenbach, who you hired to go after us?"

Adam looked stricken, and it felt sadistic, how I leaned in hungrily to that look.

I said, "Reichenbach called you? To say we were suing you? Is that standard practice?"

Rodriguez cocked her head at me.

"It's not standard, no. But, in this case, according to him, before he opened a suit, he wanted to, and I quote, 'appeal to me in good faith to do the right thing here.' Because a kid was missing. Carl R. has a soul. Who knew?"

"When?" I asked.

Palmer now: "Is that important?" An eye roll implied by the tone.

"Yes," I said. "To me it is."

Adam was staring at me. He looked grateful. The gratitude made me feel ashamed given that I was, at this moment, trying to destroy his whole sense of reality. I reminded myself that this was for his own sake, to save his son.

Rodriguez rearranged some papers she had in front of her. I could tell from how she cocked her head at me again that she was making a point of being kind and reasonable. She pitied us and didn't like the role that she'd been cast in.

"I don't remember precisely," she said. "It was after my lunch. Maybe a little after noon?"

Adam pulled himself together enough to say, "That was right before I spoke to him. Right before he pretended not to know me."

"OK," Rodriguez drawled the word out but not in a mocking way. She was exchanging a complicated look with Palmer.

This conversation was moving too slowly, too tentatively. Adam seemed more deer-caught-in-headlights than man-hurtling-alone-through-zero-gravity.

I said: "You said because a kid *was* missing. Was. Past tense."

"That's right. Carl thought a kid was missing."

"I'm totally lost," I said. "Is there news? Why are we here?"

Rodriguez said, "Look. We're trying to do this nicely. Is this a mistake, this approach?" She was speaking directly to me. "You called a lawyer on us. *After* what you and I spoke about this morning."

Palmer said, "We get you guys are going through something here, but the thing is we don't have the resources to spare for—for whatever this is. You're not making our lives easy."

Rodriguez was pulling something out now, a document from her stack, and I hoped whatever she had there was convincing.

She slid it across to us in a plastic sleeve.

"What is this?" Adam asked.

"The death certificate. For your son. Who died the same day he was born. Eight months ago."

Rodriguez was looking back and forth between us. I could see her trying to piece it all together, who was sharing whose delusion here.

She said, looking at me now, "We need you to stop. We want to help, we do, but we're not the help you need right now. You understand?"

Palmer, no master of subtlety, added: "Your son is not missing."

Adam was touching the edges of the plastic like they might burn him.

"What is wrong with you people?" Adam whispered.

Rodriguez put a hand on Adam's arm. "Mr. Bennett—" He shook her off.

"You saw the monitor footage last night!" He was looking back and forth between the two detectives. "You saw him on the screen! He was there and then he was gone. You saw it!"

Adam's eyes were bugged with frustration: a sane person trapped in an insane situation, with no way to demonstrate the mismatch. Rodriguez was now giving one of her complicated expressions to the man in the pilling sweater.

"OK," she said. "Do we have to do this? Are we here now? This is Dr. Jamison. He's a pathologist with the city. He's here to show you the results of the autopsy on your son. Your son who is not missing. Should we do this? Do we need to?"

The guy had a folder that looked mostly stuffed with papers, but as he moved it slightly, a photo slid out, just an edge, but enough to see my jangling memory staring back at me in black and white: Jack's newborn face with the eyes swelled shut. Eyes that had clearly never opened. And yet it was also clearly him, our son.

I was staring at it, so transfixed by the horror of the image rendered outside my mind, that I didn't notice at first that Adam had pushed back from the table. By the time I noticed, he was heading out the door.

The three others were watching him go without a word, looking not unhappy. Maybe they took his hasty exit as assurance that their intervention had worked, that we'd stop being a headache, no more frantic phone calls and frivolous threats of lawsuit.

"Excuse me," I said, and rushed out after him.

I found him pacing up and down MLK Boulevard, hands linked behind his head, elbows splayed.

He walked back and forth in front of me several times without seeing me. On the fourth pass, he saw me and stopped.

With his hands still splayed behind his head he said, "Is this really happening? Can this really be happening? I keep thinking it has to be a vivid nightmare, that I'm going to wake up. But I don't wake up, and it just keeps getting worse."

"It's not a nightmare."

"Julian has to be right. He's got to be. So where do we turn now?"

"Julian isn't right."

Adam had resumed his pacing. I jogged to keep up with him, but the street was crowded with pedestrians, and I kept falling behind.

"Can we get in the car?" I asked.

Adam kept walking. He looked like he was headed to the

grassy area down the block, and I followed, hustling to keep up with his long-legged strides, wondering how aware he was that I was still here with him. Then, without warning, he stopped and whirled around.

"Shit, are you OK? I completely forgot about your—what happened to you in the car? Are you OK?"

I closed the space between us. "Can we sit down? Can we sit and talk this through together for a second?"

We were only a few yards from the grassy area now. There were benches. Adam reached and, with his thumb, wiped a fleck of blood from beneath my nostril.

He said, "What I can't make out is what their angle is in this. What does it buy them, what they're doing now? We know we're not nuts. They know we're not nuts. So, what good does it do them for us to think they think we're crazy?"

"Adam, did you see that picture?"

A muscle in his jaw pulsed like a fish's gill.

"Doctored. Badly."

"If it was, it was done well, not badly."

"Fine. It was done well. What's your point?"

I took a long breath, considering my best approach. Maybe start somewhere familiar? I said, "I'm saying exactly what I've been trying to say for these past eight months—blue lips and a dangling arm. That's what I saw. He looked like that."

His hands went back behind his head. He collapsed forward then sprang back up.

"Are you fucking— Hannah, don't lose it on me now. I need you with me. I can't do this on my own."

"I'm not losing anything, I'm trying to explain. I'm trying to explain what's going on because I know what's going on. I swear to you I do, but you need to really listen. You need to really hear."

"OK. OK. I'm listening." Something in him had stilled. He

did seem to be listening. He also looked like he hated me, but that was a side effect I could tolerate.

I said, "Jack isn't missing, exactly. He's—he's disappearing."

"Hannah—"

"No, just let me speak. He's disappearing, Adam, because that memory I had, that you said never happened, that you told me to stop bringing up? It happened. It did. Just not here."

"Hannah—"

"Not here, but it happened. And I saw it. I couldn't have, I understand that, but I did. And it's good I did, it's good I can see what most people can't, other worlds, other ways things could have gone, because it's going to help us save him."

He'd started walking again. Fast, trying to get away from me. I ran to keep his pace.

"You saw that picture! You've seen the evidence—you just haven't recognized it for what it is. The detectives first, then Dr. Goodman, then Reichenbach. Adam, he's being erased. One by one, all day, from people's minds, and even from devices. Everyone's forgetting him."

He didn't slow, but he was speaking to me at least, spitting the words over his shoulder.

"This is your fucking book, Hannah. Do you realize that? You're just reusing old material. Possible worlds affecting each other in impossible ways? You're describing *Probability Lanes*."

"No, this is nothing like that. That was—" I stopped.

We were outside Julian's building. Adam was staring up at it. This was where he'd been headed all along, and why not? Julian lived around the corner from the station, and Julian was the one person Adam trusted at the moment, now that he thought I'd gone off the deep end. I wanted to keep on explaining—about the special relationship between infancy and possible worlds, about the interaction that was changing our reality, stealing our son, about the condition of too much seeing. But maybe this was better. It was a gamble for sure. I was putting a big bet on Julian having forgotten Jack by now. But I wasn't getting anywhere like this.

"Go on," I said. "Ring."

I was daring him, and he knew it, but he didn't know what the dare was, so he wavered, his finger hovering above the doorbell.

I reached past him and pressed it. No voice came over the intercom, but twenty seconds later, Julian appeared, honeycombed by the screen door.

Julian was a twice-live-sized, bearded white man. I always described him to myself with that exact phrase, "a twice-live-sized, bearded white man," because that was the description of God's first guise in an Octavia Butler story. Julian was not actually twice-live-sized, but he had to be at least six foot six, and his beard was biblical, long and flowing. He also had a good-natured God complex as a lawyer who spent his life trying to dismantle a racist criminal justice system. He and Adam had been roommates all through college.

He was smiling widely as he opened the screen door. I had taken the right bet.

"Hey, man!" He reached to grab Adam into a hug. "It's been a minute. Hannah. How you been?"

Adam stepped back, out of Julian's reach. He was easing down the steps. He was starting to understand the dare. He was starting to understand he'd lost.

Then he looked between us, turned, and took off running.

I didn't even bother apologizing to Julian. I just went after Adam. When I grabbed his arm, he turned around so violently he almost knocked me over. His face looked like a stranger's. It was barely him he was so angry.

"You're doing something!" he said, beneath his breath. Even in this state, Adam would never make a scene. "What are you doing? What have you done to make Julian pretend we haven't spoken three times today about the fact that my child is fucking missing?"

I stepped toward him, knowing he'd move back. I was angry, too, I realized.

"That's where you're going with this? That I'm in on the conspiracy theory? Me, Julian, we're all in on it?"

He was looking at me like he'd never seen me in his life. Or maybe like he wished he never had.

"You're a monster." His angry whisper was tipping toward a snarl. "You're a—there's something wrong with you. Where's our son? Who is with him right now? Do you understand how scared he must be? Do you have any sense of what you're doing?"

"What *I'm* doing?" I was shouting. Unlike him, I didn't care about making a scene. "I'm trying to save our son. I'm trying to explain—"

"You're trying to confuse me."

He looked like he might walk away again, but he didn't. That was something at least. Something to work with.

I lowered my voice and said, "No. No. Adam, no." He was listening. "You're making me into the bad guy because you need someone to be. You need to think somebody is in charge, even if they're monstrous. But no one is in charge. No one is doing this to us. No enemy, no monster. It's just happening. And I really do believe that if you help me, I can make it stop. We can."

Something was passing over his face. A look of utter doubt, utter confusion. I felt such longing. Longing to make him understand, to get him to believe me. Then he could help me. Then we could save our baby. But mixed in with these longings must have also been a longing for my mother, or any mother maybe—my own longing for someone, anyone, to be in charge here—because those dark and hungry feelings were starting up again, and I had to shut my eyes to keep the doors from swinging open. I could feel a trickle edging from my nostril and pinched my nose to stop it.

"We need to get you to a doctor," Adam said, his voice no longer so full of hate.

"No, it's just a nosebleed. Nosebleeds always look bad. You said it yourself: Think about how scared he must be. Does anything matter other than that? Suspend your disbelief for just one second because you know nothing makes sense right now. You know it."

I opened my eyes. The view was steady. And Adam was looking back at me, his face full of love, full of pity.

"Hannah, enough. No more what-ifs. He isn't scared. He can't be. That's it. We need to both learn to let go."

He had tears in his eyes, but he looked steady. The man who trucks in facts.

"I can't do this anymore, Hannah," he said in his steady voice. "This constant rehashing, the constant what-ifs. He died. That's it. That's it. What are we even doing here?"

He looked around, at the courthouse and police station across the street, the grassy space behind us, the pedestrians passing without concern or interest. He looked around as though he were genuinely confused about what had brought us to this part of Berkeley in the middle of a workday. His brain hadn't supplied an alternative explanation as quickly as Dr. Goodman's had. Maybe because he was more emotionally invested in the events he was erasing. Maybe because he was just slower on his feet. Whatever the reason, he didn't have a narrative in place yet, so maybe I still had time to get to him before a new sense of reality clicked fully into place.

I said, "Do you really not remember what we're doing here? We're having a fight. You were accusing me of being in on a conspiracy theory to kidnap Jack."

He looked at me blankly.

"Is that a joke?"

Behind him Julian was approaching at a jog.

I thought of wheeling Adam around, straight to the car, before Julian could reach us. I could bring him home, show him Jack's nursery. Although, for all I knew, the nursery had also changed or was in the process of changing. Or worse. He'd look at the nursery and be unmoved. Remember nothing. Say we'd never taken the room apart in our long grief. You could make any evidence fit your narrative if you wanted it enough. You could tell yourself that reason was in charge all you wanted, but reason was just doing the bidding of something underneath.

Maybe I had pushed Adam too hard or approached this the wrong way, or maybe this was always going to be the moment when Jack disappeared for Adam. But either way, I'd lost him. I'd lost.

"You OK?" Julian asked. He was bent over his knees and taking long, deep breaths. "I wasn't sure if I should— Do you want me to go away?"

"No. I'm so sorry about that, man. I don't know what came over me."

Julian nodded, closed his eyes to indicate the enormity of what his friend was going through, the death of his newborn. The weight of his sympathy. He opened his eyes.

"I hear you. You guys want to come inside? Pam's not home, but I could probably get together some refreshments. If that's the kind of thing—"

I said to Adam, "You go. Have a drink. Have a talk. Is it OK if I take the car?"

Adam kissed me on the cheek distractedly and handed me the keys.

I watched them go and thought, *Fuck. Fuck fuck fuck.* Because what did I do now?

Behind the steering wheel, my first instinct was to race back home. *I* wanted to see the nursery. Jack's room, Jack's things, with Jack's smell still on them. I wanted to bury my nose in a onesie, inhale the real of him, that he had been here, that he still could be. Not that I doubted. I had never been so absent of doubt. Adrenaline coursed through me. I still knew Jack. And I knew what I had to do.

I could reach my mother. I knew I could. But Adam was the only one I knew for sure could anchor me to my own world while I gave in to the dark and hungry feelings that would bring me out to her. Without Adam, who would hold me here while I reached?

I started the car and thought: Akio. Akio lived in Berkeley. Maybe he'd returned here after Lulu got her ice cream. But I barely knew him. I doubted holding on to him would give me the anchor that I needed to keep me tied to this world. I could call Grace. In the warmth of that generous office, in the warmth of that generous mind, I could imagine feeling anchored. But driving there would take more time.

There was Hannah42. But she was not entirely not myself. I doubted that would work. And Adam42, but, no, not him either, because he'd only anchor me to his world, not to mine, and an anchor to my own world was what I needed if I was going to be sure of getting back.

I was out of ideas. And Jack might only have as little as four hours left. It was 3:45 P.M. already.

I hit the steering wheel in delight. A quarter to four. The very time when, every Monday, Wednesday, and Thursday, I realized with a start, *Oh! I have my moms group* and felt a surge of optimism. A place to go! A place with other people, people who could speak. Always briefly forgetting that being around most people only ever made me lonelier. Maybe all of them, except for Adam.

But fuck it. Dr. Goodman was always saying I had to learn to share in group. Today was going to have to be that day.

Chapter Twenty-seven

I was the last one to arrive, as usual. The six other women were already in their folding chairs arranged around the bright green rug with its jaunty ABCs. The only empty seat was directly above the M, next to Ash, who was already looking angry and finishing a burrito, which was against the rules (no outside food or beverage). They hadn't started check-ins yet. They were still chatting casually in groups of two or three and fussing with the babies.

As I slipped through the door, Sola and Charmaine both looked up at me in confusion. My heart fluttered with the realization that these women had likely forgotten Jack already. Forgotten Jack and therefore forgotten me, since without Jack I'd never have met them. If this was true, they wouldn't be willing to help.

But then Ash raised her eyebrows at me as her mouth closed around her final bite and Sola said, "Where's Jack?" and relief flooded over and through me.

These women still remembered him. For all I knew, they were the last people in this world who did.

I took my seat and said, "Actually, that's what I want to talk about today. If I can check in first?"

I didn't wait for them to answer, just started speaking.

"Jack's in trouble," I said. "It's hard to explain, but trust me when I say the trouble is bad, it's scary, he's in danger." I looked around. Six stunned faces, one of them licking burrito grease from her fingers. But at least they didn't look dubious, not yet. "And the thing is, no one's in a position to help. Not even Adam. It's all on me and—"

I stopped, considering how to phrase this next part. No one interjected with a question, not even Ash. This was probably a bad sign, but I chose to accept it as convenient, since it allowed me space to think. Obviously, I couldn't describe my capability, or alternate realities, or how bad odds were now erasing all traces of my son. None of that was going to sway them to my side. So what, then? It's all on me and, it's all on me and . . .

"I need my mother," I finally said. "I need my mother's help. She's the only one who can help, but we're not—we're not in touch. It's hard to explain. But I need—I need to do something, kind of go deeply into myself, if that makes sense, deeply into myself in a way that will help me reach out to my mother. I need to go so deeply in I'm afraid I might not come back out. So I need you guys to, to, I guess just to be there with me? Be my anchors, help pull me back to the here and now when that's where I need to be. Would you be willing? I know it sounds nuts."

Through this all, as per the guidelines we'd agreed to, all six of them just listened. "A place for non-defensive, non-judgmental listening" had always sounded to me like marketing bullshit, an impossible promise, like endless shrimp, but goddamn if these women didn't do exactly that, even Ash beneath her fiery bowl cut. Their faces as I spoke had contorted through sadness, horror, fear, then frank confusion, and by now it was clear that every last one of them had decided I was not an entirely sane individual. But they had listened.

They had listened and now no one was speaking. It was possible that no one ever would, and I couldn't say I blamed them.

But then Ash said, "So am I understanding correctly what the ask is? You want us to just sort of *be* here with you, while you do this thing you need to do to reach your mother? That's what you're asking?"

"Yes. That's right," I said, trying to at least sound very pleasant, if not exactly a model of mental health. "And maybe, like, hold my hand? Maybe two of you, one on each side?"

I still wasn't sure my thinking on this made sense, but it felt plausible to me: My mother existed spread across the possibilities, but likely her attention was tied, in all worlds, to her body. Likely she still looked out through her own eyes. So I had to find those eyes. I had to find a version of her, any version of her, and try to snag her strange attention. If I could find her, if I could summon her, then she could tell me how to save my son.

Ash shrugged. "Sure. I'm game."

Sarah, the very young facilitator, cleared her throat.

"This is not really what the group is about, though?" she said. "We're a space for processing, is the thing. Not for doing. As absolutely harrowing as this must be for you, Hannah, and my heart truly breaks for you, it truly does, and I know we're all now feeling scared for Jack and hoping that whatever it is he'll soon be A-OK, but I'm not sure this group is the right place for—that. We said no to Charmaine doing her pitch for the cloth diaper service, remember."

Ash said, "I'm sorry, is this not a group for mothers supporting mothers?"

"It is, but through *talking.*"

"Sarah, no offense," Ash said, her voice already thrumming with her characteristic rage, "but you're the only one among us who's not a mother, so I think, and pardon my being blunt here, but is this not just painfully obvious? I think you have less say about what counts to us as support."

"I wrote that mission statement," Sarah said weakly, but it sounded like an admission of defeat.

It seemed like this might actually be going well.

And then Charmaine said, "I'd like to do it. I'd like to help."

"Me, too," said Kate. "I'm happy to do whatever Hannah needs."

Sola and Devaki agreed. Sarah looked like she wanted out, but she wasn't going to stop us. She wasn't even licensed yet, poor woman.

"Are you serious?" I could not entirely believe this. "You'll do it?"

Ash said, "Why not? I mean, it doesn't sound very hard. We just, like, hold your hand while you kind of, like, do a weird, intense meditation, right?"

"Right," I said, and God bless Berkeley, this might not have even been the strangest thing they'd been invited to participate in this week. I mean, Kate had invited us all to a druidic blessing of the babies at summer solstice. I'd never RSVP'd, which now I was regretting.

They were amazing, these women. They didn't care if what I was asking of them was reasonable. They didn't care if they believed me. They knew I felt I needed this, so they were willing to go along.

We all scooched our chairs in closer. Some of the babies in the center of the rug took issue with the commotion and needed to be soothed, but that was accomplished expertly and quickly.

Ash took my left hand. Sola took my right. I looked at all six of them in turn, memorizing their faces in case I needed to use these details to pull me back. Sola's small pink mouth like a candy heart and the mole just above Kate's left eyebrow, and Devaki's seriously good bone structure. The small, tight curls escaping Charmaine's bun. The intricate lattice of pale freckles across Ash's cheeks and nose. Sarah's chin sunk down into the cowl-neck of her sweater.

Then I said, "OK."

I closed my eyes. I tried to feel along my thoughts for those same doors I had found while in the car with Adam, desperation for my mother's arms and voice and smell, impressionistic and hard to grasp, but hinting at a whole lost continent of memories. One: A face coming down from above, closer, closer, laughing. Two: A warm-bellied contentment. Gorgeous slivers of recollection, and yet the feel of them was a howling, a too-much-ness, black and threatening. I braced against them and squeezed the two hands offered me as I tried to open myself to the feelings of these doors. It was like trying to coax my body to jump from a high building. I was too afraid of these dark and hungry feelings, of what they'd do to me.

I opened my eyes. Looked at the babies in the center. Thought of Jack, his loamy bread smell, his delighted squeal. I closed my eyes and tried again.

Ash was saying something, maybe about the blood leaking from my nose, but I was finding it hard to hear. My ears were rushing with a sound like the whoosh-whoosh of a fetal heartbeat on an ultrasound. I was pretty sure this was my own heart pounding.

I was bent over my lap. My whole body was trembling, and Ash and Sola were still managing to hold tight to my hands. They were doing exactly what I'd asked of them, and it was working, something was happening, but it wasn't enough because I couldn't open myself to these feelings, I was too afraid of letting go of this world and never coming back.

I opened my eyes. Stared at the babies. My mother was

going to take this, too. By making me too full of fear, she was going to take Jack from me by taking away my ability to save him. Just like she'd taken herself and ruined any chance I'd ever had before a single chance unfolded.

I started to scream.

Then I was somewhere else.

Chapter Twenty-eight

I was staring at the shimmering yellow dollop that bounced and shivered and shot off light in the very center of Dr. Goodman's generous bay window. Like an eggy glob of sunlight. Like naked strands of DNA.

I wasn't sitting in the womb chair but on Dr. Goodman's couch. I never sat on the couch. It was reserved for couples.

I looked to my left, and there was Adam. Sitting as far from me as he could possibly manage while still occupying the same piece of furniture.

He looked thin. And underslept. He was holding himself like he might bolt at any moment. Like he was here under duress.

And in fact he was saying, "I don't see what she hopes to gain from couples therapy when we're no longer a couple. I don't mean that to sound cruel. I just—I'm trying to move on as well, and this feels counterproductive to my own progress. I'd just like a clearer understanding of what we're doing here right now. Together."

"Speak to her," said Dr. Goodman. "Not to me."

I turned my gaze to Dr. Goodman. Her auburn hair was

falling in a perfect wave over one eye. Her black satin pencil pants were creased to a knife-edge point, and I wanted to lay my cheek against her crisp white shirt.

I wanted to tell Adam to give us a second here, maybe step outside, so I could explain to Dr. Goodman what was going on. I wanted her to listen, nod in her unflappable way, and tell me that she understood. That she was sorry to have lost faith in my sanity in some other possible world; that she was sorry to have lost faith in me. To have abandoned me.

But this was a distraction.

The wrong abandonment, the wrong loss. Two wrong losses, actually. Adam. Dr. Goodman. And it made sense, I guessed. It wasn't such a simple thing to ride the possibilities, to cleanly separate out feelings for one person or another.

Still, I tried to focus again on that more specific longing, a longing that was a rage against everything I'd lost—was still losing—when my mother went away. Instead of closing my eyes, this time I stared at the eggy dollop in the window.

The dollop was wavering in and out of focus.

I looked back at Dr. Goodman. But Dr. Goodman was drawn in streaks now. Black shadows passing over her. Black shadows becoming her.

I felt an awful searing behind my eyes. And then a wrenching. As though my whole body had been flung against a wall without my moving from the couch.

The view swung wide.

I was clacking down a marble hallway. My toes felt pinched. My heels were starting to blister. I was wearing stilettos. Jimmy Choos. I couldn't imagine a reality in which I'd spend so much money on shoes. But apparently I was in one.

I was in a slick corporate building refashioned from a church. Soaring windows many stories high let in a gray afternoon light. To my left was a low glass partition that I knew, without checking, looked down on an atrium far below. These were the offices of my London publisher. And the woman clacking beside me was my British editor, Maureen.

Maureen was saying, "We're all mad about it, naturally. It's so different. So surprisingly different. I had no idea you could write *scary.*"

My head was turned so that I could look at Maureen's pale oval of a face, her lips in their habitual nervous twist. Maureen wasn't being dryly witty. She was being sincere. This was a reality in which I wrote books that weren't scary.

The Jimmy Choos I could almost just believe. But that I wrote books that weren't repositories of unease was too hard to wrap my mind around. This seemed promising. This was clearly a world quite different from my own.

"I'm so relieved you like it," my mouth said, although the words were not mine. I wasn't even sure that I could move this body, make it speak. It didn't feel as though I could.

I was surprised to hear the voice that came out of my mouth. It was only a little bit like the voice I knew as mine. It was slower, for one thing. Took its time and made the listener wait. But also deeper. And louder. And somehow richer, too. It was a very good voice. Impressive. It took up more space than mine along every dimension.

"*I* like it very much. But it's as the group from marketing were saying, it's more a matter of positioning. We just want to get it right. When you have a built-in audience the way you do, what you don't want to do is put them off."

My head nodded, but, again, this was not my doing. I was feeling along the thoughts skimming beneath my own, searching for a way in, trying to understand what had brought me here, and how it could lead me to my mother. But whereas Hannah42's mind seemed to mingle easily with mine, the mind of this Hannah felt closed. This was a more distant world. A more distant version of me. I couldn't get a purchase on this Hannah.

We'd reached a bank of elevators. My body leaned against the marble wall, giving the battered feet some small relief.

Maureen was saying, "I should be cross you aren't letting me take you to lunch. I still want to talk about the other book, the motherhood as hero quest that I was promised. But Thursday?"

"Thursday," my mouth said, and I was again unnerved by the voice that greeted me, like mine but so much better.

The elevator pinged open. Maureen delivered me inside with a limp hug.

I closed my eyes. Something from this rich-voiced Hannah's mind was finally getting through now and distracting me. It was the person I was heading downstairs to meet. I was wonderfully eager to see them. I was jittery with the pleasure. It was possible, it was very possible, that this person was my mother.

I didn't want to leave, not now, not at all, but for some reason the searing was starting up again. I wanted to press my palms into my eyes, to stop the process, but I couldn't lift these hands.

The doors pinged open. A group of men got on, conversing softly. I felt a lurch, as if the elevator had shot sideways. I reached to grab hold of the wall, but instead of metal my fingers touched the wool of the couch in Dr. Goodman's office. I was back in the world where Adam and I were sharing in an ill-advised counseling session.

In Dr. Goodman's generous bay window, the eggy dollop was shooting off its gorgeous light, the late-afternoon sun streaming around it.

Adam was talking.

"—that story about when my sister had a crash driving

from Montreal? Her car was totaled. She wasn't hurt, but she was a wreck. And when she called my mom, the only thing she said she wanted was for me to be the one to come and get her. Two hours there. Two hours back. I didn't want to. I was eighteen and home from college and feeling lazy, but that's not really why. I don't know how to explain it. I just—the fact that she wanted me to so much made me not want to do it. That was all. And so I didn't."

Dr. Goodman's face was a studied neutral as she looked to me for reply.

"I know that story already," I said, because I did, although I'd never liked it.

"Does it strike you any differently, hearing Adam offer it as an answer?"

Dr. Goodman was giving me a very strange expression.

I felt beneath my nose again, but there was nothing. There was *nothing*. No nosebleed, but also no cause for a nosebleed. The door to my own world, which I'd been trying to keep propped open, had shut. I was only in this world now.

"The answer to what?" I asked, distracted by the discovery that I'd lost my hold on my own world.

"To your question. Jesus, I'm not the one who asked you to be here in the middle of the day." Adam's voice was pleasant. I generally hated when Adam said angry things in a pleasant voice, but right now I didn't care.

I'd lost the stream of information from my own world. Just like I'd feared would happen if I went through the doors that connected me to my mother. I couldn't see or hear the six women arranged around the round green rug in folding chairs. But somehow I could still feel the two hands holding mine. Anchoring me like I'd planned. Whether this would be enough to get me back I didn't know, but there was no point in worrying about that now. I just had to keep going.

"Hannah?"

Dr. Goodman's voice was trending toward alarm, although her face didn't match the sound.

This time I didn't try to focus so fixedly on the longing. I didn't try to force it. I tried instead to do what I had never managed to do with Dr. Goodman, when she said, "Don't think, just speak. What comes to mind from there?"

This time, at least, the wrenching was less violent. It was smoother, slower, and it gave me time to analyze the sensation. Like a full-body charley horse crossed with a flicker of insight.

And then I was clacking in my red and tan Jimmy Choos toward a set of large glass doors. The eager anticipation I'd felt in the elevator was even stronger now. I couldn't wait to see the person waiting for me on the other side.

What I was feeling, what *this* Hannah was feeling, was opening to me.

Like a foreign language I was finally feeling my way into, the language of this Hannah's feelings was speaking loudly now, excitedly. And what it was saying, as far as I could tell, was wonderful. Almost like a golden light glowing within me, flowing warm and comforting beneath my skin. It glowed stronger the closer I came to the doors, to whoever was waiting for me on the other side.

I pushed through the doors, feeling giddy, but there was no one. Just a busy London street.

I focused without focusing, the searing starting behind my eyes, and with only the gentlest of tugs the busy London street became a beach. I was standing knee-deep in greenish-yellow water that sparkled into turquoise just a couple of feet away.

The sand back on the shore looked pale and soft. The beach was empty except for me and Jack.

Except it wasn't Jack. It couldn't be. The child who felt to me like Jack in every way was doggy-paddling back and forth in front of me. Was six or seven years old. Was female.

"Mommy, are you watching?" this child shrieked delight-edly, water trickling from her mouth as she struggled to hold her head above the gently lapping waves.

This world. This world was wonderful. The golden light was still glowing warm inside of me, maybe slightly brighter. Maybe because of the girl. With her nut-brown skin, her high-arched eyebrows that I loved to trace with a finger, but these days only when my daughter was asleep, because otherwise she wouldn't allow it.

The light playing over the turquoise water had a certain familiar quality, a softness that seemed to clean whatever it touched down on. The curve of the shore was familiar, too. It reminded me of a beach toward the very tip of Cape Cod, where my father and I had rented the same house three sum-mers in a row, a house he'd also rented with my mother for a week when she was pregnant. It was a wind-battered old place that felt like an ancient ship and I'd loved it. Just for being a place that my father had chosen to take me, a connection be-tween our current life and the one that had included her.

I turned to look for the house. It wasn't there. And neither were the dunes in which it nestled. So not Cape Cod, then. Or not that beach.

I dipped into the skim of thoughts beneath mine, searching for a location, for some sign of my mother near, but already the searing was beginning. Already, I was leaving. Not even a gentle tugging this time. It felt as smooth as stepping between rooms.

I was standing at a kitchen counter looking out the window at a winding road lined on both sides with tall, pale grasses. I was still near an ocean. I could smell it in the air. Sharp and briny with undernotes of decomposing seaweed. In the dis-tance, seagulls circled. There were clumps of sand amidst the tall, pale grass and on the asphalt of the road.

On the counter in front of me was a blue and white ceramic

bowl filled with caprese pasta salad. I picked the bowl up. Turned. A woman was sitting at a yellow farmhouse-style table just behind me. Her back was to me.

The golden warmth inside of me flared so strong that standing here, just being, was almost too good to believe. Was this a way that people could feel? Might I have been interacting all my life with people who secretly felt exactly like this? The question sent a ripple of displeasure through the lovely golden light beneath my skin. I took a few steps toward the table, toward this woman.

She turned to smile.

"Oh, that looks lovely, sweetheart," my mother said. "Just like your father used to make. Do you remember those summers on Cape Cod? All that sand you could never get out of the sheets, and the towels always damp and Neil always somehow surprised by it, each and every time? 'Eva, this towel is wet.' No fucking kidding, Neil."

My mother had long gray hair held back by a tortoiseshell barrette. Her eyes were narrow, twinkly, alive with good-natured mischief. Her face was beyond describing. So beautiful that I almost couldn't stand it, although it was impossible to say what made the wrinkled, thin-lipped face so lovely. Just looking at it made me feel weak-kneed with joy.

I almost dropped the bowl, then caught it.

I was weak-kneed with something else now. This was what it felt like to have a mother. And for a moment, just a moment, I'd forgotten my own son.

I tried to open this mouth. I tried to speak. But this Hannah was too distant a version of me. I had no sway over this body.

And my mother? It was hard to believe that anywhere inside this twinkly eyed woman was the mute, rocking mother who was mine. That my mother, spread between the possibilities, really crouched in any corner of this healthy mind. But if I was right, my mother looked out from all her eyes in all her versions. And I had to believe that I was right; I had nothing else.

Which meant I had to find a way to get this body to speak. This body put the bowl of pasta salad on the table and took a seat.

My mother's fingers were smoothing back a few strands of gray hair that had escaped the barrette at the nape of her slender neck and were flying loose around her regal forehead. The hands moved smoothly, elegantly, the motions young and fluid. But every few seconds the head jerked to the right in a painful-looking spasm. Perhaps she noticed my noticing.

"I've got a funny crick," my mother said, moving her hands to rub behind the neck.

I could have laughed if my laughter worked inside this body. Just as Hannah42 had described it: a post-hoc justification. Maybe it was a crick, just like she said. But maybe it wasn't. Maybe instead it was my broken mother inside this healthy mind, forming her own intentions.

I couldn't shift my gaze to see what it might be that my broken mother maybe wanted to look at. I couldn't even work this body that small amount.

But it didn't matter. I'd found it now. The way to wield some sway over this body.

I was feeling the photo negative of that golden glow. How much I'd lost. How much I wanted.

It was a howling all through me, and it tied me somehow to this body, just enough. Bit by bit, I pulled the jaw down, an unhinging, a prying.

And then, in this charming room, at this well-laid table, at a cozy family gathering over bowls of pasta salad, I made this Hannah scream.

Almost a word, almost "Help," but as it might sound in a mouth incapable of forming human words.

It was a scream that could have come out of my mute and

rocking mother. But it hadn't. It had come out of this happy, golden Hannah. Right into her mother's startled face.

I'd done that. I'd done it. I had made contact.

I felt for the two hands holding mine, I lurched. I was on the green rug, which was speckled with my blood. The women and the babies had all huddled on the far side. Even Sola was only barely maintaining contact between our fingertips, the rest of her leaning away.

Only Ash was still right here. Her hand still holding tight to me. She kneeled down now, brought her face just inches from mine.

"Holy shit," she said. "Was that a seizure, or was that the thing you wanted to do? Did it actually work? Did you actually just do something completely fucking awesome and insane?"

Chapter Twenty-nine

I had done something completely fucking awesome and insane. But I had no idea whether it had worked.

And as I struggled to sit up with Ash's help, my whole body still trembling, I let that fact settle in my bones: I had no idea if it had worked.

"Your part worked," I said. "You did perfectly. Thank you, all of you, so much."

Sarah had run off to get me a wet towel, and now she returned with it. Charmaine took it from her and began to swab beneath my nose. It was hard not to cry as she tended to me, her touch gentle but not pitying.

No one was speaking. I was grateful for the silence.

The white washcloth was saturated with red. I had bled an astounding quantity, it seemed to me, but I wasn't feeling woozy. My phone pinged with a text. I scrambled over to my bag, but before I could reach it, it pinged again. And again and again. Eleven times in total.

I looked at the messages in confusion, feeling a vertiginous hope that was almost indistinguishable from having to throw up.

The texts were all identical. Unintelligible. All sent with no cell number attached, just, somehow, the message.

37.82746009721271. -122.28459071600813.

It had to be from my mother. The timing of it, the strangeness, and Grace had said it was always electronic communication. But what did the message mean? Two random strings of numbers. One positive, one negative.

I looked up at the five curious faces watching mine. Then at one, at Ash. I handed her my phone. She was a scientist, had a mind like Adam's, methodical. She'd know how to make sense of this if there was any sense to be made.

Instantly she said, "Longitude and latitude. It's a location."

I felt a laugh burst out of me. It sounded too big, and it took me a moment to understand the reason: All of us were laughing. Even Sarah, standing in the doorway with a fresh wet towel.

I'd summoned my mother. And she'd summoned me in turn. To God knew where. A star in the Andromeda Galaxy. The event horizon of a black hole. One reality amidst an infinite origami matrix of space-time. Wherever it was, I would find a way to get there.

Ash was typing in my phone.

"What are you doing?"

"Putting the numbers into Google Earth."

She held it out for me so I could watch. The little red pin dropped. I grabbed the phone from Ash's fingers and zoomed in.

This point in the universe my mother had sent me was the Home Depot in Emeryville.

Or, not exactly the Home Depot. It was hard to tell. The streets and overpasses did something weird there, near that intersection where 580 became the MacArthur Freeway. But it was close enough that I basically knew the route, and my phone would make up the difference.

Ash said, "If we beat the rush-hour traffic, it'll take us under twenty minutes."

"Us?"

"Well, yeah, I mean, aren't we—are we not coming with you?"

All six of them were looking at me expectantly. Ready. Eager, even, to help. Babies in tow. Like some squad of ancient heroes.

Like in the book that other Hannah, the Hannah with the confident voice and Jimmy Choos, had promised to her London publisher. Motherhood as hero quest.

But in the hero's quest, the hero always goes into the final ordeal alone.

"Not for this part, no," I said.

This was between me and my mother.

Chapter Thirty

As I watched my moms group grow small in my rearview window, waving me off like a band of tribal sisters, I wondered if I wasn't making a mistake. Backup would be nice right now.

I was heading toward the Home Depot in Emeryville where my mother was . . . what? Meeting me? Sending me to encounter someone or something else? To see something I needed to see? I had no idea. I was going to the spot where my mother wanted me to go, obeying the woman whose absence was a void that had been howling through me so loudly and so long that I had come to think of it as simply the sound of me.

As I eased the car into stop-and-go traffic on Claremont Avenue, the phone lying on the passenger seat lit up with Adam's name. I let the call go to voicemail. A few seconds later a text came through. I took a long, slow breath and chose not to read it. I couldn't stomach whatever was going to be there. It wasn't Adam's fault he'd forgotten that we had a son who was in danger, but it was hard not to want to blame him.

The traffic eased up as I merged onto 24. It was 4:57 P.M. so the uncongested freeway was a touch of grace. Above the few scattered high-rises of downtown Oakland, where tech companies were starting to move in, the sky was beautiful in a way I didn't like. Big, dense clouds were lit up an electric red by the setting sun, looking like a 3D movie, realer than real. Sticking out from the screen to fill the theater. A sideways world spilling across the axis.

As I merged onto 580, another series of texts from Adam lit up my phone lying screen-up on the passenger seat. This time I did glance over, curious at the flurry.

Can you call me?

I can't stop thinking about Jack.

I know it's not healthy you don't need to tell me that.

I know what Dr. Goodman says about complicated grief and guilt etc. but I keep thinking there's something I should be doing.

As though he still needs me.

Like urgently.

Like there's something I'm forgetting to do and it's a matter of life and death.

Do you think this sounds insane? Do you ever feel that way?

I know it can't be but it feels true like he's not dead like he needs me.

Can you call me as soon as you get this?

Hannah?

Reading these with quick sideways glances, I didn't notice a Tesla cut in front of me and had to swerve right to avoid rear-ending it at 70 mph. I took a few deep breaths and rolled my shoulders. It was a good reminder to stay calm, stay focused on the road, drive like I wasn't in a race for my child's life. This would be a very inconvenient time for me to die.

I took a long, slow curve onto the exit for Market Street/San Pablo, wondering if there was a world spinning off now in which I did rear-end that Tesla.

I turned onto Peralta. I'd been tuning out the commands

my phone was giving me. Now I realized I was headed in the wrong direction, to the Home Depot's main entrance. The phone was telling me to make a left as soon as I was able, and I obeyed, turning onto 40th and then making my first left again onto Hollis.

I slowed to a crawl as my view filled with a sprawling homeless encampment that spread out on both sides, filled the median, and spilled onto the asphalt. I was ashamed to realize I'd forgotten this existed behind the Home Depot. Tents, shanties, dismembered pieces of furniture, rolling hills of trash. As with most of the homeless encampments that had sprung up in the Bay Area in the past couple of years, I'd never seen a person in this curbside community, although poignant clues to its residents were all around. A mint-green bicycle tied with rope to an orange and gray tent. A stroller tucked carefully behind a folded mattress. A flower-patterned sheet spread across the sidewalk, each corner held down with a cinder block, I assumed to let it dry after a washing.

I always felt monstrous when I passed these places. That I could know they existed and yet go about my life as though they didn't. A place like this existing simultaneously with the life I inhabited, not ten miles away.

The phone was still urging me onward. A right, a left, and I was directly beneath the freeway.

"You have reached your destination," my phone informed me.

I was just beyond the overpass. I cut the engine.

It was not yet dark, but the electric red sunset had spent itself in one quick dazzle and left the sky a sludgy gray. It made the day look used up and worn out.

At least I was where I was meant to be. There was nothing to do now but wait.

No other cars had passed since I had parked. No other humans were within eyeshot.

I picked my phone up and read over Adam's texts again, trying to think of how to answer. What was kindest in this moment? It seemed to me as though something inside of him was fighting against forgetting Jack, fighting against reality for love of him. Maybe this was wishful thinking on my part, projection, but I still wanted to help. Calling seemed out of the question. I needed to remain fully alert for any next signs from my mother.

Instead I texted: *You're not insane. But you need to trust me. I'm handling the thing that feels so urgent. I'll call when I can.*

Three dots and then: *Wait what?* And then: *OK.*

I reached into the glove compartment and found a pack of Pall Malls I'd stashed there when I was trying to quit smoking. Just before we'd started trying to get pregnant. The secret car stash was supposed to be a psychological crutch, not actually available to me, but there if I truly needed it. Which I did now. I lit one quickly, not even bothering to open the window, before I could start thinking about smoke trapped in the fabric of the car seat. I inhaled deeply and felt a lively tingling in my toes.

Then jumped. For a moment I'd thought there was a face peering in the passenger-side window. It was just my own reflection hovering against the graying evening. I looked bad. Haunted, hunted. Drastically aged and yet somehow regressed, unformed. The face moved closer to the glass. It wasn't mine.

Against every instinct, I moved my face closer, too, and squinted, right foot poised to press the gas, right fingers wrapped around the key in the ignition. The face stared back, but not exactly at me. A teenage boy. I knew him. He'd been making a scene in CVS yesterday, trying to take off his windbreaker and freaking out the cops. Not a boy, not young, I remembered realizing, and now I realized it again.

Not male, not young. A face a little like my own, but not in any of the details. A face at once old and young, decrepit and unformed.

Her face. Her.

I did my breathing, counting to four on the inhale and six on the exhale just like Dr. Goodman had instructed. I was an adult, a mother, and here to save my son. I needed this reminder because this face, this body was too much. In them, I could see the beautiful woman at the yellow farmhouse table: the version of my mother I'd been sitting across from not an hour earlier, with twinkling eyes and long gray hair held back by a tortoiseshell barrette. The strong bone structure, with firm, high cheekbones, the slender, boyish build. The long aquiline nose, although this nose was crooked, broken and healed badly, maybe more than once.

The two faces came together, resolving briefly into one and I felt knocked back three decades, a small child standing in a yellow, sun-drenched room that smelled of bleach working overtime. Afraid to breathe. To call attention to myself. To draw my rocking mother's hollow eyes in my direction. Because I knew that if she turned to me, if we locked eyes, then I might see that this was really her. The same mother whose arms and voice and smell once made the world for me, the world when I was loved within it. As though, if we locked eyes, that world-making mother would be gone, erased, as though she'd never been.

This was her, and I took my hand off the ignition. My mother lifted a hand as well. Maybe waved. The effect was hard to describe except to say it looked laborious for barely any movement at all. I leaned across to open the passenger-side door.

There are certain things you expect another person's body to do. Such as move out of the way when a car door opens outward. My mother failed to do this. And so the door collided with her gently. She staggered back two steps, then stopped. I guided the door farther until it could prop open on its own.

"Hi," I said, and my voice really did sound like a child's, small and wavery.

My mother brought her head and shoulders inside the car. I resisted the urge to flinch away. It wasn't just the her-ness. Nor was it the unwashed smell of her, though that was sharp. It was how she moved; it was unnerving. Like a lazily drawn animation, most of the intervening motions missing.

"Come on, get in," I urged, and at least my voice sounded like my own voice now, adult, impatient to get moving. The sludgy gray of evening was turning to real night. We had a job to do. No luxury of time for whatever this endless moment was becoming, this silent stillness of reunion.

She wasn't getting in the car. Why wasn't she getting in the car? She was doing something else, but it was hard to say just what it was. I flicked on the meager yellow of the overhead, but this didn't help me understand what I was seeing. Maybe she was shaking her head *no*. Maybe that was it. And her mouth looked like it was trying to form words, too. Her eyes looked like they wanted to speak and couldn't get the mouth to fall in line. Every few seconds a brightness flared inside the eyes and then went out, like a fire that wouldn't catch. Flare, nothing. Flare, nothing. It was maddening. I was starting to give up hope that she could be of any help at all, that she was even really here with me, that I had made the right decision.

And then, finally, she spoke.

"This way," my mother said. "Where we can hear the music."

Chapter Thirty-one

My mother's voice. My mother's voice exactly.

Hearing it, I remembered. The memory right here, exactly where it hadn't been: this voice. Unremarkable, neither high nor low, neither pretty nor ugly. But unmistakably hers. The sound of it, the feel of it, this register, this timbre, the way it had once formed a climate that I lived in.

I got out of the car. I followed her. She was moving quickly, back toward the underpass.

The moon was nearly full. I could see well enough to make out broken glass, shiny chips bags, Slurpee cups strewn across the asphalt that gave out on dead grass. Well enough to make out every strange and jerky step that carried forward that narrow back in its blue windbreaker. My mother's back.

I walked a few steps behind, not wanting to fall beside her. It felt important to keep her fully in my field of vision, to not let her disappear.

We both stopped when she reached a mural that extended the entirety of the concrete wall. She was running her fingertips over one portion of the painting. I hung back, examining her, and the painting. It was just a standard piece of public art.

People of all ages, races, enjoying the amenities that the city had to offer. Old men playing chess. Families picnicking in a park. Laughing children riding skateboards.

My mother was palpating the giant face of one of the laughing children, and for some reason, I trusted that this was a reasonable thing for her to do. That she had a plan and was executing it. But I was still relieved when her hand disappeared into a nostril and half the face seemed to peel away, as the boy's right side revealed itself to be a door now opening outward. A narrow door, but definitely a door, definitely real. Probably for maintenance crews.

Without bothering to check if we were being observed, my mother climbed inside. I peeked my head in and couldn't see beyond a few dark inches, but what choice did I have? I scrambled through. The door swung closed behind me. I whipped my head around on instinct and was glad to see a handle flashing silver in the murky dark. Assured there was a way back out, I started climbing.

Climbing because the dark passage was stairs. The walls were so close that they brushed my shoulders. The space smelled of damp and mildew and rock, the smell of medieval castle walls. It echoed with a hollow rhythmic thumping that sounded either ancient or postapocalyptic. Not at all like what it must have actually been: cars passing on the highways overhead.

I soon was out of breath. The stairs were tough going. Roughly hewn. Randomly spaced, some so high I had to grab hold with both hands to hoist myself onto the next one. I could hear my mother making her way in front of me, but I couldn't see beyond my own two hands. Light filtered in from somewhere up above, but weakly, barely. These steps didn't seem intended for municipal maintenance as I'd first assumed. They seemed more like a mountain pass carved painstakingly with knives and axes from the steel and concrete monoliths left behind by mysterious ancestors. Like a passageway carved by some distant orphans of our race, huddling from superstorms and leveling floods and wildfires, all the horrors we'd unleashed on them.

I wondered if my mother had made these stairs herself. I couldn't seem to settle between the idea of my mother as an immensely powerful figure, able to carve secret passageways in public spaces, and my mother as inept, no possible source of hope. It was like being a toddler and a teenager at once. Like I was cramming my whole childhood of maternal delusions into one interaction.

Because of the dark, I was feeling my way with fingers, feet, hips, shoulders, angling and shimmying to fit in the narrow spaces. At one point my nose brushed against something mossy and pond-smelling. I pulled away in horror and hit the back of my head hard enough against concrete to hear a disturbing thwack and, seconds later, feel the corresponding pain radiating out from the point of impact down into my neck and shoulders. I shook off the pain and kept on climbing, sideways, like a crab.

I'd been climbing for five or six minutes before enough light reached me that I could see the outlines of a door above. With the help of sight, I was able to pick up my pace. No sign of my mother, but I trusted she was with me still, on the other side of the door I saw in outline. I didn't know why I trusted this, but I did.

And it was true: When I finally stepped through the door and out into the cool night air, here was my mother waiting for me. Here was my mother in her blue windbreaker, and here was I, on a concrete platform suspended several stories off the ground by a latticework of metal beams. There were four platforms in total that I could see, ours and three others, and their bases looked to me like transmission towers, but why they were topped with concrete platforms I couldn't say. The platforms were maybe six feet by four feet, with no walls or ledges to prevent someone from plummeting to the street below. Above us, the exchange of highways was close enough to look like a ribboned sky. Alternating bands of black night and gray asphalt carving up the space. A strange place for a rendezvous, but here we were. Here she was. Hanging on to this reality even though Grace had made it sound as though she couldn't ever be in only one. The smell of exhaust was overpowering.

"I need your help," I said. "I think you know that. I need to save my son. I think you know that, too."

My mother made no sign of having heard me. She was kneeling on a blue waffle-knit blanket spread across our narrow strip of concrete, trying to smooth the edges as though she were getting ready for Shakespeare in the Park. I kept my back pressed firmly against the safety of the brown metal door I'd just emerged through. There was a small gap between the door and the start of the concrete platform, enough for my foot to slip through if I wasn't careful. We had to be at least fifty feet above the ground. I peeked down and kicked a piece of gravel through the gap; it turned to dust on impact with the asphalt. I closed my eyes.

"What's the plan?" I asked. Actually, shouted. The sound of cars rushing in four different directions across the interchange of highways above our heads was both a celestial roar and a hum throughout my body.

This time, my mother heard me. Or, anyway, she turned to look over her shoulder. It was hard to tell if she was looking at me or just past me. She was standing so still in the changing wash of lights from the cars above—*red, white, shadowed, red, white, shadowed*—that I wasn't even sure she was still present or had left this world already. Then, without a word, she went right back to fussing with the blanket. At least my mother's movements seemed less like a badly drawn animation than they had earlier. Not normal, still stiff. But more like a person moved.

I felt I ought to join my mother on the blanket. We needed to establish some greater contact than we were so far managing. But I was afraid to leave the relative safety of the wall.

"Is this . . . is this strictly necessary, with the blanket?"

My voice seemed to disappear into the roar of the cars passing overhead and so maybe she didn't hear, or maybe she just didn't consider the question worth answering. She went on busying herself with the blanket.

"Please," I shouted. "Can you stop?"

This time, my mother did look at me. There was something touching in the expression on her face. It was the look of a hostess worrying she'd annoyed her guest. The expression was so polite.

"I don't mean to rush you, but I really don't have time to spare."

My mother nodded, patted the blue blanket.

I forced myself to step away from the door. I sat myself down gingerly on the royal blue waffle knit, already missing the firmness of the wall behind my back. The platform on its metal base seemed to sway, just slightly, each time the wind blew.

My mother had dangled her feet over the far edge of the platform, which sent a flood of acid through my stomach— could she not be more careful with her body, this body I had been waiting all my life to find again?—and now she patted the blue waffle knit behind her, where her own head would go if she lay down. When I didn't take the hint, my mother swiveled on her denimed butt and laid herself flat with her feet, in clean white sneakers, pointed toward the metal door and her head near the platform's outer edge. I hesitated, then laid myself in the same configuration. It was almost comfortable except for the phone and car key in my back pocket. I wiggled my hand beneath me and extracted them, laid them both beside me on the other side from my mother.

Our heads were almost touching, cheek to cheek. So close that the hum the traffic was sending through my body also seemed to thrum now with my mother's heartbeat, her rushing blood, her breath. A real person. Here. Inches away. I wanted to touch her. I was terrified to touch her.

"My son's name is Jack," I said, still screaming, despite our proximity. "He disappeared last night. Thank you for coming. Thank you. I need to save him, like you saved me, but I don't know how to do it."

My mother said nothing, so I went on, "What else should I tell you? I somehow feel you know exactly what I've tried and why I asked you here, better than I can say it, but maybe that's mistaken."

In fact, it seemed to me that all these words were mistaken. Maybe it was because I was shouting them, but they sounded like loose syllables, disconnected shards of sound, that couldn't possibly link up into any meaning.

My mother was pointing upward. I directed my attention to the ribbons of road above. I knew what I was looking at, and yet I didn't. I'd driven every which way over this poorly designed exchange between the 580 and the MacArthur Freeway. But from this vantage, the bands of gray against the richer black of night didn't look poorly designed, but rather ingeniously arranged toward some strange end. The ribbons of night and the ribbons of road broke up the plane so that it was possible to look and see either of them as the negative space and either as the positive. The effect was unsettling, and almost beautiful. Under other circumstances, I might have gladly stared at it for hours, exploring the many ways the view played with my vision.

But I was growing impatient.

I shouted, "I think I'm running out of time. Can you tell me how?"

The look in my mother's eyes reminded me of a dog Julian had once owned. Bugsy, who used to try to save us all whenever we went swimming. Those desperate eyes of Bugsy as she paddled after you and nearly drowned you, trying to claw you to her own idea of safety: *Just let me save you in my insane and harmful way.*

"Can you tell me how to find my son?" I asked. "I need to know what it was you did that worked. Can you remember?"

My mother said, "I want to tell you."

My mother wasn't shouting. But, quiet as it was, her voice didn't get eaten by the noise the way that mine did.

She tried again. "I want to tell you that the wave function changes in time in a way that is described by the same mathematics as a vibrating string."

I closed my eyes, willing my voice even as I shouted, "What?"

"What is oscillating is the wave function, a sum of terms each of which is vibrating, so to speak, at its own characteristic frequency."

How was it that I was suspended on a tiny, perilous platform with my mother, my own mother, who I hadn't seen since I was six years old, trying to save my son, and these were the words that she was saying?

"I don't know what that means," I yelled back in helpless frustration.

"It means they behave like a vibrating violin string."

It was cold up on the platform. It wasn't a cold night, but the winds were strong up here. I was in jeans and a T-shirt, and I was shivering. The tears rolling down my cheeks weren't helping. They felt like little beads of ice.

Fighting harder to keep my voice steady, I shouted, "OK! Vibrations! Thank you! But how do the vibrations help me save my son? How do they help me—" I paused, searching for the right words. "Do what you did?"

"The tessellation," my mother said.

She was holding real eye contact now. And this statement, said so simply, so lucidly, in direct response to me, seemed poised to set a different course for our conversation, even if I still had no idea what she was talking about. An actual give-and-take. I pressed my palms into the waffle knit on either side of me, trying to choose my next words with care, to not let this moment go to waste.

"The tessellation?" I had only the dimmest sense of what this word meant, a term I associated—maybe?—with geometry. Rightly or wrongly, the word brought to mind those Escher prints freshmen tacked up in their dorm rooms to signal they were brainy, sketches where figure and background were reversible, white birds separated by black spaces becoming black fish separated by white spaces and vice versa depending on how you looked. Kind of like the ribbons of night and the ribbons of road above us, actually. My voice was getting hoarse from shouting to be heard above the roar. "Tessellation has something to do with finding Jack?"

My mother's hand twitched beside mine.

"Please," I said. "I'm not trying to be difficult, I just don't know that I'll be able to follow the—the vibrations of the wave function or the tessellation or whatever, so if you could just tell me—"

My mother put a finger to her blanched, scabbed lips. Pointed her other hand up again, toward the ribbons of road and sky passing figure and ground back and forth between them.

This was useless. Pointless. Insanely and stupidly dangerous. I used my palm to wipe the tears off of my cheeks. They were coming fast now. From rage and impotence and sickness with myself. That I was depending entirely on this woman. That I couldn't save my son without her.

"Please, if you could just tell me—"

"I'm going to start the vibrations now," my mother said. "But I need you to be still before I do."

"Isn't there anything you can tell me?"

My mother nodded gravely.

"I can bring you out," she said. "But I never came back in."

My mother's hand was up against mine, pinky just barely brushing pinky, but the touch felt intentional, the touch felt kind.

"Come," she said. "I saw you there. I saw you make the pasta salad just like your father used to make. Come."

"OK," I said, because at least I understood this invitation. Back to the world where I had found and summoned her. Back to the world with the yellow farmhouse table. We were going to ride that possibility together.

Possibly I wasn't coming back. Possibly I was going to end up like her, spread out across the possibilities. She could take me out, but she couldn't bring me in, and that was not ideal, but I willed myself to be still just like she'd asked of me because I was with my mother and my mother had a plan. No plan was ever perfect. I'd find my own way back here. I'd do it because I had to.

She had started making a sound. A low, not-quite melodic hum like Tibetan throat singing, which I'd discovered one afternoon after falling through a clickhole. I remembered thinking then that throat singing sounded like gods or planets arguing between themselves. But this was even more . . . vibrational. Like a power drill straining toward beauty.

I turned my head to look at the face just inches from mine. My mother turned to look at me as well.

"The vibrations?" I asked.

My mother smiled.

"What is oscillating is the wave function," she said.

"OK." I looked back up, letting the sounds wash over and through me. Its own kind of tender touch.

As I listened, it almost seemed to me the ribbons of road and night were moving, vibrating with my mother's sounds. Shifting against each other and making a music of their own.

I closed my eyes and tried to recall that golden feeling, the spill of golden light all through me, a way I'd never known people could feel. That would be the door to the world with the yellow farmhouse table, if any feeling was. That and its photo negative, the wanting: black, hungry, howling.

But I couldn't recall either feeling. I was too afraid right now. For Jack. For me.

"I can't get there I don't think," I said out loud.

My mother went on singing. If singing was what you called it. That low vibration.

I remembered asking Grace the mechanism for moving between worlds, and how she'd told me, "You tell me."

"You're the one who can do it," she'd said. "And your mother's theories, on this point, make little sense to me."

If this was my mother's theory—a song that was a vibration that was the oscillation of the wave function—it made little sense to me either. And yet I couldn't deny that something was happening to me as my mother sang. A sense of my own borders dissolving, myself dissolving, but not in a way that felt like loss or diminution. For some reason, my mind filled with the image of the eggy dollop in Dr. Goodman's window.

And then I felt the snag in the corner of my vision. That golden liquid feeling.

And my mother's lips brushed against my ear.

Chapter Thirty-two

Then there I was. At the yellow farmhouse table. The dishes had been cleared. I was sitting with my mother, my beautiful, unbroken mother, with twinkling eyes and long gray hair held back by a tortoiseshell barrette. We each had a mug of tea in front of us. Oolong. The windows were black now. Several lamps around the room had been turned on, and the buttery light they cast was even cheerier than the late-afternoon sun had been an hour ago.

The air still smelled of salt and brine and now also of wood fire.

From hidden speakers somewhere in the room, Tibetan throat singing was playing.

"It's so relaxing, isn't it?" my whole and healthy mother asked. "I wasn't sold at first, but now I love it. When I'm in a certain mood nothing else will do."

My mother's elegant fingers were wrapped around an expensive-looking ceramic mug that matched the one in front of me. The mugs were teardrop-shaped and had no handle, just blinding white swirls flecked with tan. My mother, holding hers, looked poised, serene. It was hard to believe that my broken mother was anywhere inside there.

But then, just like the last time I was at this table, my mother's head jerked to the right in a painful-looking spasm.

"That funny crick again," she said.

I would have smiled if I knew how to make my smile work in this body.

As it was, it took all my effort just to slightly shift the head. But I did shift it. By focusing on the howling need that somehow connected me to this body, I wrenched the head just enough to see what my broken mother wanted me to look at.

To the right of the yellow table where we sat, there was a sideboard made of reclaimed wood stained gray. Papers lay on top of it in loose piles. Magazines, unopened mail. Above the sideboard a large painting, abstract, vivid blue and green, quite pretty. Beneath the left edge of the painting, three framed photos. I zeroed in on these: all of me, at various ages, looking happy. In one of them I was lying across my parents in a snowbank; their legs were flung up in the air as though I'd just crashed into them. We all were wearing pom-pom hats. My father was laughing.

The body I was in stood up, moved closer. I couldn't tell if I had done it. It did seem that this Hannah's mind was finally mingling with my own in drips and drops. That lovely golden warmth, letting off a constant stream of goodness, a thermostat of contentment.

I pulled my own mind back, resisting the warm pull. It would be too easy to allow myself to sink into this luckier version of myself. Like slipping into a bath or into sleep. I needed to figure out what my mother, my own one, wanted me to do here. Sitting at the table, I'd thought it was the row of family photos. But once I was standing at the sideboard, I knew it was the painting.

Not abstract at all. It depicted the same view that my own body, in my own world, was still looking at. The ribbons of

Emeryville highway, the ribbons of night, tiling the sky. Only instead of gray and black these were done in green and blue.

"Sorry, I know you hate these." My healthy mother came up behind me and wrapped her arms around my shoulders. The hold was perhaps the loveliest way I had ever been touched: tight enough to make me feel held, loose enough to in no way constrict me. "I meant to put it away with the others before you arrived."

The voice that came out of my mouth said, "I don't hate it at all. I've never hated these."

The voice was not my own, it was the better voice, the one I'd first heard from a version of my body clacking in Jimmy Choos through the halls of my London publisher. The voice that took up more space than mine along every dimension. But I had said the words. I had made them come out of this mouth. Being here was getting easier.

"Can I see the others?" I asked, with effort, and with even greater effort broke away from the shawl of my mother's arms.

We walked through a tiny formal dining room; a living room in pleasant disarray; and into a colder room, completely dark.

My mother flipped a switch and the room jumped into view. It was a sunroom, ceilings and walls all made of glass. But it appeared to be doubling for the moment as a painting studio. The profusion of colors was gorgeous and overwhelming. There were canvases set up on three easels and stacked deep all around the perimeter of the room, leaning against the windowed walls. They were all startlingly similar. Dichromes of tessellated planes, the highways and the ribbons of night sky between them done in every shade of orange, pink, blue, green, yellow, black, white, and silver. Blaring neons and delicate watercolors and precision-etched black and whites. Only I supposed, now that I was looking at them more closely, that it wasn't really the highways. The configurations varied a great deal. The number of bands across the plane, the shapes they made as they curved around one another.

My mother stood just behind me, hanging back as I continued to flip through the canvases.

"Are you really OK?" she asked. Her voice was soft but not tentative. "I don't want you to worry. I remember what you used to call these. My expulsion compulsion. And maybe you weren't wrong then. But now—" She leaned her cheek briefly on my shoulder. "I don't know. The urge just comes over me sometimes, and when it does, it feels wonderful to paint. Like weightlessness. Like letting go of some tremendous burden that it turns out has been the only thing keeping me back from flying. Does that make sense? Do you ever feel that when you write? Ed's taken to calling it my retirement compulsion. But that's his own wishful thinking. I'll retire when I'm dead." She kissed my shoulder now. "Sweetie! Don't look so stricken." She draped one silk-sleeved arm back around me. "I promise not to be mortal if I can help it."

I went on flipping through the canvases. I was beginning to notice how the bands of color almost seemed to vibrate as I moved through them. Like stop-motion art. The shapes seemed to be vibrating to the music, to the strangely perfect melding of throat singing and ocean waves that mingled in this room.

I flipped the canvases more quickly, trying to understand. Maybe the spread of possibilities was a tessellation, worlds like shapes repeating in endless variation. Maybe this was how you saw it all, everything at once, by opening yourself up to this strange vibrational music. Patterns that maybe had to do with vibrations of the wave function and maybe had instead to do with emotions, and maybe had to do with both and maybe had to do with neither, I had no idea. I had no idea how possibilities, once unleashed in a certain way, ricocheted between realities or why my son's death was swallowing his life like some slow-motion tidal wave. None of this made sense to me, but something did to her. And maybe that was all I needed.

A hand closed over mine and stilled my frantic flipping. I looked up at my twinkly eyed mother in surprise. She looked back at me as though she was trying to figure out what she was up to as very deliberately and slowly she touched my heart, her heart, my eyes, her eyes. All four of us in just two bodies.

Not the paintings, it seemed to me my broken mother was trying to say to me through this other woman's movements. Us. We were the tessellation. The two of us in endless variation: figure and background. Merging, blurring. The golden glow and the howling. Presence and lack. I still didn't understand, but my skin was prickling with the feeling that I did.

I wasn't in the golden world any longer. My mother had traveled us away from the glass-walled sunroom, with its paintings, its alien golden glow of deep contentment. I was back in my own body, on a platform beneath the 580 and the MacArthur Freeway. The lights of the cars were slashing the night and making it bleed brilliance over all the bands of road and sky, blurring their edges. My mother continued to hum the vibrations through the system of our bodies. She was back in her body, too. Her fingers, stretching from the sleeve of her blue windbreaker, reached for mine. Entwined with mine. I looked at her. I let my fingers wrap around hers, let them anchor me. Her fingers anchored me even as her humming opened up for me a wild strangeness, a sense I'd never known I had, that gave me information through vibrations. Other views were opening for me now, refracted and honeycombed, like mirrors reflecting mirrors, looking endless, and maybe this was everything, all possibilities, but the magnificence of what now spread before me didn't seem the point. The point was what we were doing together, this other form of communication. I wasn't sure yet *why* it was the point, but the feeling prickling up my spine told me that it was.

An uncanny feeling: as though there was something I knew without knowing I knew it. Another form of communication. This language of vibrations, a language that, somehow, my mother seemed to be creating for me, moment by moment, as I needed it. As though she *was* language. What, actually, was she?

"What are you?" I shouted.

The wind was fierce. My hair lashed at my face.

"Your mother," she answered.

I rolled over and flung myself against her.

To my surprise, her body conformed to mine, embraced me back. She felt so thin, fragile, but she was holding me. My own mother was holding me.

"Mom," I whispered.

The sound of the cars above was louder than before. It took me a moment to realize that what was missing were the low vibrations of my mother's singing. Without her humming, the vast, honeycombed vista winked out of view and all I saw was the concrete platform we were lying on. Another gust, the platform swayed, and I buried my face against her neck because I felt like I was falling. Not falling off the platform, but like I'd felt inside the MRI and again on Hannah42's bed. The alone-in-the-dark feeling of tumbling into endless shapeless space. I pressed myself against her tight, just like I used to wrap myself in blankets.

"Mom." I was crying. It was hard to speak around the crying. "Mom. Mommy. Mom. You're really here." I paused for breath. Started to hiccup. "Please, how do I save him?"

"You need to listen," she said, stroking my back.

"I'm trying to. I'm listening. Just tell me what to do."

"No, my sweet girl, not to me. To him."

Uncanny feeling pricking at my skin.

"Can you feel them, his vibrations?"

My stomach lurched.

This feeling like tumbling into an endless shapeless void. This dread that paralyzed my body and my mind, rendering both useless. *These* were Jack's vibrations.

Just like my mother's humming had opened up vast vistas, Jack was also trying, in his way, to reach me. We'd always shared this other language, vibrating through the system of the two of us. He couldn't speak yet, he sent his feelings into me through cries, screams, shrieks, coos, gurgles, his belly laughs, his many smiles, his small teeth biting, small hands reaching, all of which I met with corresponding action: his hunger with my milk, his exhaustion with a darkened room prepared for sleep, his cold with a blanket, his loneliness and fear with the safety of my arms. And in this way, I transformed his need into communication.

All day he'd been trying to communicate his need to me, to make me feel what it was like for him, and, too afraid, I'd failed all day to take him in.

Even now, even knowing that what had felt to me like a resurgence of my motherless childhood fears of falling into nothingness was in fact Jack pulling at me in his need, I still couldn't give in to his vibrations. It was instinctive, like flinching away from fire or gasping when you needed air.

Out loud I said, "I can't. I won't survive. There has to be some other way."

I was still clinging to my mother's neck, trying not to let my mind go tumbling toward the no-place, and so she said into my hair, "There is no other way except to ride the same vibration."

I still had only the vaguest sense of what she meant by the

vibrations or how it was we rode them. But that didn't actually matter. What mattered was my son was calling out for me. What mattered was I had to go.

So, still clutching my mother tight, I forced my mind to do what it was telling me I absolutely should not do. I gave myself up to the blackness.

Chapter Thirty-three

It was worse than I'd imagined.

Worse than anything I could have conjured, although I couldn't say exactly how, I couldn't say a thing about this place, except that it was shapeless, formless, and that I would have gladly chosen any threat with form and shape over this boundlessness. Just to be tethered to sights and smells and sounds, even pain would have been relief against this nothingness where sense couldn't get a purchase. Where I was dissolving, becoming part of the nothingness around me. I knew I had to leave. I also knew I couldn't, although I didn't remember why. The why had already been lost, devoured by this chasm. Just like I would be. I needed not to be here.

And then I wasn't. I was lying in my own backyard. Beneath the redwood. Green leaves above, arching branches, the smell of soil and eucalyptus in my nostrils. I reached my hand into the dirt, just to feel the cool soft give of it between my fingers, beneath my nails, to soak in the immense relief, the sweet solidity of my own edges. But then relief gave way to panic as I realized I had left the no-place, abandoned Jack for the sake of my own skin. I had failed him, and I was—

There again. In the no-place. Dissolving, leaking out, and I had to leave this place. Why wasn't I leaving? Was it because I knew that this formless, hostile absence was just what I deserved, where I belonged? This place was telling me the truth. That I was bad, all wrong, and that was why I was alone, had been abandoned, and I was—

In Dr. Goodman's office building. Staring at the sign on the elevator door—"We're working on it!"—taped at a lunatic angle. It occurred to me that I was flickering. Just like Jack had been all day. In and out of my own world. This meant I needed to think fast while I could, while I was here where thought was possible. What was the logic to the flickering, why these places in particular? Maybe spots where Jack was likeliest to be right now? Where in this dreadful existential Whac-a-Mole was he?

I looked around me, at the fern, the industrial gray carpet, my foot extending from a sausage leg in rainbow-striped pajamas, and I felt an excited breath burst from my lungs. Which weren't mine, but his. Somehow I *was* Jack. As though we'd merged at last in oneness. No separate me. No separate him. Just figure and ground. A tessellation? Less than ideal for the purposes of saving him, but still the relief was an immensity, almost a world unto itself. Because here he was. He was here and I was with him. And that was all that mattered: He had called to me, and I had come, and I needed to hold on to that. I needed to remember when I flickered out to—

Nothing. Back in the savage void, but now it wasn't the same. Somehow, this time, I'd held on to the thought that Jack had called, and I had come. I'd brought a thought into this place, and the thought was changing it. I could feel his cry now. It was all around me, in me, I was floating in it, falling in it. He'd called and I had come, and his cry was all around me. The undifferentiated dark was taking shape. The shape of leaves. Azalea leaves. The anemic azalea in front of the lactation center where my mothers group met! We were in the parking lot, car bumpers at eye view. We were on the curb, we were in our car seat. And maybe we had flickered here, the same as we had flickered into my backyard and Dr. Goodman's building, but this time had felt different. Less a flickering than a resolution. Like a face coming into focus in a darkened window. Almost as though I had transformed the no-place into this place with my thought. A woman gaped at us as we fell back into nothing.

And, yes, this place was awful. With its endless shapeless threat. And no, I could not move here, see here, could hardly think here. But it wasn't unendurable. I was enduring it. I'd held on to the crucial thought, and now I had another. This formless terror formed Jack's immediate experience and so the place was thick with him. Like in the middle of the night, when I slipped into the cool, whooshing dark of his bedroom for a feeding, how the whole space was alive with his delicious smell. There was no smell here, no possibility of smelling, but the no-place was alive with him just the same. Not just his cry, but all of him.

And actually now I could smell him, too. His bready sleep smell. We were back inside his crib. Jack's fat fingers grabbed a wooden slat. I could hear Adam puttering in the kitchen down below. Gray light was filtering through the curtains. I lifted up a hand, I lifted up a leg, I grabbed my foot, delighting in my edges. That dimpled hand! That plump and perfect foot! We were falling back into the no-place, but now it didn't scare me. I knew what I was doing. I was feeding myself to Jack, not my milk, but something else. My mind. My ability to withstand this and make sense of it.

Which, after all, had always been my part in our wordless conversations: taking his anguish and giving it calmly back as something named and manageable. Hunger that could be solved with milk, cold that could be solved with warmer clothes. And this? Harder to name, harder to solve, but this one could be managed, too, because we were managing, we were here again, back in his crib.

And I was relishing the way his small heart pounded. And the way his fist opened and closed, and how he stuck it fully in his mouth, sucked at the knuckles, overwhelmed, exhausted, trying to soothe himself by knowing where he ended and the rest of the world began. And how much happier he was now that he'd rolled onto his stomach. A feeling almost like the golden glow with his front pressed to the mattress, his gums around his hand, and something else, some other source of great contentment, undetectable like oxygen until you lack it. Me. His mother close.

His heart rate was slowing. His breath was slowing, too. His eyes drooped heavy, worn out by the trials of the day. He was asleep.

We'd been cohering for several minutes. But I didn't know if I could trust that we were really here to stay. I could hear Adam downstairs more distinctly than before. He was clattering at the stove, not knowing Jack was up here, not knowing Jack existed. I wished I had some way to summon him upstairs to test Jack's durability, his realness. I wished that Jack would cry. But Jack was sleeping deeply.

And so instead I waited, feeling his even breaths like weather moving through me. It was a lovely sort of agony, trapped here in his body, but I couldn't last much longer like this. Holding on to these vibrations, existing in two parts of my own world at once, was hurting me too badly. And, anyway, it was beginning to feel like trespass to share this body that, unlike Hannah42's, had never belonged to me. It was the feeling of trespass that told me it was time. Like the realization that you've been hurtling down the highway for long minutes without taking in a thing: simply here. He was simply here now.

As though he'd been here all along.

I wanted to withdraw my presence gently, like backing from his room when he was sleeping. But I had no idea how to let go of his vibrations in any way but just to close my mind against them, all at once. And so I did. I let go of Jack.

I returned to my own borders.

Chapter Thirty-four

I was back on the blue waffle-knit blanket on a narrow platform suspended beneath the highways. At some point I must have gotten to my knees because I was kneeling. My mother was kneeling with me. Her hands were cradling my cheeks, and she was staring at me, smiling. I was pretty sure it was a smile. A toothy grimace that managed to express both triumph and despair.

Maybe it was because I'd done what she hadn't been able to do, what she'd warned me she couldn't help me with. Gone out and then back in. In fact, it was hard to see what could have kept me from returning to my own body, to my own self, where I could be Jack's mother. It was hard to imagine why my mother hadn't done this. Had she been lending her mind to me all this time in order to keep me from the no-place? For nearly forty years? If so, either she'd made a terrible mistake, her sacrifice unnecessary—or I had.

I tried to stand up but couldn't manage it. I hadn't fully settled in my body yet. So I tried to reach for my phone instead. A smaller movement.

Adam answered on the first ring. He started speaking, but I cut him off.

"Go upstairs to the baby's room," I ordered. "Right now. This second."

I wasn't sure if it was the severity of my tone, or whatever psychic rearrangement he'd been going through since forgetting Jack that had led him to send those desperate texts, but for the first time since I'd known him, Adam didn't demand to understand before agreeing. He simply went. I could hear the creak his foot made on the second to last stair. I could hear him opening Jack's door. And then I heard him gasp.

"Hannah, he's, what's—"

I could hear Jack crying. Adam must have woken him.

"It's Jack." Adam was still whispering. "It's really. He's—wait, am I—Hannah, I'm so confused. Am I—? He's here, he's sleeping. He's just . . . asleep."

"Then who's that crying?"

I could hear Jack very clearly. It wasn't yet his all-in cry, but he was working his way up to it. The sound had set me trembling with a longing almost too big to be contained by my one body.

"Hannah, have I lost my mind? He's here. He was missing. And then I thought, did I really think, Hannah, did I think that he had died? Did I say that? Did I tell you that or am I— Was he even missing? Hannah? Hannah?"

His voice was coming from the concrete floor now. I'd let the phone fall clattering down. The crying was coming from all directions. It wasn't Jack. Or rather, it was, but not my own. It was other Jacks. Other vibrations. Other lines of communication that had opened to other children of mine, spread across all possibility. I sensed them all, my view so wide that every view I'd ever had before now seemed unworthy of the word. All my life, I'd sensed the universe through pinpricks. Now reality and I had finally met.

And it was nothing like a hallway. The possibilities arranged themselves around me in three dimensions, maybe more. Each world a filmy polygon of many edges, one shape endlessly repeating, tiling the space in multiple dimensions, growing smaller at the outer boundary of my view. A little like a honeycomb. Or actually, no, like soapsuds. Bubbles, just like I'd pictured them in Grace's office as she explained to me the strange way possibilities behaved when a life began.

I felt a small movement beside me and looked to see my mother on her feet.

"Hannah?" I could still hear Adam's voice coming from the concrete. He sounded like Adam42 to me, so steady and afraid, but I couldn't pin down what about his tone made me think this. I could barely think at all with these many Jacks crying out across the multiverse, clamoring for my attention.

My mother was watching me carefully. As though memorizing.

"I'm so sorry," she said.

"Why? What for? What is this? What's happening?" My mind felt like a party line in use by the whole planet.

"I love you so much, Hannah. I don't know how to choose otherwise, but I wish with all of me I did. I wish I knew another way. You need to know that."

"But what, what do you choose?"

"I choose to save you."

I was trying to focus on right here, right now—my mother's words, Adam's voice coming from the phone lying on the concrete, and with him Jack, in his crib, so close. I was trying hard to tune out all the rest of it, but I could feel these other Jacks tugging at my care, at my attention. In one world, just outside our house, a Jack having a pre-bed meltdown wriggled from my arms and started crawling toward the street. That Hannah bolted into action, swooped him up out of harm's way. The road's one lonesome pair of headlights was still far distant, it hadn't been that close a call, but her heart was racing and so was mine, and I wobbled, I stumbled backward several steps. I regained my balance just before my left foot slid off the concrete platform's edge. Catching my breath, I glanced behind me, down at the asphalt far below. If I'd have slipped, I would have fallen fifty feet.

From the phone, Adam's voice was saying, "Hannah, can you hear me? Who's that with you? Are you OK?"

"Adam!" I called. "I can hear you! Is Jack still there? Is he still with you?"

But the call had dropped, and I wasn't sure if he had heard me. I wanted to pick the phone up, call again, but somehow just wanting it was not enough to make it happen.

Beside me, my mother had started to rock.

"No! Not now, I still need you." I was shouting into the roar of wind and cars and the many Jacks pulling at my senses. "Don't you dare leave me again."

My mother folded me into a hug, kissed my cheek, then my forehead.

"I never leave you, my sweet girl." Her voice was still easy to hear above the traffic's roar. But already it was losing some of its distinctness, already blurring. "It's just that there are so many of you, and only one of me."

"What do you mean? Mom, what do you mean?"

Her eyes were blurring, too. The look going unfocused.

"I'm so sorry," she said.

"Then don't go. Please. You don't need to be sorry." I was tugging at her arm like a needy toddler. I could feel the hum deepening in her body, the vibrations.

She said, "I wish you didn't have to. I wish more than anything that you didn't have to choose the same way I did."

"Choose what? Mom, choose what?"

But already I could feel the answer. Already I knew. I'd

known, without knowing I knew, from the moment I'd first given myself up to Jack's vibrations. Maybe even earlier. Of course this was the last stage in this process. Boundless love and constant presence, an impossible ideal, but somehow, with my mother's help, I'd made it real and bought Jack's safety through it. I'd ripped open my borders, and now I was humming with a multitude, like a barrage of extra senses trained on Jacks. Jacks shimmering like jewels set in an infinite origami matrix of possibility. So many of them, and only one of me.

Jacks in their cribs. Jacks in their ducky tubs.

In my own world, I stood on a swaying platform, raw, exposed, the wind battering at my unprotected body as my extra senses battered me with Jacks. With one Jack in particular. An insistent signal, blaring. A Jack in danger. Not my Jack. My Jack was safe in his own crib, but this one was in peril, and it was so easy to step across the spread of possibility, like walking between rooms. So easy and so I stepped—into my kitchen, where Jack sits in the middle of the floor in his yellow inflatable ducky tub. Splashing, kicking, laughing. The towels spread beneath the bath are drenched. The windows dark, the room well-lit and cozy. This Hannah's body stands, her phone is ringing on the counter, and a small soapy body suddenly slips beneath the surface. Reaching for the phone, she doesn't see. But here I am. I turn her head, and he is safe. Fished out, fine. Small wet body held close against his mother's, this Hannah's heart pounding relief, regret. How close she came.

I stepped away. Back to my world, back to my body. Where my mother was saying, "Hannah, I can't. I can't stay any longer. They need me. My Hannahs, my poor Hannahs."

"They don't," I said, but I knew it wasn't true.

Amniotic in her immensity, godlike in her power, my mother was trapped. And so was I. Because once you felt them, living, breathing, dying, and you could save them, how could you not?

Another in his bath. The danger came in waves. An infinite array of Jacks slipping in their ducky baths, each held hostage to chance, to time, causation. Time relentlessly approaching, but not for me. I could absorb the impact.

A Jack choking on half a grape. A Jack rolling off the changing table. I stepped toward them, I saved them.

Impossible not to when you could, and yet my mother had to be mistaken. Surely, together, we could figure a way through this. If only she'd stop humming. If only she'd stop rocking.

"Don't go! I still need you, I do, I need you more, I need you most," I shouted, but she was gone. Her eyes already glazed as she spread out to save them.

I felt my own legs buckling. I'd been abandoned. Again. Abandoned again and I had no idea how to choose differently than she had, but I willed myself to move my feet. Wobbling, clutching my head against my extra senses, I began to make my way. Toward the door, toward Jack. My Jack.

I was trying so hard to hold on to the details of my own normal senses. The brown metal door. The scuffed silver doorknob. But I could feel another Jack in danger and how could I not? I stepped—into the car, which I am driving up the switchback roads toward home, Jack in his car seat, fussing. I'm distracted. I'm looking in the rearview at Jack fussing and almost miss the stop sign, the other car barreling from the left. But I am here, I turn this Hannah's eyes back to the road, she slams hard on the brakes, and he is safe.

I can feel her horror, shame, the hot leak of the car-swerve feeling spreading through her limbs. But already I was stepping away. Into my own world where my hand reached for the scuffed silver of the doorknob, my fingers brushed it, but already another Jack was needing me, and I was moving toward him. Such easy work but endless, this casual thwarting of fate with my attention.

As I moved between the worlds, monitoring, righting, less a person than an atmosphere, necessary and sustaining, I felt desire for my own child, but the wanting was abstract and almost trivial. One among an infinite variety of ways that I might feel about one among an infinite variety of this child.

Still, I felt it. A loosely held volition to choose differently than my mother had for the sake of that one Jack amidst this multitude. The Jack to whom I was and always would be his only mother. I could spare him what I had gone through, but the wanting was so easy to misplace, a speck in the infinitely mutable stasis of the spread of possibilities. All possibilities, exhaustive, so what was missing?

"Hannah!"

I could hear Adam's voice calling to me, too, across the multitude.

"Hannah! Are you here?"

His voice sounded near, as though it weren't coming to me through vibrations, or even from the phone still lying faceup on the concrete. Instead, it was as though Adam were calling out from just beneath the platform.

My fingers were still brushing the silver doorknob and, hard-won as that contact was, I was reluctant to let it go. But now I inched myself in the wrong direction, away from the brown door. Wobbling, shuffling, I made my way, and peered over the edge until I was looking at the road below, and there, right there, was Adam standing in a golden circle of streetlight. And strapped to Adam's chest was Jack. Even as I stepped into another world to save a Jack from falling down the stairs, I also stayed right here and drank the sight in.

Jack was dressed in a fresh pair of pajamas, the fuzzy blue ones, and Adam had also put him in a jaunty little woolen hat topped by a tassel. For extra warmth, he'd draped him in the white muslin blanket with the stars, tucking it around the edges of the carrier. With his fat cheeks bouncing, his plump feet dangling, Jack looked blessedly robust, unharmed, at least in any way that I could see. Only maybe a bit nonplussed. His brow was furrowed as Adam patrolled with him beside the mural.

Adam had both hands around his mouth as he called out for me. I couldn't imagine how he'd found me, but he seemed to know that I was here. He kept to a narrow strip below the underpass, passing into light and shadow, light and shadow as he moved beneath the bulbs. He didn't think of looking up. But somehow Jack did. Just as they were passing into another pool of golden light, his tasseled head swiveled upward, the movement sharp, an animal acting on instinct. Maybe he'd smelled me; my milk had just let down and was soaking through my shirt. It was hard to believe he could smell me from fifty feet away, but it was hard to believe that any of the last two days had happened.

He found my eyes. He met them. His face cracked open in a grin, so utterly delighted. *Why, there you are.* I tried to smile back at him, but I could tell it wasn't working from the way his arms reached up for me, trying a different bid for my attention. I was spread too thin, my focus on so many Jacks, and his features balled into a fist of pained confusion. I saw him start to cry.

I was still moving with purpose between the possibilities. Between the Jacks, all mine, all needing me. Exhaustive. Reality in its fullness. But now I knew what it was missing.

Impossible to be a person and an atmosphere at the same time, but the choice was actually so easy.

I looked back at my mother. Exactly where she had been. Where she maybe always was. Rocking, humming beneath the highways in her blue windbreaker and too-big jeans, her blindingly white sneakers. Carrying out her endless task of saving endless variations of her child. Of me.

What, actually, was she?

A saint. Responsible to all. A monster—responsible, unforgivably, to no one in particular. To this particular, to me.

And I? What was I?

I was helpless.

Because all I wanted was to be here, with him. And to love him in the most unextraordinary way, which was to say with an immensity that couldn't be contained by the laws of logic, morality, or nature. Which was to say, my fingers finally closed around the silver knob, and I left my mother behind.

Chapter Thirty-five

The door swung open with a smell of mossy stone. It was as dark as I remembered. I couldn't see beyond the second step. I stepped inside and began to pick my way down the damp stairway, toward where my child and husband waited.

I could still feel the other Jacks, calling, dangling, needing.

I felt them as I shimmied through the narrow spaces, bracing with my shoulder as I lowered step to step. I felt them as I came barreling through the hidden door in the laughing child's face and scanned the space for Jack and Adam.

Would I always feel them?

I closed my mind against the question, against the possibilities, against the stakes of what I'd chosen.

Because there they were, their backs to me, at the far end of the mural. Adam was still calling out my name, and the distance between our bodies was suddenly unbearable. I ran. Adam heard my steps and turned, and now he was running, too. Jack's face had been a pinched, red welter when they turned, but it went slack in the commotion. He looked afraid, or maybe just confused and rudely jostled. But then he saw me. His mother running toward him, smiling, and he began to laugh.

"Hannahbelle! Oh my God, you really are here. Are you OK?"

"How did you find me?"

We'd collided and were leaning against each other more like two collapsed structures than a reunited couple. I was kissing Jack's cold cheeks, and he was squirming with gleeful impatience.

I had been forming theories about how Adam had tracked me. Adam riding his own vibrations, tapping into mine, finding his own strange capability as he fought against forgetting. But he held his phone up, and my theories looked ridiculous. How had I forgotten that he used to track my phone when I went out running after dark?

Adam was trying to unhook the straps from the carrier because Jack was straining to get to me. His straining was making it more difficult to release him.

As Adam struggled with the straps, he said, "What are you doing here? Where even are we?"

Jack was finally loose, and now he lunged into my arms.

"I'll explain the whole thing later," I said.

I had no idea if this was true. Would I actually explain it? This seemed too big a question to answer on my own. We'd have to answer it together. Whether we could love each other while loving Jack, both of us giving in to helplessness, not in defeat, but in triumphant surrender.

As we walked toward the car, I laid my head on Adam's chest, and he wrapped the muslin so that it wound around all three of us, encasing us like a delicate new skin.

Jack was snuffling against my neck and I breathed in the smell of him—that bready smell, loamy and delicious.

"He might still be hungry," Adam said. "I only gave him half a smoothie before we came out looking for you."

But he wasn't trying to nurse. He was doing the same thing I was. His tiny nostrils taking in the smell of me. Inhaling me, and I closed my eyes and didn't care what it made me that I had chosen this, chosen to be here with him.

Jack stopped his snuffling and pulled his head back to get a fuller view of me. I took in the view as well: his thick, black lashes, his gummy grin, six tiny teeth, widely spaced, standing at bright attention. A twinkle in his eyes that seemed to say *Hi, you.*

"Hi, you," I said. "We're home."

Epilogue

The babies in the moms group were finally walking. Or, rather, they were running. Right now, they were tearing through the playground, terrifying and thrilling three large dogs who were running with them. The whole park seemed alive with their expansiveness and their will, as they made their intentions known on the world around them.

Charmaine grabbed at my wrist as her daughter, Nia, careened into the path of a big kid on a swing. But Nia changed trajectory in time, pink ruffled butt now chuffing toward a rainbow-frosted cupcake she'd abandoned near the slide, and Charmaine released her grip on me.

"You know what treat *I* want for surviving her first year?" she said. "A year without her. I mean, not really. Obviously. But also maybe yes. If someone could stop time for her? And not for me? That could work out nicely."

Then she took off in pursuit as Nia headed back in the direction of the swings.

We were here for Nia's birthday. The official group had ended at the one-year mark, but we'd decided to keep meeting weekly on our own, for outings like this one.

Ash wandered over to stand beside me, her gaze on her son, Ezra, in the sandbox, pouring a thin stream of granules into another child's hair. Somehow Ash was already midsentence when she reached me.

"Also, did you ever notice how it seems like he's revising his bio every time he opens his mouth? You just know he thinks of himself as *the biologist Matthew Ishida.*"

She seemed to be continuing a conversation we'd begun last night when Adam and I had Ash and her husband over for dinner, a surprisingly enjoyable occasion, the mix of personalities blending well against all odds.

I was half listening to her and half focused on Jack, who was racing up and down a wooden ramp pushing a toy shopping cart missing two out of four wheels. He was wildly happy, high on sugar and the power of his own limbs. His birthday had been two weeks ago, and a week before that, the vibrations from the other Jacks, which had been getting progressively less insistent, had finally gone silent. I assumed the quiet meant the end of my capability, my powers all dried up, although I hadn't actually tried to travel since the night I got Jack back. Knowing I had likely weaned myself from my ability brought relief, but also guilt, regret, and terror. The guilt and terror was toward the Jacks, the other Jacks and also mine, whom I could not always keep safe now, but the regret was for my mother. Two days after fighting my way off it, I'd returned to the platform beneath the highways to find her gone. I planned to keep returning, because maybe one day she'd be back there, but it seemed more likely we'd said goodbye.

"Why actually do people do that," Ash was saying, "use the definite article like that? *The* biologist so-and-so. It's never *the* auto mechanic. *The* line cook. There's a clear implication of a hierarchy of human mattering in that small— Oh, fuck."

Where one of the wheels was missing, the shopping cart had caught on the ramp's lip, and now Jack was toppling over the edge. It was a good four feet to the packed dirt of the ground.

I was close enough to lunge in his direction, and far enough to know even while I did that there was no way I could catch him. For a moment, I longed for what I'd given up, immunity to chance.

Instead I watched, unable to stop what was unfolding, as Jack gave himself over to the fall, his small body succumbing without protest. He landed with a painful-sounding thud on his left shoulder, and came up looking uncertain. I kneeled beside him, ready to offer comfort, but when he found my eyes and saw that I was smiling, he laughed and clapped three times, then turned and went on running.

Acknowledgments

For invaluable feedback on drafts of this book, Ayelet Waldman, Beate Lohser, Chelsey D'Arrigo Lesser, Dena Freundlich, Emily Pronin, Helena Echlin, Lydia Kiesling, Kara Levy, Edan Lepucki, and Kate Milliken.

For equally invaluable discussion as I was trying to make sense of the project I'd taken on, Molly Antopol, Lee Bowman, Claire Jarvis, ZZ Packer, Kaylis Moskowitz, Julie Orringer, Heidi Pitlor, Emily Raboteau, Jonathan Shedler, and Susana Winkel.

For answering a series of very strange questions, Catherine Mallouh, Scott Aaronson, and especially Sheldon Goldstein.

For writing what has to be the most perfect book on the psychology of motherhood that will ever be written, the late Rozsika Parker. It was from this masterpiece, *Torn in Two,* that I borrowed the metaphorical use of the scientific term "umbilical radius," which appears on page 184. I am also indebted to the work of Joan Raphael-Leff, Alison Stone, Lisa Baraitser, and Jessica Benjamin, not to speak of Melanie Klein and Wilfred Bion, who I hope would not be horrified to see projective identification transformed into sci-fi.

For being my forever consultation group, Natasha Oxenburgh, Ben Diamond, Sullivan Oakley, Sophia Norman, Mara Gerson, Andreas Stocker, Ariella Gould, and Ying Zhang.

For being my forever mothers group, Cynthia Nguyen, Kim Rohrer, and Elizabeth Valley.

For immense kindness in a moment of great need, Susan Carey.

For teaching me that co-parenting can be beautiful even when it doesn't go as planned, Marco Lopez and Trish Crawley.

For being the Peacock Hotline and quite often my only tether to sanity, Elissa Strauss and Ruth Whippman.

Sarah Burnes has the loyalty of a mafioso and the mind of a novelist, and I cannot imagine a better agent. Caitlin McKenna has made this book so much stronger with her incisive edits I almost feel she should be listed as a co-author. I am immensely grateful to everyone at Random House including Andy Ward, Rachel Rokicki, Windy Dorresteyn, Madison Dettlinger, Maria Braeckel, Christine Johnston, Rebecca Berlant, Sandra Sjursen, Debbie Glasserman, Rachel Ake, Michelle Daniel, Cara DuBois, whose careful attention to this manuscript was much appreciated, and Noa Shapiro, whose practical and literary instincts were a great boon.

And for more than I can name, Rebecca Newberger Goldstein, Steven Pinker, Danielle Blau, Kai Blau, Eliza Block, and most of all Solomon Lopez, who made me a mother and continues to teach me how to be a human being.